The Brawler

A History of the World's
Unluckiest Soldier

By
Lewis MacLeod

This book has been published by its author

This work is a work of fiction. With the exception of
historical figures, the details of characters described herein
are inventions of the author and not intended to resemble
actual persons, living or dead. Historical events are the
result of several thousand pages of public-domain research,
well-documented in gross dimension, while minor details
may be the contrivance of the author for the sake of the
narrative.

The Brawler copyright © 2016 by Devon B Nickerson

ISBN 978-1533472038

published in the United States of America

August 2016

My friend, you would not tell
    with such high zest,
To children, ardent for
    some desperate glory,
The old lie:
    Dulce et Decorum Est
Pro patria mori.

Dulce et Decorum Est
        Wilfred Owen 1917

Friday, 13 February 1981, Northern Manitoba Province, Canada
I ALMOST GET KILLED IN A PLANE CRASH

A s a general rule, I don't believe very much in superstitions. Knowing this, some particularly mischievous sprite of the Unseen Universe was about to hand me a big surprise.

What happened was, a teeny little stainless-steel coil-spring, whose purpose in life was to maintain tension on a metal linkage-rod which connected a fuel-supply needle-valve to a solenoid actuator, was just about to give up the ghost, so to speak. To the extent that coil-springs possess ghosts to give up.

You see, this part had for years and years been in-place within the fuel supply system of the starboard-side turboprop engine of the CanadaNational Airlines aircraft in which I was riding. I had the dubious fortune to be occupying a cramped and poorly padded seat within the plane's frighteningly thin-walled fuselage, a window seat which commanded an excellent view of the starboard wing. It was upon this wing that the particular turboprop engine in question was throbbing and straining in order to keep my aircraft racing along at five hundred knots airspeed, twenty-five thousand feet above a million square miles of uninhabited, frigid, snow-shrouded boglands in the northern stretches of Manitoba. "Poinggg!" the coil-spring mournfully intoned, its swan-song utterance as the minuscule vital component fractured neatly across its slender, wiry middle.

The starboard engine gave a throaty cough. A thin white streak of poorly combusted vaporous avgas, clearly visible to Yrs Trly and a number of other starboard window seat occupants, started to stream aft from the engine's exhaust port. "Oh shit!" murmured the pilot into his throat mike. He had forgotten to silence the intercom after his last optimistic announcement of our flight status, so all us passengers heard this particular update as well. "Hmmm...Friday the Thirteenth," I noted to myself. I believe it probable that all twenty-seven other passengers took a similar mental note at that instant.

As they say, all's well that ends well. Our competent pilot, after a brief stretch of panic and fervent prayers to an unhearing Almighty, made a number of adjustments to fuel flow, engine rpm's, propeller blade angles-of-attack, trim tabs and elevons and various wingy, ruddery things, then made placating announcements to the rest of us about a 'minor mechanical problem', and then put the aircraft into an alarmingly steep descent, considering we only had the one portside engine still working properly, slanting down out of the Arctic sky toward the nearest satisfactory landing site. This turned out to be the Northern Manitoba town of Churchill, smack on the ice-clogged shores of Hudson Bay, about halfway up that frigid body of salt water's western shore.

Well, I knew quite a little bit about Churchill! I must explain what I was doing in Canada's Frozen Northern Wastelands. In those early days of my checkered professional career, I was a young but well-trained specialist in soil geology. My particular specialty dealt with the bearing-strength of saturated soils as regards such structures as building foundations, roads, airfields, above-ground pipelines, and railbeds. As you may already know, most of northern Canada is one great big peat bog, underlain at no more than half a meter's depth, on average, by permanently frozen soil. If you drain the water off some of this boggy land, dump gravel or dirt or household garbage or anything else semi-dry and quasi-solid on top of it, compact it with crawler tractors and spiky-wheeled thingies, then lay down a foundation slab or a roadbed, and then build a supermarket or apartment building or highway or oil pipeline or train track on top, the first thing that happens is that the drained-away water leaks back in. Northern Canada is all real flat, and seventy percent of the terrain consists of shallow lakes and muskegs. The second thing that happens is that, in winter, warmth from the building's heating system or, in summer, heat from the sunshine shining on that highway, or on that railroad track, or whatever, gets conducted down through all those nifty construction materials straight into that layer of permanently frozen soil, and causes it to *un*freeze, turning it into mush for the first time since the late Mesozoic. It goes without further explanation what happens to that well-intentioned foundation and whatever structure has been built on top of it. Okay, okay…by way of further explanation, the structure tips and tilts and heaves and cracks and sinks and breaks up into pieces and collapses. Well, that's where I usually came in! My expertise lay in the area of how to salvage the damage, or better yet, how to avoid the damaging situation in the first place. The farther north you go, the more pronounced this whole problematic mushy-soil syndrome becomes.

So I had been sought out frequently, and at a lucrative daily stipend, to supply aid and advice to a Canadian governmental agency called "DOT"…the Department of Transportation. I had visited Churchill on a number of occasions. Churchill, Manitoba, lying on the shores of Hudson Bay, was the northern terminus of a Canadian rail line which supplied almost all the needs of the northeastern portions of the Canadian territories. This included the Province of Manitoba, to be sure, but also included all the far northern parts of the territories up there in the Arctic beyond the Provinces. Specifically, the Keewatin District of the Northwest Territories. In more

3

recent years, a decade or so *after* the forced-landing of my CanadaNational turbojet, this territory became, by bill of Canadian legislation, *Nunavut*, a portion of the Canadian North administratively ceded to the local governance of those First Peoples known as the Inuit. Please remember NOT to refer to these gentle people as "Eskimos"...it's a rude, inappropriate, outdated, pejorative term that these folks have had to bear, undeservedly, for a number of centuries. The word 'Eskimo' does NOT derive from any Inuit language or dialect, but rather from those Amerindian tribes southward, speakers of proto-Athabaskan-derived tongues, with whom they did not particularly get along, back in the Old Days. I'm told it means, derogatorily, 'Those who eat uncooked meat.' In recent decades, Canadian citizens have strived to purge the word 'Eskimo' from their vocabularies. The least the rest of us can do is to attempt the same.

Interestingly, Churchill is widely known as a haven for vast numbers of Hudson Bay polar bears. The critters come into town for handouts. Or to raid landfills. Or to turn over dumpsters or garbage cans in search of age-ripened ursine delicacies. It's all pretty shameful and degrading from the bears' standpoint. But it *has* spawned a bit of a tourist industry for Churchill, because where else besides a zoo or a difficult-to-get-to, snow-covered wildland Northern Arctic destination can you go on a nice, comfortable Canadian passenger train to see and photograph polar bears outside of cages, firsthand and up-close?

Well, so I was on that turboprop airplane returning from a pretty-successful meeting with DOT highway construction engineers in Yellowknife, Northwest Territories, on an all-day flight returning me to Ottawa, thence home to Boston on a connecting flight, when a five-gram spring snapped in two, and forced our aircraft to

4

make an emergency prang-in on the tarmac at Churchill, Manitoba.

Later That Evening...
NO ROOM AT THE INN

After us passengers got shuttled out of the icy-cold twilight air and into Churchill International Airport's miserable excuse for a terminal, we all faced the same problem. It was Friday. The Thirteenth. Kind of late in the day. That disabled aircraft out there being ignominiously towed to a repair hangar was NOT going to be replaced any time soon by a substitute aircraft flown in from Lord knows where. We were going to have to wait for it to be repaired. Our aircraft had been manufactured in France. It was to be several hours before the pair of aircraft mechanics on-staff who normally took care of such things, who had already clocked out and taken off for the weekend, and who had already consumed several liters apiece of fine, strong, inexpensive Canadian beer, had been located and forcefully dragooned into overtime engine repair duties. It was to be several *more* hours before the two mechanics were to locate the broken spring within the complex interior workings of our ailing aircraft turboprop engine. By that time, it would be the wee hours of 14 February in Churchill—St. Valentine's Day—and the pre-dawn hours of that same day (a Saturday) in Toulouse or Lyon or Paris or wherever in France the damned replacement spring was to be found collecting dust on a warehouse shelf. Both French and northern-Canadian unhurried paces-of-life being what they are, it would naturally be a matter of a couple days before the replacement spring would have made its leisurely way to Churchill, Manitoba, there to undergo installation at the hands of the two dipsomaniacal mechanics responsible for repairs. So the problem all us stranded passengers faced was: Where in the tiny town of Churchill Manitoba were we to put up for the interim? Beyond furnishing us with chits exchangeable for whatever local lodging and meals each of us might be so fortunate as to find, the terminal staff pretty much left us to our own devices.

I'd become familiar with Churchill's cramped, primitive public guest house on a previous business mission. It does the establishment no kindness to call it a 'hotel.' If you did the math, you will note that there was me, twenty-seven other passengers, a lone, young, innocent, virginal, cornflower-blue-eyed female flight attendant fresh out of one of the prairie provinces, a pilot and a copilot on that airplane…thirty-one stranded travelers seeking lodgings. I believe the guest house had eight rooms, each just barely suitable for a lone occupant. No "public" spaces at all. No bar. No restaurant. No business center…although in 1981 a "business center" would have been a laughable affair, since there were precious few computers of a personal nature, no cellphones, no Internet hookups…no Internet *at all*, for that matter. There was no gym and no spa and no sauna. No library. No TVs or telephones in the rooms. No mini-bars. No swimming pool (unless one were as cold-resistant as a polar bear, and didn't mind sharing the pretty much iced-over coastal waters of Hudson Bay with a large number of those same, the planet's largest and most ravenous terrestrial apex predators)…assuming you could even *find* an open reach between diverging slabs of ice big enough to insert your body into. Well, however, I'd been made comfortable in *other* Churchill accommodations on other prior occasions as a guest of the DOT! Since mine was a DOT mission gone bad, perhaps I could avail myself of this fine agency's hospitality! I hunted down a public phone and made a call.

The DOT receptionist transferred my call to Charles "Call me Chuck!" Townshend, who bore the title of Regional Equipment Depot Chief, shortened in the whimsical Canadian fashion to "RED CHIEF". Chuck's bailiwick, the Regional Equipment Depot, was a large garage facility (known in informal Canadian parlance as "The Gradge") where diesel trucks and heavy construction equipment were brought to undergo repairs and maintenance in a warm, dry environment...far more conducive to effective mechanical attention than would be rendered if repair staff were dispatched into the field to stand Wellie-deep in muck and slush with cold, snow-laden winds whipping around their ears while attempting with frostbitten fingers to tinker with the innards of a diesel engine. I identified myself to Chuck and described my predicament.

"No worries, Mr. MacLeod!" Chuck assured me. "It's *Lewis*, if I remember right. I seem to remember we've put you up before, haven't we? The DOT Hilton, no?" This was a long, stretched-out three-story residence building with some fairly nice amenities, only a few years old, divided into one- and two-bedroom apartments, which accommodated DOT personnel as a perquisite of their employment. The DOT Hilton mostly housed single employees or those accompanied by spouses, plus perhaps one or two children at most, during their three-year tours in Churchill. Churchill was widely regarded as an End-of-the-Earth posting.

"Yes," I assured him, "I was housed there for a couple weeks in 1979...when the preliminary design work was going on for the new train station."

"Well, the DOT Hilton's all full up!" he laughed, with something suggestive of having, after a hopeful buildup, gleefully deflated me with disillusionment, a bleedin' Yank for all my sometime usefulness in the sparser-populated parts of the Dominion. "But!" he continued, "we've got a couple single chaps housed in two-bedroom units. Would you mind bunking in with one of those fellows? A spare bedroom of your own...I promise!"

Better than nothing. I gratefully assured "Red Chief" Chuck that, beggars not being choosers, this would be gratefully acceptable. Anyway, the arrangement was likely to be only for the one night, since I supposed that CanadaNational would whisk us out of the Canadian Arctic sometime tomorrow on another aircraft, dispatched to our rescue. Sheer optimism! Little would I suspect it would turn out to be six days and nights before I returned to more clement southerly latitudes!

He promised to get back to me in half an hour, after he'd made a few phone calls and secured me a billet. Before our cordial telephone conversation came to an end, I mentioned that there were thirty other stranded travelers in the same predicament as I, and if the DOT had additional accommodations on hand, any of them might be most grateful for DOT hospitality. We both rang off and I went to see if I could locate one of those hoppy, high-alcohol Canadian lagers.

The barman in the airport pub had just slid the second foam-capped schooner of Molson across the counter to me when a CanadaNational counter clerk strode up. He stumbled a bit with my name, but got it close enough that I realized it was truly me he was seeking. The guy glanced at a note in his hand. "You have a phone call holding at the CN counter. Somebody from DOT. Would you kindly follow me?"

We scuttled back to the CanadaNational check-in counter. "Yes...is this Chuck Townshend?" I said into the receiver.

"Good news!" he crowed. "Things are pretty full up, but I got one of my diesel mechanics to let you stay in his empty second bedroom. His name is Hans Raufer. He's in Unit 218...that's second-floor with a nice view toward the river."

"The name sounds German..."

"*Ohhh* yeah! Hans is *real* German, eh! You'll find out, I bet. He's married. His wife is Anna...she's Inuit.

Very nice lady, works day shift at the Regional Health Authority Hospital here… quite an expert OR nurse. Very quiet but not particularly shy. Her English is better than her husband's, but she doesn't speak a word of German that I know of, and Hans doesn't speak a syllable of Inuktitut…that's the Eastern Canadian Inuit dialect. You gotta be *born* Inuit to do that! With Hans, it would help if you sprecken-zee Doitch, eh? He'd like that. Do you, by any chance?"

"*Ein bisschen…meine Grossmutter war Deutsche*" I replied, straining to summon up the long-disused phrases.

"Um…okay…." Chuck observed, apparently *nicht verstehend*. "Well…anyway, Hans is a great big guy, about three times Anna's weight, a head-and-a-half taller. Could pick her up with one hand. Absolutely top-notch diesel mechanic. A little rough in the social skills, one might say, but he's lived an…um…*eventful* life. Ask him where he learned to work on diesel engines! Well, I'm having my receptionist zip over to the airport as we speak, and she'll drive you over to the DOT Hilton. Tomorrow evening if your plane's still grounded , my wife and I, we'll have you come to our place for dinner, and—"

"I don't want to be any trouble, Chuck," I protested.

"What's trouble? So you'll come to dinner! I'll pick you up about six. Oh yeah…my receptionist left maybe ten minutes ago, she should be there any time. I told her you'd meet her out front…look for a banged-up dirty white DOT Toyota pickup. Her name's Mary Lou. The receptionist, not the Toyota, eh?" The phone clicked off.

In due time, an aged and battered, dirty white DOT Toyota rattled up to the Arrivals curb. The side window came down a couple inches and a face peeked out, uttering my name.

"You're Mary Lou?" I inquired. She was indeed Mary Lou, and she shoved the passenger-side door open for me. I levered my smallish travelbag in, and quickly followed, out of the snapping-cold Arctic air and into the stifling interior of the vehicle. I've always found that Northern Canadians in wintertime tend to make up for the perilous frigidity of the Arctic Outdoors by keeping the Arctic Indoors at ninety degrees or thereabout. Mary Lou bumped the vehicle's blast-furnace heater another notch in order to deal with the frigid air that had entered the car along with me. Then she ground the shift lever, selected a gear almost at random, popped the clutch and we lurched off into the darkening evening.

A short way from the airport we traversed a short block which appeared to be the 'business district'. I spied a shop, obviously a liquor outlet, probably Churchill's one and only 'Provincial Liquor Store', since this item of trade was still somewhat regulated by the Government. "Mary Lou, would you mind stopping there for a moment? I think I ought to take a little something to the Raufers as a house gift. Some beer ought to do it, don't you think?"

The DOT driver grinned quizzically. "Beer! An excellent choice!" she remarked. "Get plenty!" I assumed by this that Mary Lou meant a six-pack, rather than a nice quart or something.

I shoved into the stiflingly hot interior of the liquor store. The way liquor stores worked in almost all of Northern Canada—certainly all the Territories—is you asked for what you want by brand and quantity and the proprietor would fetch it from the back room. Other than a few empty bottles here and there on high, wall-mounted shelves, either for decorative purposes or to demonstrate definitively the nature of the enterprise herein, no actual merchandise was on display. "What beers do you stock?" I asked the guy behind the counter.

"Three kinds. Molson, More Molson and Still More Molson."

"Um...could I have a six-pack of Molson, then? Pints, please...bottles, not cans."

"We only stock cans." The guy looked at me like I ought to have known that simple fact. Then the fellow vanished for a moment into the stockroom. He returned carrying my six-pack like it was a basket of precious eggs about to hatch. He named the price. "Half liters!" he informed me. "You must be a tourist. We don't do 'pints' in Canada!"

While the fellow had been gone, I'd conducted a brief inventory of my wallet's contents. Ooops! I was running a little low on Canadian currency! "Can I give you US dollars?" I asked. I laid down a twenty-dollar bill.

"Yankee Dollars are fine. You're American, eh?" the guy asked, squinting at the banknote. "You one of those folks stranded on that CN flight?"

Sheepishly, I admitted the truth of it, as if somehow I had been partly to blame for the engine failure. "The Department of Transportation is putting me up for the night, out at their residences."

"Oh! Well then! That's not so bad, mate! I bet they got you squeezed in with one of their employees...the DOT digs have been running full up for months on end. Those chaps come in here on a regular basis...I pretty much know them all. Who they put you in with?"

"Well...I haven't met him yet. A fellow named Raufer and his wife."

The liquor store guy considered this data with raised eyebrows, studying me like I was a particularly rare and unfortunate genus of bug. "Hans, eh?" he murmured. Without another word, he reached over and snatched back the sixpack I'd intended to buy. He spun on his heel, and pushed his way back through the swinging door into the storeroom. I was left standing at the counter, wondering what I had said or done to queer the transaction.

Fortunately, the guy came right back. He had a cardboard carton under each arm. Each one, a twelve-can case of Molson half liters. "Here you go, mate! A couple twelvers is…ah…more suitable, shall we say, considering it's Hans!" He swept my twenty-dollar bill off the counter. Change did not appear to be forthcoming. I hefted a case under each arm and struggled out the door.

Ten short minutes later, I stood in an overheated hallway outside a door numbered 218, two cases of Molson clutched awkwardly under one arm, my travelbag under the other. I'm pretty much okay meeting people for the first time, but the situation seemed stranger and more fraught with potentialities than most. I plopped my travelbag at my feet and gave the door a knock.

The door to Apartment 218 slowly swung open a few inches, creaking theatrically as if a cobwebbed crypt full of dusty bones and mummies lay on the other side. A massive body blocked all light from the room beyond. I ratcheted my gaze upward…then upward some more. The head, and the face upon it, was…terrifying! On top, there were lank wisps of unkempt blond hair. Huge flapping outsized ears protruded sideways, the right one missing a sizeable chunk of cartilage. Forehead and right cheek a landscape of ruddy ridges, the mementos of a long-ago ill-healed burn. A livid scar started just at the corner of the right eye, wandered down a ruddy, pockmarked cheek, hooked its way onto the bulge of a chin where a week's grayish stubble was rooted, thence down the neck to vanish into a loosely buttoned shirt collar. The eyes, the *eyes*! They were ice-blue, sunk in rat's nests of wrinkles…devoid of emotion… wintry … appalling! On the left hand, a digit apiece was missing from the little finger and ring finger. The horrible apparition's purplish-vermillion lips writhed, flecked with spittle, probably working up to a wolf shriek or a banshee howl or a vampire snarl. Or a hideous, leonine roar of rage.

The Horrible Herr Hans Raufer gave utterance. "*Ja?*" his deep voice rumbled. "*Wer bist du?*"

I gulped audibly. "*Guten Abend, Herr Raufer,*" I tried. "Errr...*Ich bin Lewis MacLeod.* Umm...*Herr Townshend—mit das DOT?—ihr hast getelephoniert Sie, Ich glaube?*" I was rapidly running out of German and I was pretty sure I was making serious grammatical errors. Raufer's terrifying visage showed no change of expression.

I remembered the Molson. Sheepishly, I hoisted one of the cases into Herr Raufer's view. "*Ich bringe Sie ein klienes Bier,*" I explained, gratuitously.

A massive, craggy, beaming, radiant, toothy smile spread over the entirety of Hans's face, banishing all—or *almost* all—my initial impressions of that face's fearsomeness. I passed over the case. Then I hoisted up the second case and proffered it as well. One look at that second case of Molson and Hans's smile widened at least four more inches, becoming an openmouthed grin.

It was the beginning of a beautiful friendship.

3
And after a few beers…
WE DISCOVER SOME COMMON ROOTS

So, there in the doorway of Apartment 218, with one arm Hans Raufer seized both cases of Molson, and with the other arm scooped up my travelbag and grabbed me by the sleeve, and then dragged me into his roasting-hot apartment. There was a very small woman hiding behind him. I had not noticed her at all, so far, because Anna Raufer was *very* small, and evidently had retained her Inuit capacity for remaining still and unnoticed whenever potentially perilous circumstances threatened. That would have been me.

"You must be Anna," I suggested.

"Yah! I suppose I must!" she agreed. I was blessed with an enormous toothy Inuit smile of welcome, which nearly banished the masses of eye wrinkles from her neat, triangular face. "Come into the kitchen and I will fix you something to eat, Mister MacLeod." She pronounced it "Mack-LEE-odd", like most people do. I suspect Chuck Townshend may have misinformed them when he'd telephoned a little while earlier. No sense trying to lesson these nice people just now on the proper pronunciation of a common Scots name: "Muh-CLOUD," despite the spelling. So I suggested she and Hans just call me Lewis.

Within ten seconds, Hans thrust a beer can into my hand, the tab deftly pre-popped by his spatulate thumb. He scooted a chair out from the battered Formica table for me to sit. Within ten more seconds, an oversized bowl of pretzels appeared in Anna's grasp, which she placed between me and her enormous husband. She skittered away down the length of the long galley kitchen and started clattering pans, giving her retreat into her private sanctuary some legitimacy, while Hans tipped up his own can of Molson and slurped the half liter of beer dry in one

15

sustained slurp. *"Prost!"* he bellowed, after the fact, slamming the empty onto the tabletop.

I raised my can to my lips and took a comradely swallow. Nearly choked. The mouthful of beer approached room temperature. The room temperature hovered around ninety-five Fahrenheit. An interesting, new sensation for me, hot beer…I was very young and naïve back then.

Well, we made small talk for awhile, until a massive plate of bratwurst and spaetzle and rotkohl— traditional south German fare prepared with whale fat, a subtle Inuit twist—was thrust under my nose. Hans must have already been fed, for a comparatively meager sandwich snack (consisting of a twelve-inch baguette housing a sixteen-inch wurst and oozing dribbles of pungent, grainy mustard along with strands of kraut) was all the provender Anna Raufer evidently decided her husband deserved. Masticating a dry sausage stub herself like it was meat-flavored bubblegum, Anna again retreated into her kitchen. It would seem Inuit sensibilities held that when someone eats, *every*one eats.

"Und so! How comes it you speak the German?" asked Hans.

I made a deferential gesture. "Only a little. *Nur ein bisschen."* I admitted. "My grandma was German. I picked up a little bit when I was a kid, because Gramma and my mom always resorted to German when they didn't want us kids to know what they were talking about."

"Hah! Kids are not so dumb! You *spreche* like a kid! *Nein,* the words sound *sehr gut,* but it's like you only know like what words a kid of six years would say. You learn just from your *grossmutter?"*

"Not entirely…I took a year in High School. And then, I had a girlfriend in College…exchange student from Berlin. Picked a lot up from pillow talk, you know."

"Oho! *Jawohl*!" Hans agreed. *"Unglücklich*, it doesn't work with the Inuit!" From the depths of the kitchen, Anna softly emitted what might have been an Inuktitut swear word, or maybe just a generalized, pan-cultural noise of disapprobation. Hans reddened slightly, then asked, "So what about this German *Grossmutter*?"

"Well...she wasn't exactly born in Germany. Born in the United States, but only by a matter of a few weeks after they got off the boat. She may well have been conceived in Germany! Her momma was carrying her in her belly...Gramma's parents emigrated to the Dakotas in 1874, and she was born there."

"Aufrichtig? Where from, in Germany?"

"Near Leipzig."

Raufer choked on beer and goggled. "Leipzig! In Saxony! Me, I'm from Saxony, too! Dresden!"

"Well...actually, her family were farmers on a tiny bit of land some ways east of Leipzig...a town called Oschats. Do you know it?"

"Oschats! Sure! That's even closer! Only about sixty kilometers from the part of Dresden where my parents lived! *Guter Gott, mein Freund,* we are *neighbors!*"

I patiently explained that I'd never been within four thousand miles of Germany in my life. And that my grandmother, *née* Freida Zacher, who had passed away a decade earlier, had never been within *seven* thousand miles of Germany in *her* life. And that *her* parents, brothers, sisters, and other emigrant familial hangers-on had not been back to Germany since the year eighteen-hundred-seventy-four. And that by eighteen-hundred-seventy-*nine*, every one of them had become loyal, English-speaking, patriotic citizens of the United States of America and the Dakota Territory and the Greater Township of Bismarck. And that the US Government, by way of the Homestead Act, had given—given! free!—the Zacher kin a hundred and sixty acres of level, fertile Dakota farmland, which was twenty

17

times as much acreage as they'd been trying to eke a living out of, back in Saxony, and in time the clan had bought up adjoining land to the tune of nearly four thousand acres, which was approximately six times the area of the entire town of Oschats, back in Saxony. And that the other three-fourths of my two-generations-previous ancestors went spiraling back to Scotland and rural England and Ireland and God-knows-where-else. Point being, as with many another immigrant family, the ties to the Old Country were a little tenuous.

Didn't matter. We were homeboys. Maybe cousins. Hans popped another celebratory Molson and thrust it into my hands. He popped an eighth Molson half liter for himself. There was no sign of him slowing down.

"So...tell me what it was like, growing up in Dresden?" I asked. It was sort of like pulling the wrong brick out of a four-hundred-foot-tall dam. Hans started narrating and I just sat there and listened.

14 February 1920, Dresden, Saxony (Southeast Germany)
A STOUT GERMAN BABY-BOY IS BORN

At three o'clock on St. Valentine's Day morning in the Year Nineteen-Twenty, a baby was born to Trüdl Raufer, age thirty-eight, the exceptionally homely wife of an impecunious Saxony brickmason. It was not an easy delivery. Nonetheless, the presumptive father strutted and grinned with pride while his exhausted wife lay abed grimacing with post-partum throbbings. She lay in a welter of knotted sheets, bloodstains, and birth fluids in the sagging bed of their own cluttered, tiny bedchamber wherein for all the preceding night, the soon-to-be mother, unassisted, had labored long and painfully until, with infinite difficulty orchestrated by her own groans and shrieks along with her husband's ineffectual, importuning curses, she had eventually given birth to a robust boy child. The baby's plump, broad-set shoulders and cannonball head had done its mother's meager birth canal no favors. Now in the pre-dawn hours as the swaddled newborn howled shrilly, the swaggering father strode the slivery bedroom floorboards as if he himself had pulled off the delivery. Fired with the dual blazes of self-importance and schnapps, the bricklayer roared "We shall name the boy **Hans**!" Since the simple-minded father's name was Freidrich Dortmund Raufer, the infant would, in due time, be christened *Hans Freidsohn Raufer*.

A prophetic name, that. *Der Raufer*, in German, means "The Brawler."

THE YOUTHFUL YEARS OF HANS RAUFER

Hans suffered, in addition to the adversities of a barely functional family, from having been born into a time and place wherein his nation and people endured the oppressive Versailles-imposed hardships of the decade following the Great War. But a child who has never known any other regimen barely notices the travails of political turmoil, poverty, rampant inflation, shortages, unemployment, and the collective mental burdens of blame and shame in reparation for the violent vicissitudes of Teutonic military adventurism, played out in the trenches of the Western Front. All of that martial madness pre-dated the boy's birth by a small handful of years, anyway. He lived a childhood which was at least as carefree as the next youngster's. Hans was favored with animal vigor, genetically disposed to good health, a stout physique and an above-average stature. By age eight, he was half a head taller than his cronies, a bit of a tyrant, pushy and physical, within his little neighborhood coterie, although companionable enough. He cared not at all for the educational rigors imposed by his local school, and incorrigibly ducked out of his classroom whenever he could manage. Rather, his enthusiasms ran toward hardscrabble games and adventure, and worship of his neighborhood's star athletes, those teenage and grownup sportsmen, amateur or professional. He particularly admired pugilists and wrestlers. For their own part, Hans and his boyish chums would get up ball games in a weedy lot or in a street, using whatever improvised sports gear came to hand and employing ill-understood rules, or those of their own devising, or no rules at all. Sides were fluid, baselines or goal markers nonexistent, periods or scorekeeping haphazard...only the clash of competition mattered. Or, barring sports, they would choose up sides and play out their youthful war fantasies: medieval knights against Mongol invaders…space warriors versus grotesque alien monsters… cowboys fighting off hordes of savage redskins, make-believe of course, since no childish participant was docile enough to have such a reprehensible role as aboriginal American savage thrust upon him, even temporarily. Or, best of all, the whole mob of Dresden tenement-boys would become a trenchbound squad of Kaiser Wilhelm's fierce and heroic troops wielding broomsticks representing rapid-fire *Maschinene-gewehr 08*s or bayoneted rifles, and fist-sized stones masquerading as Model 24 *Stielhandgranate* "potato masher" grenades. The boys would slaughter imaginary windrows of Frenchies and Tommies and Yanks who advanced in their imaginary thousands, faceless and timorous, across a cannon-cratered, barbwire-cobwebbed, corpse-strewn, reeking, vaporous no-man's-land on the killing fields of the Somme. Young Hans entertained none of the collective burden of his nation's angst for the *actual* earlier violences these boys' games mimicked. Nor did he suffer any of the vexing national chagrin for the onerous costs of reparation, nor the pride-wounding injuries to national prestige and glory imposed on the German Fatherland, the Defeated, the Betrayed. Hans only felt the simple, belligerent boyish pride born of a natural masculine aggressive nature—and that was about all.

Ah, but then the rise of the German Nazi movement and the blossoming of Hitler's regime was soon to teach him otherwise!

The instrument of Hans Raufer's re-education was named *Hitlerjugend*—The Hitler Youth!

Commencing in 1933, when Hans was thirteen years old, there was no other youth organization recognized—nor legally permitted to exist—in all of

National Socialist Germany. Adolf Hitler had said, "Give me control of the youth and I shall have control of the nation!" Accordingly, his regime had terminated all traces of the Boy Scouts, the only significant national/international organization offering rivalry to Hitler Youth, and had merrily plagiarized most of the Scouts' activities, structure, uniforms and rhetoric. All boys in the entire nation were automatically enrolled in Hitler Youth as of their fourteenth birthday, and so thus was young Hans Raufer on St. Valentine's Day, in the year 1934. Boys aged 10 to 14 had the option—actually, more of a semi-compulsory obligation—of enrolling at age 10 in a junior version, the *Deutches Jungvolk* ("German young folks"), but Hans's mom and dad, not particularly engaged parents, had not pushed the issue on him, since less than a year after the instigation of the *DJ*, Hans would reach his fourteenth birthday and elegibility for the Hitler Youth.

Hitler-Jugend, Bund Deutscher Arbeiterjugend ("Hitler Youth, League of German Worker Youth"), as the organization was officially named, was organized along distinctly military lines. A local region or city would host a *Bann* of some 2400 members or more, divided into four *Stämmen* of 600-plus members...curiously like the brigade/battalion structure common in most nations' armies of that time. The youth organization required attendance at weekly meetings, but these meetings were hardly burdensome for adolescent boys! There was an educational objective, of course, but it hardly dwelt on academic topics! Instead, indoctrination focused on spirit, physical activities, vigorous competition, running, jumping, shooting guns, waving flags, marching, camping out, emulating the organization's handsome, manly, uniformed, valiant, powerful adult leaders and celebrity role models, singing bold songs, undergoing lessons of Nazi-German national pride...stuff like that.

...And lots of anti-Semitic racism.

22

All of it inspirational music to a young boy's heart!

Late Winter 1938
SOLDAT RAUFER SERVES THE REICH

recisely on 14 February, 1938, St. Valentine's Day the world around, young Hans Raufer received, instead of a scarlet, lace-fringed paper heart with sweet sentiments, a very official-looking packet of documents from the *Wehrmacht* national central headquarters in Berlin. This day was Hans's eighteenth birthday. In anticipation of receiving these orders, or something very much like them, Hans had already been subjected to a battery of physical inspections as well as the issuance of uniforms, equipment, and insignia of a very junior enlisted man in the Nazi war machine. The orders, terse, formal, but quite as expected, directed Hans to board a train in two weeks' time, and travel south to Munich. There, in a sprawling military camp devoid of almost all normal comforts and conveniences, young Hans would undergo twelve weeks of rigorous indoctrination in strenuous physical regimen, close-order drill, lethal use of various infantry weapons, thorough grounding in the discipline and expected behavior practiced within Hitler's massive, growing engine of war, and the latest nuances of Nazi attitude—social, political and racial.

Well, looming international circumstances resulted in Hans Raufer's twelve weeks of indoctrination being somewhat curtailed.

In Berlin, the wheels of intrigue had been turning for many months. The Führer's policymakers were appalled—righteously appalled!—by the ill treatment of millions of ethnic Germans just across her southeastern border, in Austria. Many—no, *nearly all!*—of these fine Teutonic sons of the Greater Germanic Sphere had recently announced themselves ardent supporters of the National-

Socialist cause, and had even taken up Party membership. To boot, the entire nation of Austria, after all, was like a strayed-away little sister to the German Reich! If not for the evils perpetrated upon Germanic folk by the Versailles Treaty a score of years earlier, the two nations would have long-ago become reunited like the unwillingly estranged siblings they were!

Das Führer demanded that the Austrian Chancellor Kurt von Schusschnigg hold a plebiscite within his nation on the issue of reunification with Germany. Von Schusschnigg waffled, then sensing an inevitable calamity looming, he resigned and slunk away from the hotseat of public life. His replacement dissembled and procrastinated. Public sentiment in Austria was undergoing a gradual shift toward Austrian Nationalism, and a significant Jewish population was agitating resistance to unification with an openly anti-Semitic Germany. With a little stalling on Austria's part, perhaps the outcome of a plebiscite was no longer foregone in Germany's favor. Hitler, for several weeks toward the end of winter having graciously offered the loan of German troops to "quell disturbances and restore order in Austria," finally lost patience with the whole diplomatic approach and ordered his armies to forcibly occupy his smaller, less-militarized neighbor.

"Training Brigade Two-Nine-Six Alpha!" Raufer's training camp *Oberstleutnant* bellowed to six hundred young uniformed men assembled on a sandy drillfield in the predawn gloom of 12 March. "Your *Führer* requires your immediate participation in a field action of paramount importance to the Fatherland! You are as of this instant no longer mere trainees, but fully qualified troops in the *Wehrmacht* of the Reich! Each of you will unquestioningly obey every order from your company officers! You will be issued field rations, weapons and ammunition. Comport yourselves with glory! *Heil Hitler!*" Six hundred amazed tenderfoot recruits extended their right arms, palms outstretched, in vigorous salute, echoing their officer: "*Heil...Heil!*" they chorused.

In less than two hours, Hans and nineteen other brand-new *soldaten*, mere youths all, were crammed onto bench seats lining the back of an open truck bound for Austria. The date was 12 March, 1938. The precipitous military action that Adolf Hitler had ordered became known as *Der Anschluss Östereichs*, the "Re-annexation" of Austria, a lovely euphemism for "hostile military invasion in overwhelming force with heavy infantry, tanks and artillery."

Hans was a bit less than four weeks beyond his eighteenth birthday. At this time, the German Reich regarded age eighteen as the minimum age for induction into active duty...the days of fourteen-year-old Storm troopers toting single round *Panzerfaust* rockets was a few years into the calamitous future final throes of the Third Reich. So at age eighteen years and twenty-six days, Hans Raufer was one of the youngest and most poorly trained of German soldiers to participate in the *Anschluss*.

The truck bearing Hans's squad joined a massive convoy streaming out of Munich toward the Austrian border. Eastward they traveled, north of the pointy westward elongation of that doomed nation, traveling along the east-west highway that would enter Austria to the north of Saltzburg, a highway which eventually led to Vienna, hundreds of kilometers to the east. By nine o'clock the lead trucks entered the German town of Simbach-am-Inn, swung left, and ground their way up onto the vehicle bridge spanning the River Inn. This river marked the border between Germany and Austria. As their truck rolled across the span, to their left the troops, chilled and huddling in the morning air, could see a second bridge bearing rail tracks. Across the iron-girdered highway span the trucks growled, then down into the town of Braunau-am-Inn, the village immediately on the Austrian side of the river. Troops of the leading element piled out of their trucks, relieved the unsuspecting Austrian border guards of their weapons, their duties, and their liberty, then manhandled the red-and-white painted heavy pipe border gate up and out of the way. This event made excellent photographs for the press at every point on the Austrian border where it was repeated. Propaganda officers' flashbulbs popped, young storm troopers grinned and struck heroic poses. Austria was irresistibly coming back into the bosom of the Reich!

The truck containing Hans Raufer was well back in the column. As they crossed into Austria, one of Hans's cronies, a simpleminded farmboy named Rolf Kaustenberg, had his head down. The lad had been occupying himself for the last twenty kilometers honing a long, fearsome bayonet. This weapon was a gift from an uncle upon Rolf's departing for military service. Both uncle and bayonet had miraculously survived the murderous trenches of the Great War. The weapon was nowhere near official issue, and its possession would have earned Rolf a day of hard labor in the disciplinary stockade had his platoon sergeant known of its presence in the boy's pack, but Rolf's uncle had sworn the historic bayonet was destined to draw blood when in his nephew's hands. Rolf had come by a pocket whetstone somewhere, and was rhythmically stroking the blade when their truck passed through the border crossing.

Up in the cab, the driver craned out his side window and gazed at the fun time being had back there by the troops and press agents around the border turnstile. His attention was diverted from the trucks ahead, which had momentarily come to an abrupt stop. This was because a military convoy usually advances bumper-to-bumper in fits and starts, like the jostling segments of a cartoon millipede, rather than racing fluidly down the open road as its commanders might envision that it would.

27

Hans's truck slammed into the one in front. No great harm done to either truck—they were stoutly built and the speed of impact was modest. Hans Raufer, however, flew forward like a soccer ball, along with most of his comrades. *Soldat* Raufer was neatly impaled through the right ear on *Soldat* Kaustenberg's ersatz bayonet. In its passage the bayonet also opened up a fearful gash across Hans's right cheek and temple, severing shallow arteries which gushed fountains of blood. This unfortunate event occurred eighty meters inside the Austrian border, less than forty-five seconds after Hans had crossed the frontier on a military mission to reclaim this errant nation for the German Fatherland.

Ah, there was blood in streams! There were bellows of rage, pain and confusion. NCO's and *Unteroffizieren* came running from both directions. Curses and threats flew, aimed primarily at the inattentive truck driver. It was quickly determined who was the sole injured party in the back of the truck from the fact that Hans Raufer's ear was the only appendage spurting gore and Hans Raufer himself was giving off bloodcurdling yells. Rags were solicitously wrapped about his head, to little avail, and eventually he was bundled off the truck and into the sidecar of a motorcycle for medical evacuation. The cyclist—a four-year veteran of such military fiascos as this convoy—spun his heavy bike around and commenced negotiating a jarring route back toward the Inn River Bridge and Germany, a short distance back the way they had already come. Rough going, since the motorcycle was relegated to the road ditches and the bridge's footpath. *Soldat* Raufer, quite possibly the *first*, the *youngest*, and certainly one of the *very few* German casualties of the entire *Anschluss*, was delivered up to the single elderly doctor of a tiny hospital, the only medical facility available in Simbach-am-Inn, back on the German side of the border.

A *veterinary* hospital.

28

A FEW CLARIFYING REMARKS

"So they patched you up, the Army medics?" I asked him. I imagined that perhaps the notch in the rear portion of Hans's right ear and the hideous, livid, wormlike cheek scar with its parallel rows of stitchmarks were the result of this particular misadventure.

"*Nein...nein*. No Army medics. We only had two medical staffers in our column, I found out later, and they were six or seven kilometers back in the convoy. The...the *animal doctor* took care of me."

"The veterinarian?"

"*Ja*. Well, after he stitched up my cheek, he had started to trim my ear with a big dull pair of snippers—you see, it was all ragged where Rolf's bayonet went through, and I guess he wanted to smooth it out—and I was yelling and bellowing, because it hurt like *scheiss*! So, the doctor decided to use a little anaesthetic. He's got no nurse or surgical assistant, and he's only got animal medications, so he puts a rag over my face and starts dripping some bad-smelling stuff from a can onto my nose. I'm thrashing about because the stuff smells awful and it's making me choke. Then the place blows up."

I goggled at this, certain that if I remembered my history correctly, scarcely a shot had been fired by either side during the *Anschluss*. "Austrian artillery?"

"*Ach, nein!*" Hans grinned. "It was those anaesthesia fumes! That *verdammt* pig-doctor was smoking a cigar while he worked, and he lit the anaesthetic fumes off himself! See these scars on my forehead? I got cooked like a *schnitzel*! Hospital took fire and burned to the ground! But before I fried completely, I got out under my own power, still streaming blood, hair crisped off, forehead blackened like charcoal. Dove straight through a window. Then I sat on the roadside until afternoon, clutching a rag against my ear and picking slivers of glass out of my arms. The medic truck finally arrived. They stitched me up…crappy job of it! No anaesthetic at all! I got shipped back to a regular hospital where I spent a few weeks in bed, mending. By the time I got out, the *Anschluss* was history and Austria was a happy part of the Third Reich. Well…the *German* Austrians were happy. That, *mein freund*, is the story of my first military service to *Führer* and Fatherland."

I shook my head in disbelief. "What a series of bad-luck occurrences!"

Hans Raufer shrugged his massive shoulders and made a face. "Could have been worse…a few millimeters to my left and that bayonet would have skewered my skull straight through my eyeball. Would have killed me for certain! Now, what happened when we invaded Czechoslovakia…*that* was bad luck!"

14 March 1939

SOLDAT RAUFER AND 140,000 OTHER GERMAN SOLDIERS INVADE CZECHOSLOVAKIA

Hitler's 're-annexation' of Austria was, at least, perpetrated against a Germanic nation. But there was a larger, a much larger plan, and its next step was *not* a Germanic nation, but Czechoslovakia, just north of Austria.

The Nazi dictator went about it like this. First, his machinery of propaganda trumpeted the ills and insults aimed at 'expatriate' Germans living in the fringes of the western part of Czechoslovakia: the Sudetenland. In short order, during the spring of 1938 following the *Anschluss*, these grievances were blown up to the magnitude of a rationale for war.

The Czech, British and French governments had no appetite for war. As National Socialist demands became more strident, British Prime Minister Neville Chamberlain made placating public statements that the grievances of Sudeten Germans were perhaps justifiable. When Hitler and the Czechs both mobilized for war against each other, the British pressed Czech President Beneš to submit to mediation. The result was the Munich Agreement of 29 September 1938. Germany, Britain, Italy and France signed the document. The following day, perceiving the inevitable, Czechoslovakia capitulated. The Sudetenland was ceded to Germany. Wehrmacht troops swiftly took possession.

…But it was not Adolf Hitler's intention to stop there.

Through the winter of 1938 and on into March 1939, the remains of Czechoslovakia were in political turmoil. Its high command realized the nation's borders had become indefensible, since its mountainous fringes and its strong chain of fortifications had been lost with the cession of the Sudetenland. Presidential elections, interference from influential European nations, and the machinations of ethnic Germans created an atmosphere of querulousness and uncertainty. In mid-March, newly elected President Emil Hácha, successor to Beneš, was summoned by Adolf Hitler personally to come to Berlin. The *Führer* informed Hácha that German forces were under orders to invade Czechoslovakia within twenty-four hours. But first! The *Luftwaffe* would bomb Prague to rubble. All this unpleasantness could be avoided, Hitler explained cordially, if Hácha would instantly order all Czech military forces to lay down their arms. Hácha's response was to suffer a heart attack on the spot. Skilled German physicians kept president Hácha conscious long enough to give in and accept Hitler's terms of surrender...although history reports that the Czech president's signature on the documents of acquiescence was shaky at best. In the early hours of 14 March, a tsunami of German troops and armor poured across the German and Austrian borders into the country no longer known as Czechoslovakia. The Germans encountered no resistance whatsoever from the Czechoslovakian armed forces. Well...*almost* no resistance whatsoever.

So what role did *Soldat* Hans Raufer play in this treacherous act of Nazi aggression? Following the unfortunate accidental encounter a year earlier, back in March 1938, with *Soldat* Kaustenberg's bayonet (not to mention the fiery destruction of the veterinary clinic in Simbach-am-Inn), Hans had spent six weeks mending in a rural medical clinic just outside of Mühldorf. In Munich, only eighty kilometers farther west, there were full-service hospitals and university-staffed clinics, far more qualified facilities for repairing and minimizing the burn scars left on

Hans's face as he healed, or for that matter, performing the minor reconstructive surgery necessary to give him a reasonably intact right ear. But the ambulance medics who hauled Hans's bleeding, scorched carcass away from Simbach-am-Inn and his abortive participation in the *Anschluss*, had simply dropped him off at the *first available* military medical facility. In Mühldorf. Eighty klicks shy of Munich. The clinic's nursing staff changed Hans's dressings every so often, made up his bed once weekly, and saw to it that he received sufficient nutrition and a nice bedpan to pee in. After six weeks of this lackluster regimen, adequately healed, Hans had been discharged.

Soldat Raufer possessed no great ability in any particular specialty or skill which would merit keeping his soldier's berth open, and so his unit commander had ordered-up a replacement for him—little more than another half-trained, warm, young body—shortly after Hans went into hospital for his injury. Consequently, the *Wehrmacht's* manpower apparatus had no specific reassignment in mind for the eighteen-year-old trooper, once he was declared fit and discharged from hospital. If one wonders why there seemed to be no particular urgency getting this young soldier back on duty, it would help to remember that, although the German Military Machine was going through significant expansion in 1938, Germany was not actually *at war* anywhere. Not yet, anyway. With the possible exception of clandestine participation in the Spanish Civil War, on the Loyalist side.

Pronounced fit for duty but not yet reassigned, Hans hung around Mühldorf, sleeping in whatever empty cot he could find in the town's military recruit transit barrack and existing on such wretched provender as he could afford on a measly few pfennigs' daily subsistence allowance. Eventually after a couple weeks, the brass sent out orders temporarily assigning him to a field vehicle maintenance unit in eastern Bavaria, up close to the Austrian border.

Hans reported to a gnarled *Unterfeldwebel* mechanic by the name of Schnelling who was the tyrannical boss of the maintenance unit's diesel engine servicing section. This grisly sergeant eyed his new *Soldat* up and down, was not very impressed, and decided Hans Raufer would serve as fetch-and-carry lad, greasepit troglodyte, general dogsbody, and unit whipping boy…at least until an even less qualified candidate came along to embrace these menial functions.

Hans learned how to clean up spilled engine fluids. Then he learned how to scrub oil, mud, filth, grease and grime off of the underbellies of diesel engines, using a bristle-brush and a caustic solvent that dissolved skin as effectively as it dissolved petroleum products. Then he learned how to apply a wrench to the loosening of fuel line connections, and how to blow crud out of clogged lines without getting too much diesel fuel in his mouth. Then he learned how to properly replace glowplugs, fuel filters, air filters, coolant hoses, and fan belts. By being exceptionally observant, he absorbed a very small amount of comprehension about the servicing or replacing of bearings, connecting rods, head gaskets and coolant pumps…but he never actually got to *participate* in these meticulous, exacting tasks, all of them considered by *Unterfeldwebel* Schnelling to be far above Hans's pay grade. By the end of June, if one were willing to stretch the truth very nearly to the snapping point, one might have gotten away with calling Hans Raufer a Junior Apprentice Diesel Mechanic Trainee of Limited Expertise.

Well, there chanced to be an Infantry Regiment not very far away that just happened to have a request in to the Central Staffing Command for a half-dozen experienced diesel mechanics! *Soldat* Hans Raufer was somehow considered "close enough" experience-wise, and so in late October 1938 Hans found himself ordered to report to the Field Headquarters of the 84th Infantry Regiment of the *Wehrmacht* 8th Infantry Division, stationed in Poysdorf,

Austria, a hundred kilometers east of Vienna. Back over the Border into Austria went Hans in the poorly sprung rear of a troop truck. As the truck passed the spot where Hans had been accidentally stabbed in the ear half a year earlier, he tried to see if there might have been a bloody puddle still visible in the mud on the road shoulder…he'd gushed an *awful* lot of blood from that speared earlobe!

The base at Poysdorf proved to be a grubby tent camp stuffed with more than twenty-four-hundred young troops. The field officers and command staff had comfy quarters in a nearby former school building which the army had commandeered upon occupying Poysdorf. If Hans had actually gotten reassigned as a diesel mechanic, he might have fared better than a sweltering canvas hovel he shared with five other troops, since specialists such as vehicle maintenance technicians were somewhat prized. But, on reporting for duty to the unit's Personnel Officer, Hans had again been eyed up and down, thought a lot too roughshod and youthful for diesel mechanicking, and had been enrolled instead as a basic infantry rifleman. He was issued a Karabiner 98k bolt action 7.98mm rifle, one of nearly fifteen million such rifles manufactured for the *Wehrmacht* during the war years. And then he was assigned to Company 'B', 2nd Battalion, 84th Infantry Regiment, *Wehrmacht* 8th Infantry Division, where he spent the next few months drilling, polishing his gear, and policing up cigarette butts, in all nations and times the traditional employments for idle soldiers of low rank. Unbeknownst to anyone except the higher-up Central Command in Berlin, the troops being concentrated in northeastern Austria during the winter of 1938-39 had an appointment in Czechoslovakia, very soon.

So when, on 14 March 1939, the brutally intimidated nation of Czechoslovakia capitulated to Germany without, or pretty nearly without, firing a shot, the Poysdorf elements of *Wehrmacht* 8th Infantry Division boarded-truck and dashed northward. Hans Raufer's age on that cool spring morning was nineteen years, one month, and two days. The convoy crossed the Czech border into the province of Moravia. Ninety kilometers eastward, the convoy's trucks, motorcycles and halftracks screamed through Brno. Thence further eastward to Vyskov, and then a swing north to Slatinice. Once again eastward for a total dash, start to finish, of about 160 kilometers to their destination: the town of Mistek. Mistek stands only a short distance from the Polish border, on the road leading to Krakow, which was in March of 1939 one of the major centers of Polish government, second only to Warsaw. The High Command had a little secret something in store for Poland!

In March of 1939 the town of Mistek was home to 'Czajánek's Barracks', a training facility for the Czech Army. A certain Captain Karel Pavlík, assigned to the barracks, served as Administrative and Training Commander of the 12th Company of the 8th Czech Infantry Regiment. Captain Pavlík was a true patriot. He, like many Czechs, had watched the doleful events unfold between the German tyrants and his beloved motherland, and had felt a growing rage. On 14 March 1939, in spite of having gotten the word about the laying down of arms, Pavlík decided he would be damned if he'd let German troops take over his nation and not do anything about it. As news bulletins reported the advance of a *Wehrmacht* column on his home town, Pavlík deployed the 260 men of his company in defensive positions around the barracks buildings and ordered them to aim their weapons down the road whereupon the Germans would be advancing. He made sure they were well entrenched and had plenty of ammunition close at hand. The men were enthusiastically ordered to open fire the moment the German trucks appeared.

Oh wait…was it made clear that Pavlík's unit was the 12th *MACHINE-GUN* Company?

Wow! All of a sudden, this was *war*! The Mercedes staff-car leading the *Wehrmacht* column into Mistek was blown to flaming bits by a massive surprise burst of machine gun bullets the moment it rolled into Captain Karel Pavlík's cleverly-laid ambush. German officers quickly realigned their thinking from an It's-Just-Another-Convoy-in-the-Countryside mental sensibility to an Ohmygod-Someone's-Actually-Shooting-at-Us point of view. Troop trucks scrambled left and right off the blacktop, troopers were ordered out, infantrymen threw themselves behind cover, clips of ammunition were hastily seated in rifles, helmet chinstraps were buckled, pants were involuntarily wet with urine, conflicting orders were screamed, and eventually, a modicum of German gunfire began to be returned. In an instant, a couple hundred young troops—Hans Raufer among them—morphed from Young Recruit Soldier-Boys into Combat Warriors.

In the Czech positions, Captain Pavlík got his men calmed down, retargeted a number of forward machine gun crews from their ambush crossfire aiming points until they were firing toward German concentrations and hotspots, and ordered ammunition-preserving burst firing instead of the entire-belt panicky paroxysm gunfire with which his untested troops had first greeted their Nazi guests. On the German side, more and still more troops bailed off of trucks back a ways in the portions of the column holding the leading battalion of 8th Division. These troops dashed forward and spread out in an attempt to flank and envelop the Czech gun positions. Light artillery and crew-served large-caliber automatic weapons were a considerable distance back in the convoy, so for the first half hour it was

German bolt action rifles against Czech machine guns. But also, it was the better part of a German Infantry Battalion, capable of unrestricted, agile maneuvering, against an entrenched, immobilized Czech Company. The outcome would seem to have been foregone.

After the first hour, Captain Pavlík withdrew the combat squads of his company back into barracks buildings. Sporadic gunfire exchanges continued into the night. Ultimately, frantic radio signals from Czech higher command were successful in ordering Pavlík to cease fire. The frustrated Czech captain was running low on ammunition anyway, so reluctantly he complied with orders. He and his troops were rounded up and put under guard. The Czech soldiers were treated honorably as the first and arguably the bravest opponents that any unit of Germany's *Wehrmacht* had yet come against. Only two soldiers of the 12th Machine Gun Company had been wounded in the battle, none killed. Eighteen soldiers of the German 2nd Battalion had been killed. Dozens of German troops were wounded...*Soldat* Hans Raufer one of these, as it turned out. Upon surrendering, the Czech soldiers were disarmed, held for a few days as prisoners of war, and then released.

Almost immediately after the German occupation of Czechoslovakia, Captain Karel Pavlík became active in the Czech Resistance, a founding member of the *sub rosa* group *Za Vlast* ('For the Country'). He aided in the clandestine escape of skilled Czech aircraft pilots, many of whom became aces with the British RAF or the Russian air-combat service. Later in the war, he turned his attentions to sabotage and assassination, until he was captured by the Gestapo, sent to Mathausen Concentration Camp, questioned under torture, and executed by means of a single bullet to the skull. His remains were never located, having in all likelihood been converted to bone meal or ersatz soap, but he is regarded to this day as a Czech national hero for having commanded the only organized opposition to the Nazi military takeover of his country. Pavlík was, arguably, commander of World War II's very first organized armed resistance to German military might.

For his part, Hans Raufer took a machine gun round to the point of his right shoulder. The Czech bullet struck him at a funny angle, and bored right on through his entire shoulder apparatus, and then evidently kept on going until expending its energy in the dirt a hundred meters beyond the action. The distal process of Hans's clavicle was somewhat shattered, and a neat round hole was punched right through his scapula. He lost a lot of blood before a comrade could stuff rags under his tunic, fore and aft, and stanch the gushing. Hans and a handful of his injured mates were considered Heroes of the Reich, being virtually the first German soldiers wounded in combat against the Enemies of National Socialism. Consequently, he and his wounded buddies from Mistek were given top priority medical aid, ambulanced 360 km to Prague, then airlifted another 360 km in a captured Czechoslovakian Air Force Fokker Trimotor, almost uneventfully, heading all the way back toward a first-class military hospital in Berlin. Upon eventually reaching this hospital, Hans received what passed for excellent reconstructive surgery in *Reichsheer* military hospitals. While he lay abed postoperatively, groggy with painkiller, he was awarded the Iron Cross, Second Class, for exemplary valor under enemy fire.

9

WE SWITCH TO SCHNAPPS WHILE HANS EXPLAINS THINGS

So it seemed to me that Hans Raufer was possibly the first, maybe the *only*, German casualty of the *Anschluss*. And one of the first half dozen German casualties of the invasion of Czechoslovakia. "Iron Cross!" I enthused. "Quite an honor, no?"

"Well they passed them out like salted peanuts as the war progressed. Something like five million of them, by the end of the war." Hans sloshed more schnapps into my glass. We had run out of beer a while ago. Anna, not particularly interested in re-hearing old war stories, had padded off to bed some time since.

I shrugged off Hans's modesty. "Well, for exemplary courage under fire! That's something, isn't it?"

"Hah! Courage! I didn't turn tail and run...a lot of the guys did! Instead, I cowered *courageously* in the wet bottom of a road ditch until the shooting stopped. Never fired a shot, myself! Then, it stays quiet for a little while and I'm thinking it's all over, so I stand up, and...POW! Right through the shoulder!"

"Well it could have been worse! They could have easily killed you!"

Hans laughed outrageously. "Yeah...like when the airplane crashed!"

"*Whaaat?*"

"It's a *Czech* transport aircraft! Trimotor, made in Holland back in the 'Twenties. Wings were mostly wood, spars and struts and so forth, so they said. Covered with corrugated tin...except the parts that were covered with *fabric*! None too reliable a flying record! So there we are at the airdrome in Prague, stretchered onto this aircraft. A couple of hotshot *Luftwaffe* pilots jump in the cockpit of that big Fokker—*Hah!* A big Fokker, all right!— and all us wounded fellows in the passenger compartment, stacked up on our stretchers like slaughtered hog carcasses, high as kites on morphine. Those pilots look at all the dials and switches labeled in Czech, shrug and say '*Was zum Teufel!*', then fire up those three big rotary engines and sail off in the general direction of Berlin. Sure enough, all goes fine until about fifty kilometers south of Berlin. That's when the main fuel tank goes dry, and one by one those big motors slow down and cough and stop spinning. The pilots are frantically flipping switches and yanking on levers because they cannot read the Czech labels so they cannot find the right controls to switch over to the reserve fuel tanks...hundreds of liters of fuel they cannot seem to get at. We are just going down and down, and when they have maybe a couple hundred meters of altitude left, they start thinking about where they are going to try to make an emergency landing. They pick out this tiny hayfield that's all plow-ruts and mud. The plane prangs-in good! Wheels snap off, props bent into corkscrews, plane sliding and bumping on its belly, smashing through fences one after another. Everyone inside flies about. I slam my wounded shoulder into a seat stanchion, and the blood comes gushing and I feel the broken bones grinding together in there. Now *that* little escapade could have killed me for *sure*! Hah!" Hans tossed off his schnapps and laughed.

What amazing bad luck as a soldier! "So what happened in the hospital?"

"Ah, not that much. They fixed me up. I was young, full of vinegar. Healthy like an Aryan Superman, you know? I got better...took about three months. Then, about the twentieth of June, they shipped me back to my outfit in Mistek. And then..."

"And then...what?" I asked, foolishly not remembering my history for the moment.

"And then things got interesting."

10

WE KNOCK OFF FOR THE NIGHT

Go on," I encouraged. "You were saying that things got interesting then?"

Hans leaned back in his chair, stretched his fists high, yawned. "It's getting *verdammt* late!" he observed. A glance at my wristwatch confirmed it: a bit after two o'clock in the morning. Hans waved vaguely down the hallway. "*Ach*, I'm a terrible host to keep you up past midnight! I show you the guest-room."

"But—"

"*Nein*, tomorrow I tell you what happened after they fixed up my bullet hole. *Kommen Sie mitt!*"

I followed Hans down a short hallway. He gestured into the open door of the apartment's only bathroom, so I'd know where it was, Hans not recalling that I'd made several trips to the facilities already. The influence of five or six half liters of Molson. Next door down, half ajar, was the spare bedroom, made up nicely for me. Anna must have given the room her personal attention before she'd retired.

My travelbag squatted lumpishly on a six-drawer bureau, awaiting my attendance. Hans clicked a doorside wall switch and a nightstand lamp came on to a dim setting, revealing a tidy bedroom, bed neatly made and turned down. The décor was Inuit! Momentarily, I was taken aback. The room was more like an intimate display in a museum of Cultural Anthropology than a seldom-used guestroom.

Hans bid me good night as he left, closing the door behind him. I turned my attention fully to the art and artifacts which adorned the room.

A row of stone carvings illustrating aspects of traditional nomadic Inuit life adorned the wide windowledge. There were framed, embroidered scenes on the walls, executed on felt or fabric, showing parka-clad Inuits going about daily doings in villages of split plank dwellings and traditional ice-block igloos. But one partcular sculpture captured my gaze.

It was a large sculpture, in a place of honor on the bureau. A composite of stone, ivory, antler, bone and fiber. The base was gray stone, showing two long-tusked walrus heads, diagonally opposed, worked outward from a single thick slab of stone, the flat-topped center part representing perhaps a chunk of sea ice. The walruses' downward-thrusting tusks glowed a pale, luminous white in the lamplight. They were doubtlessly wrought from genuine walrus ivory to give the creatures naturalism and spiritual authenticity. Centered on the ice floe, standing on its hind legs, a bear of the same grey stone. Even lacking the distinctive coloration, it was clearly a polar bear. Unlike other bears, the animal possessed the unique characteristics of *Ursus maritimus*, its species: long legs, long neck, lanky body, head tapering to an extended muzzle. This particular creature hugged a large, perfectly spherical stone ball in its forepaws, the ball's surface scored with claw marks. The bear appeared about to drop the ball directly on the head of one of those walruses. Later, I learned from Anna that the stony material from which the majority of the sculpture was hewn was *soapstone*, a variety of crystalline schist naturally impregnated with a high percentage of talc. Soapstone is found as occasional chunks in ancient glacial eskers and morainal depositions, or in more contiguous deposits of baserock outcrops here and there. Overall, the material is not too abundant in the high Arctic. The stone was highly prized as a soft yet durable carving medium by the Inuit. Anna's family had knowledge of a small surface vein several days' travel from their home village, out in the trackless tundra where her forbears had kept its very existence a precious secret over immeasurable time. One of her uncles journeyed out to this clan soapstone quarry every autumn, and would bring back a sled loaded with chunks. Soapstone had been the favored Inuit sculpture medium for thousands of years, and Anna's uncle, a traditional caribou hunter, spent his idle time housebound during the long, dark winter months sculpting pieces like the one on the bureau. So had Anna's father, before he'd passed on. As to the strange motif, Anna explained to me later that polar bears are clever, rational, magic beasts, and they are known sometimes to use their claws to scratch out a large, heavy ice ball, and to use this as a weapon to bash walruses in the head. These huge, placid sea-mammals are far too large for polar bears to kill in their conventional way, snatching them out of the sea with fangs or claws and giving them a good shake to break their necks, the way the great, predatory bears do with lesser pinnipeds. Many years later, a University acquaintance of mine confided that the entire polar-bear/ice-ball/walrus story was thoroughly unfounded in the annals of wildlife biology, and was likely an example of the quixotic Inuit sense of humor regarding what kind of preposterous falsehoods they can put over on *qalluna'aq*—gullible White Men. Like myself.

The bed was spread with what looked like a woven wool counterpane. But when I gently passed my hand across the fabric, I recognized it for what it was. *Qiviut!* The wool of musk-ox! These tundra beasts are so odd and so endangered, the Canadian government protects them assiduously! Yet, their wool is long, alluring, irresistible, soft, light-brown, lush. It spins into perhaps the most amazing yarn on the planet...like textiles from the finest Alpaca or Vicuña, or even rarer woolbearers...or something altogether not of this Earth. No one, not even the clever, resourceful Inuit, can keep musk-ox domestically! No one could succeed in harnessing a musk-ox or two to a sled. No one could round these crazy-wild beasts up at some foregone season of the year and shear them of their *qiviut*! But, obligingly, Arctic musk-ox start feeling itchy when the frigid northern winters give way to spring. The small herds find themselves a nice copse of dwarf willows on which to scratch off their shedding winter coats. Inuit families have jealously-guarded traditional gathering rights to particular willow copses, and collect up the *qiviut* once the musk-ox are done with it. The strict Canadian wildlife management laws permit this liberty, but only for card-carrying Inuits! Many years ago, Anna Raufer, it transpired, had spun her annual share of *qiviut* into fine wool yarn, and had hand woven this luxuriant bedspread on the bed I was about to occupy. As I crawled under its embracing warmth, I fell asleep within the space of three breaths.

I awoke to the scent of potatoes and onions sizzling in a pan. Dressing quickly, I wandered down to Anna's kitchen where mountains of breakfast provender were being prepared. Hans waved me into a chair and handed me an enormous enameled earthenware beer-stein which, mercifully, contained steaming hot, black, deliciously aromatic coffee rather than Molson. Moments later, Anna handed me a large plate mounded with fried potatoes, four barely-singed eggs sunny-side-up, and a fish. It all muddled together excellently in the eating process, and was far more flavorsome than I would have predicted.

"Well so!" Hans effused when at last he took a break from shoveling it in. "A message from the CanadaNational! Come down to the airport around nine o'clock and they figure out how to get you home to Boston!"

I glanced at my watch. "I'd better call a cab, then." I recalled that there was only a single cab in the entire town of Churchill, and it ran, if at all, on a thoroughly unpredictable schedule.

"*Nichts*! I drive you!" Hans insisted.

Hans owned a corrosion-eaten, mud-caked and much battered Mercedes powered by a purring diesel engine. The engine seemed far too good for the dented rustbucket body it inhabited. This of course must have been a testament to Hans's skills as a diesel mechanic. We rattled over icy roads eastward away from the river estuary in the direction of Churchill International. I was pensive with reflections about the complex yarn Hans had been spinning the previous evening. "If they get me on a plane sometime today, I guess the rest of your war history will have to save until another time, my friend," I said at last.

"*Ach nein, nein!* They won't have you out of here today, not at all! And tomorrow's Sunday...even less likely. They might get you on the train, but not until Thursday at the soonest! There's only one train a week. No, *mein Freund*, you are stuck here! We talk to the airline fellow, then we get some beer and go back to the house! Tonight you go have dinner with the boss. Maybe this afternoon we go to the movie—I'll find out what's showing. A war movie, maybe, with John Wayne so we can make rude remarks and throw pop-bottles at the screen when they make stupid with the history. After the airport, we sit in the kitchen and I tell you what happened back in 1939 after I get out of hospital, and we drink beer and maybe some schnapps. Anna spends Saturday playing cards with a flock of lady friends, so I don't have to bear her giving me scornful glances."

This confused me. "I didn't see any—"

"*Ach*, she's so subtle, that woman! You watch out the corner of your eye, you see her lips tighten. Maybe she squints a bit. Now and then, she gives a small sigh. She mumbles something in Inuit, very quiet. That's how! It's because she thinks I drink too much, *Freund* Lewis!"

It was certainly possible. Hans had worked his way through at least sixteen half liters of Molson and the better part of a bottle of schnapps. But, in his defense, I'd not

46

detected much in the way of overt inebriation. No slurred speech, no mood change, no staggering about...perhaps a little flush to the complexion, is all. But then, Hans was German, practically born drinking beer. And he was naturally pretty ruddy in the face.

My focus shifted to my present difficulties with Arctic travel as we arrived at the terminal. Hans cavalierly abandoned the Mercedes at a red-painted curb and we pushed into the stifling hot lobby. Signs over the ticket counter indicated no choice of airlines at all...it was CanadaNational or nothing. The guy behind the counter was the same agent I'd talked to the night before. I identified myself.

"We are making progress on repairs to the turbojet, Mr. MacLeod. We should have the part in by tomorrow. Oh wait...tomorrow is Sunday. By day after tomorrow. Then give us a day or so, and we will have the flight up and running!"

"No other flights scheduled?" I demanded, with a trifle of impatience I must confess.

"I'm sorry, no."

"Wait a minute...how do you get *aircraft parts* into Churchill!?"

"Oh, in emergency situations, they come in by charter carrier. Not licensed for passengers, I'm afraid. Usually just a little one-engine Cessna, anyway."

"What about all the other passengers that came in with me last night?"

"I'm afraid they are also enjoying a brief, unscheduled vacation here in Churchill."

"And so there's *no* way for me to get home?"

"No, not until the aircraft is fixed. Or you could take the train on Thursday. If it comes in on schedule. But I'm pretty certain we'll be up and flying before then. And...and there's always a chance for the weekly Monday-morning round trip from Winnipeg."

"The—! Didn't you just say 'no scheduled flights' and now you're telling me there's a flight from Winnipeg every Monday? Returning south, I presume? Later in the day?"

The gate agent reddened with embarrassment. "Well, yes. On paper. But they usually cancel if there's not enough passengers northbound, Winnipeg to Churchill."

"And how often do they cancel?" I asked, dreading the answer.

"Oh...most weeks."

"Can you give me a number?"

"Er...I'd have to say...seven out of eight weeks, they cancel."

Hans interrupted the exchange. "So! You stay with Anna and me a while longer! No problem! We have some beer, I tell you the rest about my miserable adventures!"

"Well thanks, Hans...that's very kind. Just let me get this straight about these Monday flights." I turned back to the CN agent. "So how will I know if there's a flight *this* Monday?" I insisted.

"Chrissakes, Mister MacLeod! It's a great big airplane! You'll *hear* it flying over when it comes in! *...If* it comes in."

Hailing from a significantly larger town than Churchill, I had not considered that circumstance. But my ire seemed to be holding sway over my amusement, if only by a little. "You just be certain to give me a phone call! At Herr Raufer's apartment!"

The agent assured me that a phone call would be made. He even promised to send a car to pick me up. No problem—the plane, if it materialized, would not be cleared to leave Churchill without my being comfortably on-board. Up until that point in my life, I had never had an airline promise me a personal pickup. And I *guarantee* I never

have since! "Well then, fuck it! Let's go buy some beer!"
I suggested to Hans.

"*Sehr gut!*"

Ten minutes later we stood at the liquor outlet counter where the night before I'd negotiated the purchase of some Molson. The same clerk was on duty. The guy smiled broadly as Hans pushed his way through the front door. "Hey Hans! I see this skinny Yankee out-of-towner tracked you down. Just a minute!" Then the guy vanished into the Store-Room of Earthly Delights. He popped back out lugging *three* twelvers of Molson, plumped them on the counter, then vanished again.

In a moment he came back toting a large cardboard shipping carton, its lid flaps already torn open, which clinked as he set it on the counter next to the beer. The carton bore markings identifying the contents as 'special order—Hans Raufer, Chuurchill Manitoba.' "What's this, Hans?" I asked my friendly host.

Hans had already flipped back the carton flaps and was checking the inventory. "Jägermeister..." he intoned, lifting a green bottle out and handing it to me. I scanned the label, which informed me that the spirituous liquor therein was flavored with thirty assorted Old-World herbs and was rated 70-proof. "Kirschwasser..." Hans continued, lifting out another bottle. This one had been inexpertly decorated around its stem with red satin ribbon, probably by the liquor store clerk. A hand-inked gift tag with the ribbon read '**Anna & Hands Rowfer**' in block letters. The misspelling, no doubt, was creditable to the clerk as well. "Sometimes Anna will take a teeny little glass of this stuff! So, I give her this bottle. It is Saint Valentine's Day, eh? She pour herself a thimbleful and she spend an hour sipping it...or maybe she just let it evaporate. She give the rest of the bottle back to me, since it's also my birthday! Then you and me, we got to take care of the rest." He handed the kirschwasser bottle to me, and I read its label. Distilled rocket propellant made from rare European cherries. Eighty-six proof. Hans, meanwhile, had moved on to the third liquid treat in the carton, which was evidently his birthday present to himself. A squat bottle of at least a full liter's contents made an appearance. "And here's some peppermint schnapps…you are already familiar with this stuff. We drank all the rest I had, last night." Crystal-clear high-test liquid lighter fluid, refined from snake venom for all I know. One hundred proof! Hans, evidently reaching the end of the inventory, produced one more bottle. "Slivovitz!" he exclaimed enthusiastically. "I developed a taste for this stuff in Czechoslovakia!" Clear liquid extract of galactic supernova, the label explained. From plums so ripe with fermentable organic molecules as to be completely unpalatable unless first distilled into liquor. I squinted at the label and found the proof figure. *"One hundred ten proof!"* I goggled.

"Ach, nein!" Hans grinned. "In Czechoslovakia, they call it *slivovice!*" Carefully for my benefit, he pronounced it: 'Sleeve-oh-VEE-chay!' And, you don't want to buy it from any *verdammt* liquor store! Find some country farmhouse with a plum-tree out front where there's an old *babička* and *dědeček* making their own home-brew *slivovice*! That homemade stuff will go closer to one hundred *thirty* proof!"

"Wow!" I muttered, amazed. "That sounds dangerous!"

"Well sometimes, yes! If those old fools let the fermentation go too long, and then they are careless with the temperature during distillation, they get lots of ethyl alcohol all right…but they get a certain amount of *methyl* alcohol as well."

"And that's harmful if you drink it?"

"Oh, not so much if you're lucky…it gives the booze a real kick. Well…I guess it *can* make you pretty sick. Or go blind. Or sometimes kill you."

Chastened, I handed the bottles back to Hans and he repacked the carton. It came to me that there were *twelve bottles* of highly potent liquor in that case! *Three* of each species.

"Well Hans," effused the clerk as we settled up. "That should hold you and Anna for a while! See you in a couple weeks, then?"

A couple weeks!

11

1 September 1939
HANS STARTS WORLD WAR II

This is not to say that Hans Raufer was *personally responsible* for the commencement of hostilities ...it's only that he was *present and involved*—on the field, as it were, at the instant of kickoff.

We got back to Apartment 218 without incident. Anna had left a note that, instead of cards with the ladies, she had been called into the RHA Hospital to assist an emergency surgery: an Inuit boy from 'way upcountry had been helicoptered in with a huge, throbbing, infected appendix in his belly. It was thought that Anna's linguistic skills as well as her expert surgical assistance would be called for. Hans rifled Anna's refrigerator for something for us to eat and I schlepped the rest of the beer and the carton of more potent beverages in out of the hallway.

"Und so!" mumbled Hans, around a beer-moistened mouthful of seal flipper *schnitzel* and *rotkohl*. *"Und so* you want to hear about the summer of 1939, after I got back to my unit! Here, have another Molson and I tell you!"

+ + + + + + + +

Hans Raufer was nine weeks in hospital, recovering from the bullet wound to his shoulder. Army surgeons found the shattering to his collarbone less cataclysmic than they had feared at first examination. They pinned the bone fragments together temporarily with stainless steel nails, and let him knit. Corrosive antiseptics were poured into the pulverized tissues punctured by the bullet. After six weeks, they made little slits in the skin and meat of his shoulder under the half-hearted influence of a local anaesthetic, and pulled the bone pins back out with pliers. This procedure was considerably more painful to Hans than any other part of the treatment for his wound, or, for that matter, the wounding itself. The hole in his shoulderblade was held to be of no consequence...it could heal up or it could remain a hole, as it wished.

He was discharged from hospital on 20 June, 1939. Large numbers of truck convoys were forming up and taking off for occupied Czechoslovakia or for the eastern parts of Germany. Hans Raufer was bundled onto one of these trucks, along with his personal packful of gear and weapons, and dispatched eastward. A sealed packet of orders was thrust into his hands, but the address typed on the outside read:

Company 'B' Bn 2 Inf Regt 84 Div 8 Mistek Cz

so Hans knew he was being sent to rejoin his former outfit. Other than that, no one bothered to tell him what was up.

Hans's route of travel took him through Dresden, his home town, which he had not seen for a year and a half. The trucks did not so much as slow down, so all Hans got to do was wave weakly, left-handed, at familiar sights as they rushed by. The trip to Mistek was more than seven hundred fifty kilometers...three or four days' travel in the best of times. A train would have made for a smoother, faster trip, but currently all train traffic was crammed solid with higher-priority passengers and cargo, so *Wehrmacht* logistics staff had relegated him to truck travel, slow and uncomfortable. Add to that, the Berlin convoy he'd been put aboard only went as far as Prague, and then branched off toward the city of Hradec-Kralove, of which Hans had never heard. This maneuver took place at two o'clock in the morning while Hans nodded and jounced on his hard wooden bench, sound asleep. So when he woke up in

Hradec-Kralove deep inside what had earlier in the year been the remains of Czechoslovakia, all Hans could do was show his orders to a very impatient SS *Hauptmann*. This officer took Hans by the scruff of his neck and frogmarched him into a dispatch office, where it was decided that the most likely way to get him to Mistek was to send him back to Prague where he might be redirected on another troop convoy after a few days, maybe.

Hans languished in Prague for the better part of a week. He was assigned a saggy cot in a transient barracks and made to scrub an endless conveyer belt of filth-crusted cooking pots in a steamy mess hall scullery. After a while, he began to feel like Charlie Chaplin, tightening bolts on a too-speedy assembly line. At least he got to eat a few semi-palatable meals in the low-rank section of the mess hall in whose scullery he labored. Eventually he was crammed onto an already fully loaded troop truck which, after a long, arduous journey, conveyed him successfully to Mistek.

Reunited with his unit! And it was apparent things were shaping up for something big! Through the summer of 1939, new units flooded into northern Moravia. Entire regiments! Whole infantry divisions! And heavy artillery! Each day, flights of heavy bombers and squadrons of Stuka dive bombers came over, loitered aloft in wide, circular holding patterns, then descended for landing at some airfield a short distance to the north. In mid-June, Company 'B' was ordered to provide eight truckloads of troops— ninety-six men!— on a daily basis to be driven the short distance north to Ostrava, a work party put to unloading railcars of pallets loaded with artillery rounds, crates of light ammunition, 50kg bombs, field rations, and other miscellaneous supplies of war. Whole trains of flatcars bearing Panzer III Medium Tanks with 37mm main-guns pulled in onto parallel trackways and were unloaded by heavy cranes. Tanks, armored scout cars, halftracks with twin 20mm guns…innumerable vehicles of war were offloaded in the Ostrava railyards and towed away to be hidden in nearby sheds and warehouses. After a few weeks of back-and-forth commuting, Company 'B' and two other companies of infantry moved lock, stock and barrel to temporary barracks in Ostrava where every day, in shifts, they comprised permanent, round-the-clock unloading details at the railyard.

"Where are they taking those panzers?" Hans one morning asked the sergeant overseeing his work detail.

The NCO waved airily. "They're brand new, half of them! Diesel engines never been turned over! They got to get serviced before anyone can use them! Now get back to work!" the sergeant gruffed.

Diesel engines needing servicing! thought Hans. He decided to take a risk. "*Herr Feldwebel…*" he asked. "Do you suppose they are in need of more maintenance personnel? I have experience with diesel mechanics."

The sergeant eyed Hans Raufer suspiciously. "How much experience?"

"Lots and lots! I'm very expert!" Hans lied.

Inquiries were made. It proved that the maintenance staff was overwhelmed by the influx of tanks and vehicles. From the usual nine-hour workdays, the Brass had upped the duty hours for their mechanics to fourteen a day, six days a week. Consequently, skilled workers were starting to drop from exhaustion. No questions were asked of *Soldat* Hans Raufer. He was, after all, a twice-wounded, decorated hero of the invasion of Czechoslovakia! Arrangements were made to temporarily detach Hans from Company 'B' and reassign him to the shops in Ostrava. No more arduous unloading details for him!

The ensuing eight weeks may have been the most enjoyable in Hans's life up until that moment. No longer drudging to unload railcars, he was sociably taken in by the experienced panzer mechanics as if he were a member of a mystical Brotherhood, a visiting colleague from an affiliate Chapter. The modest limits of his prior experience with diesel maintenance meant little to these veterans, and were overlooked. They left him to his own devices on the simpler tasks he had already mastered. They stepped him through the performance of any new task he wished to take on, no matter how complex or exacting. He learned a bit about the arcane skills of interpreting repair manuals and deciphering technical drawings. His newfound cronies shared secrets and shortcuts with him, unauthorized nuances of the craft they had acquired over decades of practice. Nothing pleased Hans more than, after hours of fiddling and servicing, to jump into the cab of a truck or dive into the bowels of an armored, gun-studded behemoth, fire up its engine for the first time, He loved to see the black, sooty diesel ignition smoke pouring from the exhaust stack turn a paler color as the great powerful engine spun up, its rumble transitioning into a throaty roar of pure energy. Everyone nearby would cease their labors for a moment and give a cheer, and another machine of war would clatter out of its service bay.

One afternoon a thought came to Hans as he labored shoulders-deep in an oily engine compartment: *Our unit alone must have processed four or five hundred tanks and halftracks in the last eight weeks...they keep driving them off and hiding them under tarps and in warehouses somewhere. Why Ostrava? Why not in Mistek? There's railheads there, and lots of industrial buildings. Or why not Prague, or back in Austria, or Germany, even?* A tentative answer occurred to him, and it was the correct answer: Because Ostrava is only ten kilometers from the Polish border.

On 27 August, official word went out to all 8th Infantry Division personnel. Anyone on detached duty like Hans Raufer, or on anything longer than a twelve-hour off-base drinking and whoring leave, or malingering in barracks with minor ailments (anything up to a broken leg was considered 'minor') was the target of this official word. The order was to report immediately to one's assigned unit, there to make oneself clean, spotlessly turned-out in full *feldgrau* (field gray) uniform with appropriate insignia and webgear, one's rifle, sidearm (if any), and/or other assigned weapon gleaming and flawlessly operational. Personal packs to be inspection ready with ample capacity left for field rations and ammunition, issue of which to be forthcoming. Consumption of alcohol was to cease at once (this of course did not include the liter of good German beer issued with the midday and evening meals…this traditional beverage was considered 'indispensible dietary necessity' rather than 'recreational drink'). No soldier below the rank of *Oberleutnant* was to absent himself from his assigned quarters with anything less on his person than individually typewritten orders, signed by his Company-level or higher commandant. The charge for violating this directive would be 'desertion,' a summary firing-squad offense.

What was up? The more astute of Hans's colleagues had been listening to the radio. Diplomatic relations between the Fatherland and Poland were rapidly deteriorating, nearing collapse. The Polish border was a five-minute truck ride away. Two and two added up to four. Hans, as many another young German soldier, apprehensively gave his rifle another good going over. If *Das Führer* had it in mind for them to take a crack at Poland, it was *not* going to be the cakewalk they'd encountered in the recent past, when they had gone waltzing into Austria or Czechoslovakia.

At loftier levels of the military hierarchy poised to have a go at Poland was *Generaloberst* Gerd von Runstedt commander of Army Group South. Under von Runstedt, *Generalmajor* Wilhelm List was in command of the Fourteenth Army, comprising one-third of von Runstedt's command. Army Group South was only about half the forces primed and itching along the Polish border, a force totaling some sixty Divisions of infantry, artillery and armor, not to mention innumerable elements of miscellaneous warplanes, ordnance supply, intelligence, medical, maintenance, and other support branches too various to enumerate. One-and-a-half million troops. Nine thousand artillery pieces. Two-thousand-eight-hundred armored vehicles—heavy panzers, medium panzers, tiny little mini-panzers. Two-thousand-four-hundred aircraft. General von Runstedt's field headquarters was in constant, frenetic communication with Berlin. The bureaucrats and underlings who served the Führer protested to the world's press that every effort was being undertaken to avoid conflict and come to an amicable resolution of affairs with Germany's stiff-backed Polish neighbors. But flying in the face of all that, the time and date had already been set for invasion. The date had been set for a long, long time.

Four-forty in the morning, Berlin Time, on the First of September, 1939.

A small biographical aside: General Gerd von Runstedt was in command of half the German forces invading Poland...approximately 800,000 troops. After Poland, he was given command of another Army Group for the invasion of France. Then he was made commander of yet another Army Group for the invasion of Russia, where his forces brought off the largest encirclement, slaughter, and capture of troops in all the long history of warfare: the battle for Kiev. Following that, he was promoted to *Feldmarschal* and elevated to Commander in Chief for all German-occupied Western Europe. But after the Allies' successful landings at Normandy in June 1944, and their followup liberation of France during the ensuing summer, von Runstedt was fired by Hitler. He was lucky he wasn't *shot* by Hitler. However, Hitler thought twice about matters (probably after nearly all Hitler's alternative candidates for CinC Western Europe had been implicated and executed for the July 1944 plot to assassinate him!). The *Führer* reinstated von Runstedt as CinC Western Europe, which position he held until, under his command, Germany had thoroughly lost World War II and been reduced to heaps of smoking ruins and vast piles of mangled corpses.

At Nuremberg in 1947, von Runstedt was charged with war crimes. However, he never faced trial. His defense lawyers pleaded his poor health, as well as the usual defense: "he was only following orders." The *Feldmarschal's* orders—those he received and enthusiastically obeyed, and those he issued—were directly responsible for the deaths of perhaps eight million people: European civilians, Polish, Russian, French and Allied soldiers...and German soldiers as well. Von Runstedt died in his bed six years later at the age of seventy-eight.

Generalmajor Wilhelm List similarly had an illustrious career in high military office during the War. Also, following the German surrender, like von Runstedt he was charged with war crimes, chiefly the vicious reprisal killings without trial of Eastern European hostages following local partisan activities. List was tried and convicted, sentenced to life imprisonment. He served 5 years of this 'life' sentence—and lived a further 19 years after his release, dying in his bed at age 91.

The invasion of Poland was code-named *Fall Weiss*, 'Case White'. It had been meticulously planned long in advance. A scant week before 1 September, Germany had callously signed a non-aggression agreement with the Soviet Union, its bitter ideological enemy. This treaty, the Molotov-Ribbentrop Pact, removed Russia, for a time at least, as a "second front" worry, and thus cleared the way for Germany's attack on Poland.

There are conflicting stories about what happened next. Let us recognize that history is written by the victors. Ostensibly, on the night of 31 August, a special SS squad is said to have staged a faked border incident, which has become known as the Gleiwicz Incident, after a nearby village in which a radio station and broadcast tower stood. The squad clandestinely slipped across the border into Poland dressed in Polish Army uniforms, then crossed *back* into Germany. Thereupon, they used explosives to destroy the Gleiwicz radio station. For authenticity, the SS killed several Dachau concentration camp inmates with lethal injections, dressed them in Polish Army uniforms, transported them to the site and then shot their corpses full of bullet holes before posing them convincingly around the scene. This incredible fabrication 'proved' the Poles wanted war with Germany, and on the following day, war they got.

The 1 September assault began with *Luftwaffe* bombing sorties targeting Polish border towns and Polish capital cities. Then, great masses of German land forces lunged over the border in the morning hours of 1 September, just behind the rolling advance of heavy artillery barrages. Panzer units churned forward, interspersed with truckborne columns of infantry.

The Poles knew this was coming. They were dug in defensively, and not without artillery, armor and aircraft of their own. It is a matter of record that the world press exaggerated the imbalance between Polish and German forces, probably to make better stories of the Little Guy versus the Big Brute. But it was not so much a matter of soulless heavy panzers scything through gallant but doomed horseback cavalry charges...like the egregiously misreported Charge at Krojanty midmorning on the first day of the invasion, when a couple squadrons of mounted Ulany 18th Polish Lancers, horseback assault troops armed with rifles, pistols and anti-tank weapons rather than cavalry lances and sabers, successfully routed elements of German infantry, only to be caught in the open and slaughtered, horse and rider, by German armor. No, it was more a matter of the Poles having less than two-thirds the Divisions the Germans fielded, Divisions more poorly-equipped and lacking the hands-on experience the Nazis had garnered in Spain, Austria, and Czechoslovakia. The Poles had one-half the artillery as the Germans. One-third the tanks...and all of them twenty years out of date, as mechanized armor technology goes. One-sixth the aircraft, many of them *thirty* years out of date, and *all* the Polish combat fighter aircraft only capable of two-thirds the airspeed as the corresponding German craft. Five thousand six hundred kilometers of borders to defend, almost none consisting of broad rivers or rugged mountain ranges, or guarded with pre-emplaced fortifications. Poland is a country composed of tabletop-flat terrain, well roaded and easily traversed by tracklaying and wheeled vehicles, at least in times of good weather. Poland had an attack-oriented High Command at a time when defense orientation would have served the Poles better. Given these imbalances, the most valiant of Polish resistances was doomed.

If you trace upwards through the organizational levels, you find that Hans Raufer's Company 'B' belonged to the Eighth Infantry Division. This Division was part of the Fourteenth Army, commanded by *Generalmajor* Wilhelm List. List's orders were to advance east-northeast, more or less following the broad agricultural valley of the Upper Vistula River, overcoming and clearing away all Polish resistance in their path. The prime objective was to seize the city of Krakow, second largest city in Poland. It was expected, in the detailed German war plans, to take somewhere between seven weeks and three months to achieve this objective.

It took the Eighth Division five and a half days.

+ + + + + + + +

"So that's the *big* picture. What happened to *you, personally?*" I urged Hans.

Hans pondered a bit. "Our trucks rumbled on up the road. Each Company went out by different routes, at different times, you know? So we would not be all bunched up in a convoy a thousand trucks long. Staff cars and radio cars interspersed, all elements keeping in close contact. Oh, we weren't advancing *cautiously*, exactly. *Nein*, the drivers had their gas-pedals to the floorboards. Far to the front, we could see aircraft pounding the *scheiss* out of any Polish village so brave as to have fired a shot or waved a Polish flag at our advance. Stukas dive-bombing targets, elements of Heinkels dropping bombs by the hundreds. But my Company? We encountered nothing! Until, late on the first day, we drove right into a Polish ambush. A Company of Ulanys, maybe two hundred of them. Small-arms and a couple machine guns, both sides of the road in patches of woodland."

"Sounds like the Mistek ambush all over."

"Well, to our advantage, we'd already had the experience of *that* one, so we were better prepared for *this* one. A few trucks in the lead of the column caught a lot of fire, but the rest of us bailed out, spread left and right, kept our heads down. On this trip, we had some light artillery accompanying us, 20mm crew-served guns, and a bunch of 8-cm *schwere granatwerfers* in our own heavy weapons platoon ...mortars, you know. We got to tearing up those woods pretty good. Then us ground-pounders fixed bayonets and waded on in. It was over in about five minutes."

"Did you drive the Polish soldiers out?"

"Not that so much. We killed them all, I think. It was the first time I saw heaps of dead. Heaps, Lewis! They were the enemy, of course. But they were nineteen and twenty and twenty-one year old boys...kids really, just like me. Just like *all of us*! Later, I got to thinking about what it was that made them my enemy, and I couldn't come up with a *verdammt* thing. Although, I could understand why *they* regarded *us* as enemies: after all, we were invading *their* country. The Führer told us over and over that they were our enemies—Slavs, *untermenchen*—but I must have missed the convincing details."

I thought about this for a moment. "Dangerous thoughts, given the times...don't you think?"

"Ohhh yes! Don't worry...I never shared my radical thinking with anyone else, not for a long, long time!"

We both gazed out the apartment window at a bleak morning, Northern Canada's patented mix of sleety rain and wind-driven ice pellets striking the glass like birdshot and dribbling downward in streaks. "Was that the only combat incident you were in?

"*Ach, nein!* Same thing, five or six times a day, every day. The Poles were falling back alright. Sometimes running back, full tilt. But they didn't often throw down their arms before they ran. They made us earn our advance...they made desperate, brave stands at every patch of woodland and every dip in the terrain. The Stukas would pulverize them, and then we'd overrun them with artillery and panzers and superior numbers, picking up our wounded and dead before advancing. A lot of the soldiers in my Company carried on like it was a soccer match or something...yelling for joy as we continued dashing eastward, ecstatic over savoring the feel of victory after each bloody encounter. Every night when we'd halt, they'd celebrate and sing patriotic Nazi anthems, those aggressive Party-member types. I guess they were not bothering to count up the heaps of bodies we created each day. Or the little clusters of farmhouses we'd pass, the walls blown outward and the roofs collapsed by a well-placed artillery round. Or the bloating carcasses of horses lying by the road. The villages, turned to rubble heaps by the Stukas, bloody arms and legs sticking out of the piles of brick. Anyway, we kept heading east. The officers would find a nice defensible position for us to go into *lager* for the night, and we'd dig in. Next day, more of the same. I tell you, it was so different from Austria or Czechoslovakia! Suddenly, genuinely, we were at *war*! On the third day, word spread that Britain and France had come in on the side of Poland and formally declared war against Germany. There was wild speculation about British airplanes showing up and strafing our columns. But it never happened. Nothing changed."

Hans explained in detail that on the first day of the invasion, his brigade, in columns of trucks interspersed with medium panzers, followed a good highway to the Polish border, then proceeded eastward on secondary roads, or often on foot in the tracks laid down by the swarms of panzers, through the flat, rich farmlands of Upper Silesia. They encountered more resistance like the Polish Ulany ambush he'd just described, and rolled through burned villages and bombed towns. Their route stayed north of the Upper Vistula until the location where the river's course swings northward. Company 'B' effected a crossing of the Vistula eight kilometers south of the Polish town of

Oswiecim, a place that was to become infamous later in the War by its Germanic name: *Auschwitz*.

"Did you ever get wounded, at all?" I asked.

"*Nein*. Polish bullets would whistle past, and a couple times I felt or heard bits of shrapnel bounce off my helmet with a little *ping*. I never got so much as a scratch, until the Company, on our feet for most of the previous two days, was advancing over a Vistula River bridge into the smoking ruins of the Krakow suburbs."

"So that's the day Krakow capitulated, wasn't it? What happened then?"

"I got run over by a halftrack. One of ours!"

Hans just never lost the ability to astound me! "Er…say that again?"

Hans attempted to paint a picture of the event by waving his hands around in the air. "We are strung out left and right, advancing across the walkways on both sides of this narrow bridge at the same time vehicles are streaming one-way over this same bridge, into Krakow, down the middle of the roadway. Ordnance trucks, motorcycles with sidecars, fuel trucks, ambulances, big stretched-out staff cars carrying high-rank officers. Panzers of every size! Troop trucks, covered with mud, tarps shot full of holes…some crammed with troops, some with tarped-down loads of *Gott weiss*. And halftracks, most of them towing a trailer or an artillery piece. Actually, this cavalcade is not so much *streaming* as *creeping*…there's the world's biggest traffic jam up ahead where the bridge feeds into the city streets. Half a dozen motorcycles rumble past me, followed by a beat-up halftrack trailing a field gun. A Sd.Kfz. 10."

"What does *that* mean?" I blurted.

"*Sonderkraftfahrzeug* model 10. 'Special Motorized Vehicle.' Gasoline engine, so I hadn't usually worked on any of them. I'm a *diesel* mechanic! Anyhow, as I said, this one's towing an artillery piece, and the load in its truckbed is all tarped down. Probably rounds for that howitzer. Anyway, I glance away for an instant, out across the beautiful Vistula with the sun sparkling on it, and behind me there's a big crash! Because: convoy's lurching along, convoy stops, motorcycles stop, halftrack *doesn't* stop. *Crash!* So *I* stop! I'm getting all ready to go up ahead there and lend a hand, you know, help sort out the mess and see if anybody's injured, and I've got my feet placed sort of awkwardly as I pivot around, and the *verdammt* halftrack driver puts his machine in reverse, you know, to back away from the piled-up motorcycles and their drivers. And he backs right over my foot, half the length of his track!"

The thought of a segmented, cleated steel tank-tread rolling over *my* foot made me wince. Then I considered that obviously the halftrack couldn't have run over Hans *entirely*, or he'd have surely been killed outright, and here he was in his own dining room, alive and talking, all these years later, and.... Well, you get the idea. "Did it crush your foot pretty bad?" I asked Hans solicitiously.

"Well, *nicht so schlecht* ...the vehicle only weighed about four thousand kilograms, payload included, and I got run over by the *tracks*, which are maybe twenty-five or thirty centimeters wide each, and there's maybe three meters of track on the road surface, so that's about 250 grams per square centimeter pressure under the track. And besides, I was wearing pretty sturdy boots."

I did some very rough approximating, using English units of measure, and got 4000 pounds per square inch! Impossible! Then I did a better job of the mental math, and came up with 3 3/4 pounds per square inch...like maybe a cinderblock or two sitting on your foot...ouch, but not really as bad as one would think. "So it didn't smash all your footbones outright?"

"*Nein*...but I promise you, it *really hurt!* I'm yelling like a bear in a leg-trap, and that *Gott-verdammt* driver slams on the brakes and dismounts! Comes back to see what all the yelling is about! Then, after he sees me with my foot pinned under the middle of his *ficken* halftrack's *ficken* track, he goes again forward and climbs back into the driver's seat, *reverses direction again*, and pulls ahead, continuing to roll track over my foot until at last I pop loose! I fall over backward in the slop-filled roadway gutter and just lie there shrieking in pain, clutching my leg at the knee, until a medic comes along and sticks me with a needle full of morphine. So, a few broken foot bones. I'm evacuated to a field hospital, then jounced about until I'm chopped schnitzel, lying on the floorboards in a truck as they haul my ass back to civilization. Guess where? All the way back to Ostrava! Back over the 150 klicks we'd covered pushing the Poles back to Krakow! Closest place outside of Poland with decent medical care."

"Well at least you didn't get killed!" I observed, like the obedient straight-man I am.

"Not by that halftrack...no. But partway back to the Polish border, that ambulance nearly got shot to smithereens by a strafing Stuka pilot with a hot trigger finger! It was clearly marked with a big black swastika in a red circle on the roof, that ambulance, but the pilot must have been blind or crazy. If he hadn't quickly run out of 7.92mm, he'd have slaughtered us all for certain! Later in the War, Ju-87's were equipped with 20mm, then 30mm, then 37mm wing guns, and any of that heavy stuff would have blown that ambulance to atoms, and me along with it."

"And so, ignominiously wounded again, that was the end of your Invasion of Poland?"

"That was the end."

Both of us popped another Molson and took a big slurp. "Oh. By the way...." I lifted my can to my host. "Happy birthday!"

+ + + + + + + +

At the end of 'Case White,' Germany had suffered more than 16,300 soldiers killed and 30,000 wounded in just 27 days of fighting. Germany lost 285 fighter aircraft to Poland's 333 lost—pretty even—all in the first week of the invasion. This tends to contradict the notion that 'the *Luftwaffe* destroyed the Polish Air Force on the ground in the first hours of conflict.' The invasion of Poland was no cake-walk for the German Army *or* Air Force.

At the end, though, Polish military casualties were four times as many killed as the Germans, five times as many wounded. The number of Poland's civilian dead during the September invasion was nearly beyond reckoning, being by most accounts figured at more than two hundred thousand. During the ensuing five-plus years of German Occupation, Polish civilian deaths would total up to five and a half *million*...ten percent of the entire population of pre-War Poland. More than half of these fatalities would amount to outright murder in the gas chambers of German concentration camps.

12

14 February 1981
BIRTHDAY PARTY

S peaking of Hans's birthday, our lopsided seminar on the doleful events of World War II was interrupted by the telephone. It was for me. Chuck Townshend at the DOT vehicle maintenance 'gradge.' Reminding me of my dinner obligation later in the evening. "Ahh...by the way, Lewis," Chuck prevaricated, "Would you mind if this little get-together has expanded a bit?"

"I suppose not," I agreed with my usual gullible complacency. "What's going on?"

"Er...we thought we ought to invite your travelling companions as well. It's become more of a, well, buffet instead of a sit-down dinner. Or, a party, like. Apt to be a certain amount of drinking."

Travelling companions...that would be the entire marooned planeload. Thirty guests. I had exchanged maybe fifteen words with the guy sitting across the aisle from me. Other than him and maybe the ingénue Flight Attendant, I hadn't spoken so much as a syllable with any of my other fellow fearless flyers. Oh well. "That's very kind of you, Mr. Townshend. If—"

"And a few townsfolk and DOT people."

"Uhhh...well then—"

"And the Raufers, of course. I will leave it to you to bring them along. Tell Hans I insist!"

"Er...the Raufers?"

"Yes...that's one of the little surprises for the evening! It's Hans's birthday, don't you know!"

"Well that's coincidental because just this minute I was wishing him—"

"His sixty-first! He's incredibly shy about parties and social occasions, but my wife baked a big cake and everything. Don't let him weasel out of it! Okay, Lewis?"

"You can count on me," I promised boldly. "What time?"

"We are going to get started early! Four o'clock! No gifts necessary, but have Hans bring a couple of heels if he's got any. See ya!" The phone clicked off in my hand. I imagined Hans would know what a 'heel' would be.

The Townshend home was a nice big place, fortunately for the sixty or seventy people already swarming its highly overheated rooms when we arrived. There was a spacious great room, furniture pushed back to the walls to afford more elbow room. The entire west wall was floor-to-ceiling windows with a generous view of the river estuary across a hundred yards of marshland. The early evening parade of polar bears was already on duty over by the water. At least a dozen of them, assorted sizes, evidently on the *qui vive* for fish carcasses or other morsels of an edible nature, swatting and squabbling among themselves for pre-eminence of place. You could discern the non-Arctic stranded-travelers by the proximity of their noses and their bulging eyeballs to the glass of those big windows, by their avid attention to those bears. The locals had long ago grown jaded on polar bear antics. Interestingly, many of the 'locals' were Inuit, perhaps as many as half.

Anna Raufer, in whose life social doings like this party were not too frequent an occurrence these days, was as fidgety and delighted as a fifteen-year-old debutante at her first cotillion. Earlier, I'd made a strategic decision and, privately, first broached the subject of a party at the Townshend House to Anna. As I had guessed it would, it required a lot of cajoling from both Anna and myself to get Hans on board with it. But he eventually acquiesced. On agreeing to come, he had set down his current Molson unfinished, evidently aware that serious drinking would be expected of him later on. When party time approached, he'd actually dressed in pretty decent clothes for a social affair, up to and including a necktie. When we'd arrived at the Townshend's, Hans wore the only necktie in the room. He quickly shed his neckwear and stuffed it in a pocket. After that, he was all smiles and affability upon entering the mob scene of a revelry already transitioning into full swing. He had not yet perceived that he was to be honored in the matter of his birthday; the decorations, somewhat understated in the Canadian fashion, were more slanted toward honoring Saint Valentine and sweethearts the world over. No birthday cake was in evidence, nor tableful of congratulatory cards, nor brightly wrapped gifts with big puffy bows. As we entered, Hans surrendered a grocery bag clinking with liquor bottles to the possession of our hostess when she greeted us at the door.

I lost contact with the Raufers as I was swirled into the mob of guests. Scores of introductions were made, but almost all of the names spun away from me without sticking very well. A pink-faced young woman thrust a can of Molson into my hand, then latched herself firmly onto my free arm. *Guess who?* Mary Lou, my DOT driver from last night! In brighter light and in party attire, she appeared as if she couldn't have been more than nineteen or so. She seemed delighted at our reunion, prepared to make instant, intimate friends with me. A few minutes later, another pair of youthful Churchillian damsels squealed from across the room at their friend Mary Lou's successful acquisition and, threading their way through the mob, boogied and wiggled up to the two of us. Both new girls found free space on my person and latched on as well. We all engaged in free-form acquaintancing, joked and flirted, yakked at high speed about inconsequentialities, slurped drinks and accepted refills. After half an hour of this, with substantial elbow-bending consumption of Molson and other intoxicants in spite of a lot of resolute arm clinging by my feminine hangers-on, I was beginning to feel like a solitary bull elk must feel when a determined pack of hungry timberwolves grasp onto his extremities. These three young sweeties were almost certainly aware that they had in their clutches a young, single, available, well off, professional Bostonian. Each of them, individually and in her own youthful heart, no doubt felt trapped in the isolated, polar-bear-infested small town icebox that was Churchill, Manitoba, and was clinging tenaciously to my arm, full of desperate hope, waiting for me to indicate my choice with the merest crook of my finger. I began to hallucinate that there might be *more* such ladies waiting to glom onto my as yet unclaimed appendages as the evening progressed, many more, swarms of them…five or six more, or a dozen, or scores…engulfing me, suffocating me, rendering me unable to move, my lips unable to reach the blissful consolation of my Molson….

"Excuse me, girls," a welcome, liberating voice said. "Lewis, could you get me a glass of heel punch?" It was Anna. She'd evidently seen my peril and had taken it upon herself to come to my rescue.

I freed myself, naturally with courteous and profuse apologies to the girls, and made off toward the refreshment tables in the direction Anna had pointed. Centrally placed, there was a huge punchbowl full of brownish, foamy liquid with small blocks of ice floating in it. An extremely miscellaneous array of empty liquor bottles festooned the rest of the table surface—easily sixty or eighty booze bottles. Ah! Heel punch! Evidently in Spoken Canadian, a 'heel' was the contents of a bottle of liquor reduced to a small residual amount, hardly worth mixing into drinks, stored disconsolately in a liquor cabinet somewhere. Get a crowd of people to scrounge up their heels and then congregate, pour a lot of these all together in a big bowl, stir well, add ice, and *voila*! Heel punch! Different every time, often vile in flavor but sometimes not so much, always satisfactorily intoxicating. I ladled Anna a glassful in a clear plastic cup and made my way back to where I'd left her. She thanked me, accepted the proffered glass, took a suspicious sniff, wrinkled her short, turned-up Inuit nose. She slipped her arm through my elbow and steered me toward a row of folding chairs, and we sat. Anna set her heel punch on a small chairside table and never went near it again. "You have to be careful in town here, Lewis! There are a lot of single girls. They are all desperate and hungry! They are the wolves, you are the prey!" Uh-huh...exactly the mental image I'd been conjuring.

"So..." I began. "Me and Hans have been babbling away nonstop, two days now, and you and I haven't had a chance to talk at all, Anna! I don't even know if you are a lifelong Churchillian, or from someplace else!"

"Churchill...oh goodness no!" Anna laughed. "I'm from Qamanti'tuaq, way north of here!"

"Qua... Qua...." I tried.

"I say it slow for you. 'Ka-mahn-TEE-too-ack' ...means, 'Place-where-the-river-gets-wide.' When they come there in the 1800's, white explorers decide to name it 'Baker Lake', but it's not so much a lake as a big, long, wide stretch of the Thelon River."

"I don't think I've ever heard of it," I admitted.

"Yah, only a little hamlet! But, very noteworthy, my village! Absolutely the only Inuit community in the whole Canadian Arctic that is NOT on the ocean! Baker Lake is, oh, three hundred kilometers inland from Hudson Bay."

"I'm quite intrigued with Inuktitut, Anna. Do you think a *qalluna'aq* like me could learn the language?"

Anna's tolerant, regretful smile was answer enough. "*Qalluna'aq* is a lot of you...*qallunaq* is just one of you," she explained.

"Ah, I get it...the extra syllable on the end makes a word plural."

"Yah, sometimes. But sometimes no...there's other ways of making a plural. And, there's a bunch of dialects.

Never mind…too complicated. Lots of Inuktitut words are really a whole bunch of words strung together, like my real name."

"Yeah! Like German words, or…! Oh, sorry…you were saying, your *real* name?"

"Yah. My Inuit name. You ready? It's 'Tiriaq Utkuhiksalingmiut'"

"Wow!"

"Okay, no laughing! 'Tiriaq' means ermine…lots of traditional Inuit first-names are from nature. It turns out, Ermine is my Spirit Guide…the wild creature that watches out for me and gives me advice, all those old traditional beliefs. *Tiriaq*, like my name. Then the family—or clan—name is a mouthful, you bet! It means, "The people who have soapstone cooking-pots." I say it nice and slow: "Oot-koo-heek-SALL-eeng-mee-oot."

The nice tidy syllables notwithstanding, it sounded to me like Anna had pronounced some of them with odd combinations of her lips and tongue accomplishing clacking, trills and growls, or from her glottis, or her uvula, or from other weird far-back corners of her mouth, or with the participation of various sinus cavities and nasal passages. In fact, even such a simple syllable as her take on the English word 'yes', which she pronounced 'yah', not surprisingly like the German word '*ja*,' she spoke with what linguists call a *retroflex*, an *indrawn* utterance instead of breathed-out. Go ahead, try it! Years later, I heard the exact same pronunciation by indigenous speakers of the *Hawaiian* language! "I'll never master that name unless you write it down for me, Anna!" I confessed.

"Yah, okay! I'll do it later." she agreed. "And, in case you cannot handle traditional Inuit names, when I was born, the Canadian government gave me another one: it's 'E3-909'"

"What? Numbers instead of a name?"

74

"Well it's called a Disc Number. They started giving them out in about 1900 I guess. The Canadian government officials couldn't write down Inuit names properly, and when they tried, later on other officials couldn't read them or pronounce them right, not so any Inuit could understand. And so they couldn't connect with the Inuits whose names they'd written down. There was no written form of Inuktitut, and anyway, there probably wasn't a single Inuit who had any comprehension of writing, to give them any advice. So the Canadians just gave up on it and made up these brass discs with a letter, E, S, W or N, for what part of the northwest territories a particular Inuit lived in, then a number or two for what settlement they lived in, which didn't work too well because more than half the Inuit in those days were completely nomadic, then three or four numbers for a particular person. I'm E3-909…Eastern Keewatin, village 3—that's Baker Lake—person 909. You had to keep your disc with you all the time, so most Inuit just wore them as a necklace." With this, Anna groped around inside the collar of her blouse and fetched-up a bright brass disc pendent on a fine chain through a ring inserted in a tiny hole in one edge. The symbols were almost faded and rubbed-out with the passage of years. Anna had been given her disc upon her birth, in 1923.

"Like a military dog-tag!" I exclaimed. Only, shaped like a *dog* dog-tag, my sensibilities a bit offended. "Didn't you resent it?"

Anna laughed. "Goodness no! We thought that was the type of name *all* white Canadians had! We were proud to be given Canadian names of our own! We didn't know anything about numbers, back when I was born! You look at some of those soapstones in your bedroom…on the bottom, the artists signed their works with their disc-numbers! I was baptized 'Anna', a nice Canadian name like most Inuit after about 1918 when a lot of Canadians

75

came back from the Big War in France. But in the family they called me Tiriaq when I was little. When I finally got out of Baker Lake, age fifteen, and was sent to Ottawa for high school and then nursing college, I used my disc-number for a couple years before I got on my high-horse of Inuit Pride and went back to using Utkuhiksalingmiut! Takes five times as long to write! I used to write it in Inuktitut letters just so no one could read it…not even my relatives back home in Qamunti'tuaq!" Amused beyond measure, Anna gave in to a fit of giggles.

Our conversation was interrupted by a pair of Inuit women dashing up to Anna, squealing with delight and anticipation. The two of them engaged in a high speed conversation with Anna, all in Inuktitut. It sounded like a threesome of insane tropical birds, macaws perhaps, having a high-pitched argument in some psittacine take on human speech. From facial cues, it appeared the two newcomers were trying to convince Anna of something and were having a tough go of it. Finally it appeared that Anna had caved. She turned to me. "I've got to go do *katajjaq*," Anna groaned.

"What's *katajjaq*?"

"You'll see!"

The great room crowd split and pulled back toward the walls, leaving a wide stretch of mid-room floor. People jammed in from the other rooms, stood in doorways, or took spectator position on the stairs leading down from the second-floor bedrooms. Smoke and masculine laughter emanating from Chuck's den indicated that there was a subset of menfolk back there, uninterested in *katajjaq*, busily enjoying stinky hand-rolled cigarettes or vile Canadian rum-dipped panatelas, probably playing poker and drinking something tastier than heel punch. Out on the floor, one of the women who had hijacked Anna from our *tête-à-tête*, a cute, short, slim, long-haired little thing with carved ivory earrings and crimson-tinted lips, introduced Anna to the assemblage. Anna seemed perfectly composed, but was blushing furiously with the embarrassment of the spotlight. The woman emcee called out another name, and a youngish Inuit woman, perhaps in her late twenties, slipped out of the crowd and into the circle. The emcee hustled off the floor in my direction and came to a stop at my left side. The room fell hushed.

Anna Raufer Ook-too-whatever and the new girl approached each other face to face. It looked as if we were in for an *a capella* duet, perhaps a traditional Inuktitut folk ballad. The two women grasped each other's arms just above the elbow. Their faces were very close together. Abruptly, Anna began and the other woman instantly followed.

It was not singing, exactly. Anna uttered a very short, abrupt syllable, tonal but not exactly musical, and the other woman echoed a contrasting syllable snappily, in a similar tone. Anna repeated, very rapidly, and so did the other woman, and again, and again…like an antiphonal monosyllabic chant. Both women swayed slightly, in rhythm to the chant, eyes locked on each other, trancelike, hands gripping arms. It was the most uncanny, eerie thing I have ever heard, unlike any tonal sequence I've ever imagined hearing from the mouths of earthly humans. The alternating pace accelerated to frenetic levels, each woman uttering her syllable then gasping a short breath. The tempo sped, then slowed, then sped again. The tone or phrase each woman chanted became altered in subtle, unpredictable ways. Their pitches climbed and fell.

"*What is this?*" I whispered to the woman next to me, the one who had done the introductions.

"*Katajjaq!* It's a contest the women do. It's very ancient! Just watch!" The adorable young emcee-lady involuntarily clutched my arm in her excitement.

The chant went on and on. Suddenly, the younger woman broke off, pulled away from Anna and collapsed in a fit of giggles, gasping for breath.

"You see? Anna wins!" whispered the little woman clinging to my left arm. The spectators clapped and cheered. The woman next to me let go of my arm, then stepped out and gave Anna a congratulatory hug. Then she called out another name and another Inuit woman came forward to give a round of *katajjaq* a try. This contestant lasted all of ten seconds.

In the next twenty minutes, Anna Raufer, *nee* Tiriaq E3-909, vanquished all comers: seven more Inuit women, interspersed with three blonde, blue-eyed non-Inuit Canadian women (including the innocent young CanadaNational flight attendant we'd flown in with). Also, a forty-five year old woman from Alabama, a fellow stranded passenger who, like myself, had never before heard of *katajjaq* but was intensely keen to give it a try. And one very drunk male French-Canadian diesel mechanic who also had obviously never done *katajjaq* before, except possibly in the shower. Not an entirely gracious loser. Contest over, Anna Raufer unanimously triumphant! The crowd went wild with accolades. This was not a surprising outcome, the cutie emcee merrily confided in me, once again clinging to my arm and bouncing on her tiptoes with vicarious victory. Anna, Miss Emcee explained, had begun learning *katajjaq* at a very tender age from an elderly Baker Lake crone, herself in past years a renowned champion of the sport. Anna had practiced diligently for at least eight years, and had become practically unbeatable in Baker Lake and the outlying circle of settlements and villages. My diminutive *katajjaq* mentor hugging my arm punctuated her enthusiasm with a nice little celebratory peck on my cheek while the crowd hooted and cheered for Anna. Not satisfied with the peck, my arm-clinger wrenched my chin around and fastened her

78

plump, shapely, crimson mouth on mine for a much more comprehensive and lengthy kiss with a little surreptitious tongue in it, tasting of heel punch. I cannot say I minded too much.

Events following become gradually less distinct in my recollection as the evening wore on. Some frenzied dancing was partaken of. And a general team exercise, men versus women, involving competitive drinking. The men won, hands down…to our masculine detriment in view of the ratcheting up of our intoxication factor. More dancing to slow, teary country-western slowdances with the lights turned low. I seem to recall a sequence of partners, but I'm pretty sure Miss Cutie Emcee cropped up frequently on my dance card. Then a hilarious bout of karaoke duos and doo-wop groups, for the latter of which someone had provided an anthology cassette of Diana Ross favorites, along with a trio of outrageous Supremes wigs and sequined bras. A bit later, a small fistfight between an RCMP corporal and a minor city official (from the Sanitation Department I seem to recall). No big thing, easily defused. Whatever the issue, it was forgotten with the erstwhile combatants raising large mugs of heel punch and orating profound apologies and heartfelt protestations to the renewal of life-long amity. A little more cheek-to-cheek snuggly close-dancing with some kissing involved— pretty certain it was Miss Cutie Emcee again. Then, a while later, I somehow found myself in the den with the guys. A long, intense, inebriated conversation with Chuck "Red Chief" Townshend about horrible examples of frost-heaved structure foundations each of us had known and coped with, along with our respective experiences with a particular natural frost-heave phenomenon exclusive to the Arctic called a 'pingo', a virtual mountain of soil and ice often rising three or four hundred feet above the general level of the tundra, a phenomenon of permafrost run seriously amok. Our little two-person symposium was interrupted by a call for toasts. Someone had produced a large bottle of very nice Islay scotch, tasting of telephone poles and railroad ties as all your finer Inner Hebrides scotches do. (But, as a descendant of many fine, bold Scots myself, I assure you: the predominant flavor *is* creosote-like, but not in a *bad* way! It comes from peaty water, not discarded railroad ties wrought into whiskey barrels.) And it seemed the only way to assure this scotch's immediate consumption was toasts. We raised bumper glasses…

To the *Townshends* for sacrificing their home to this memorable party!
To Hans Raufer on his sixty-first birthday!
To Anna Raufer, Queen of *Katajjaq*!
To Queen Elizabeth, God save the Queen!
To the forlorn passengers of CanadaNational!
To Lewis Macleod, present herewith, and thus most forlorn passenger of them all!
To the Canada Department of Transportation!
To Polar Bears, God love and prosper them!
To the Children of Churchill, God save them from polar bears!

Following the toasts running a little thin, a round of cigars. Up until that very moment I had resolutely been a lifelong non-smoker, a resolution I have also maintained all the *rest* of my days since that notable evening. But in that convivial, smoke-polluted den, I found myself with one of those panatelas everyone else was smoking clenched in my jaw, pensively chewing its mouthpiece while someone—Hans, I think—solicitously ignited the thing's business-end. I remember inhaling. I remember coughing like a terminal tuberculosis patient, and then snuffing out the rest of my little cigar in a half-full glass of that very nice Islay scotch. I remember that act not being regarded by my cronies as a problem so much as a sin, there being plenty more scotch in

80

the bottle, and still more in a *second* bottle that had been sequestered in case needed for continued drinking. I think I remember some peppermint schnapps passing my lips. And something *really* strong, yet delicious, that might well have been *slivovice*. There are vague scenes of a cake-cutting ceremony out in the great room, with maudlin speechifying. Then, a large glass of something horrible which could only have been the remnants of the heel punch, as I distinctly remember Hans informing me that entirely polishing off this celebratory tipple was the indispensible culminating climax of any such evening, unless the party had gone uncontrollable and someone had dumped the rest of the heel punch over the hostess's head, or thrown the bowl and its remnant contents through a picture window. I distinctly remember being well and truly kissed good-night at the door by a small, bubbly Inuit cutie who could have only been that *katajjaq* emcee, lots of gentle, risque hand-caressing and curvy body contact involved, and a name that sounded like Quilliq or Miquiliq or Kome-hiir-quik insinuated into my ear along with a warm wet tongue tip. Also a whispered phone number not a single digit of which I could remember, even so little as ten minutes later. I remember thinking *no worries, Anna will know*. I distinctly remember a little visual vignette: glancing over the neat round raven-haired top of Miss Quilliq's or Miss Milliquik's or Miss Suchlike's head and spotting Mary Lou and her two girlfriends already huddled into their parkas, the three of them resolutely arm-in-arm, glaring daggers at me and my pocket sized, bug cute Inuit lady friend. Then, next thing I know, I was out in the ice-cold night air. I seem to recall Hans and me helping each other toward the Mercedes by the simple expedient of leaning our respective drunken torsos against each other at the shoulder, and then helping each other up off the snowy, muddy ground when the leaning failed to work and we had fallen down in the slush, both of us incapacitated by laughter, the starry Universe spinning out of control over our heads, painted with flickering aurorae. I remember leaning against a car door, and taking in brief snippets of a tense, *sotto voce* argument between Hans and Anna about exactly who was going to drive the Mercedes home, punctuated by Anna's observation that her husband was too drunk to so much as find the keyhole with the car key, and Hans's observation in riposte that, for all her exemplary skill as an OR nurse and *katajjaq* champion, Anna had never so much as driven a *dogsled*, not to mention a valuable, complex, and temperamental vehicle such as their highly prized *Mercedes*. Hans wound up driving us back to the DOT Hilton, very painstakingly at 15 mph, under Anna's constant, meticulous scrutiny, lest he inadvertently drive into the river and drown us all, or get himself arrested for operating a motor vehicle while drunk. But everything came out all right since the entire Churchill contingent of the Royal Canadian Mounted Police had been in attendance at the Townshend's little *soirée*, and had departed the premises no less inebriated than Hans and Yrs Trly.

On the following morning, Monday 15 February, 1981, I woke up, much refreshed and only a trifle hung over, in the Raufer guest facility, snuggled under a snuggly *qiviut* counterpane. All's well that ends well, don't they say?

When I wandered out to breakfast in a borrowed bathrobe, Anna handed me a mirror-shiny frying pan from off a hook above her stove. "I think the bathroom is free, Lewis," she whispered. "You ought to go wash."

I regarded my image in the frying pan. Generous, overlapping kiss prints in bright crimson lipstick, all over my face!

82

13

22 June 1941
BARBAROSSA

Hans joined us at the breakfast table, wandering out in a great fluffy bathrobe like a brown bearskin. Anna issued him two liters of coffee in an Oktoberfest beer stein. Surprisingly, Hans seemed unaffected by the previous night's revelry.

"Nice party," he opined.

I agreed. "Very nice. Lots of nice people here in Churchill."

Hans quaffed coffee. Anna patted my hand. "I give you her phone number," she assured me in a confidential whisper.

"Oh...you mean, Quilliq?"

"Qilqiq Sidney. Her Canadian baptism name is Sally."

I'm sure I blushed crimson. Like Qilqiq's lipstick. "Kill-quick...?" I tried tentatively.

"*Qilqiq!*" she said carefully, like she was swallowing the consonants, or maybe gargling them. "*KEEL-kick!*" Anna pronounced more precisely in response to my goofy, puzzled face. "It means, 'fuzzy ptarmigan chick.'

"Uhh...does it have a couple of 'Q's?" I asked.

"*Three* 'Q's! Start, end and middle! Inuktitut, every time you hear a 'K' sound, it's a 'Q'. Well...*almost* every time. Well, *some of* the time. Not enough letters in the English alphabet. Never mind, I write it for you. Better: you call her 'Sally'"

Hans elbowed me in the ribs. "*Und so dann!* Our boy Lewis makes kiss-kiss friends with nice Inuit girl! Hah! Hah-hah!"

We all three munched on a hearty north Canadian breakfast in companionable silence. Anna finished her modest plateful first, and shuffled off to tidy her kitchen. Hans vanished to the Raufer bedroom to dress for the day. I swallowed the rest of my coffee and scuffed back to the guest-bedroom/art-gallery to do the same.

When I returned to the dining alcove, Hans was shrugging himself into a massive parka. He held out a second parka for me, obviously one of his own, twelve sizes too large for my scrawny frame. "It's pretty sunny outside. But cold...ten below, I think. Let's go watch the bears."

"Okay." I struggled into the down-filled coat. "'Bye, Anna," I said. She gave me a conspiratorial smile as she slipped me a scrap of paper with a local exchange number on it, then shooed us both begone.

Hans fired up the Mercedes and drove us out around the south end of town. The recently plowed road curved back northward toward Hudson Bay, out between a maze of frozen lakes and bogs. The perpetual winds had scrubbed much of the bedrock ground surface between the lakes clear of its thin scrim of snow. One could see the deeply ice-scored Laurentian rocks which make up the lion's share of the North American Arctic terrain, thinly layered with peaty soil and deep, lush lichen in the low places. The outcrops were of ancient, flat metamorphic baserock scoured clean of its soil, its forests, its entire Cenozoic fauna, its river valleys and mountain ranges. The agent of that scouring was millions of years of continental glaciers, two or three miles thick, irresistible movers of earth, only departed from this northern land quite recently...if one were speaking in geologic time.

Hans directed my attention out the left-hand windows to a metal-grey twin engine cargo aircraft parked on the bedrock where neither road nor runway ran. "Miss

84

Piggy," he informed me, indicating the stranded airplane with a jut of his chin.

"Like the muppet?"

"Well…no—like the big fat-belly airplane. Also, they say, it actually transported pigs for a while. It crashed here about two years ago."

"What happened?"

Hans glanced at me nervously. Considering my recent circumstances, maybe there were details to the story I'd rather not hear. "Took off from Churchill International. The…uh…the starboard engine quit, just a short while after takeoff. A hundred klicks out over the Bay. They turned around and tried to make it back to the airport, just over there about a kilometer. They didn't quite get there. As you can see."

Starboard engine, huh? "What happened to the engine?"

"Some tiny little component failed. Engine lost oil pressure, quit running."

Sounds eerily familiar. "Anyone hurt?"

"Only three people on board. No one killed. Plane's belly kind of ripped on impact. Aft loading ramp flopped open. Cargo pallets broke loose and contents spread far and wide. Pilot and copilot injured pretty bad. Well though, what the *Miss Piggy* was carrying, was crates and crates of pop bound for Chesterfield Inlet up the coast. Splattered pop and broken bottle glass all over the tundra! Polar bears came and lapped it up for weeks!"

"Soda pop in glass bottles? Not half liter cans?"

"Bottles. It's only beer has to be in cans. Don't ask why…it is a Canada thing."

We continued up the rocky coastline to a place where the flat terrain extended out a ways into the iced-over surface of Hudson Bay. In warmer months, a picnic ground. There was a cluster of stout timber picnic tables and stone firepits with heavy iron grills, dusted with snow and looking forlorn, waiting for summer picnickers to arrive. Recently, slovenly idlers had dumped plastic sacks of household garbage here, and a half dozen polar bears were meticulously examining the pickings. Hans parked, and the two of us walked over and sat ourselves on a tabletop, once we had brushed it free of its dusting of snow. We propped our feet on the ocean-side bench. The bears took no particular notice of us, either in our capacity as nosey spectators or as possible bear breakfast. Pack ice crunched and ground against the gravelly shoreline.

Hans groped in a parka pocket and produced a half-full bottle of kirshwasser in case either of us was still thirsty after the revelry the night before. It was damned cold, but the down parka served pretty well. I found the cold, austere beauty too compelling to let the icy air bother me.

Hans was more uneasy than I'd yet seen him. "So..." he said finally. "So...you want to hear more of my war stories, eh Lewis?"

"Very much."

"*Ach*...I don't like Anna to hear about this part that comes next. I am...I am even more sickened of this part than of all I saw and participated in, with my invasion of Poland...and also of all that came along later. You were a soldier too once, I think. *Ja*, Lewis?"

"Three years. 101st Airborne. I-Corps. Viet Nam combat tour in 1970-1971."

"Pretty rough?"

I made a deprecating so-so gesture.

"Firebase Ripcord?"

How did he know *that* place-name? I flashed back to the siege: July 1970. Me a Pfc rifleman, nineteen years old. Twenty-three days of nonstop attack by hordes of North Vietnamese Army regulars. Pinpoint mortar fire, 122mm rockets, and constant nighttime assaults on the perimeter. No sleep, no rest for three weeks. Seventy-five

86

American KIA. Outnumbered ten to one by NVA. At the end, a mad scramble to evacuate in Chinooks and Huey Gunships. Then the whole ridgetop and whole damned valley was carpet bombed by B-52's after we got the hell out...killed NVA by the hundreds, and we told ourselves that this was *victory*. Last major FUBAR of the Viet Nam War, at least as far as we American troops were involved. A toplevel FUBAR still awaited South Viet Nam's armed forces...and all of its civilians. April 29, 1975—the Fall of Saigon. Everything we and the South Vietnamese fought and sacrificed for since 1960 or so, come to naught on a single hot springtime morning. But I didn't tell Hans any of this. "I was there," I told him simply.

Something was decided as if with the closing of a circuit breaker in Hans's brain. He deliberated only a moment longer. "Let me tell you about Operation Barbarossa, then," he said, with uncharacteristic gravitas.

"You recall I was injured on the sixth day of our Poland invasion? Back then, we had to remember to call it our 'annexation' of Poland if we didn't want a good flogging and a reduction in pay. Recall I got my foot run over by one of our own halftracks? Well, they hauled me back to Ostrova, in Czechoslovakia. I was put in a pretty good orthopedic ward, along with a hundred or so guys whose legs or arms had had to be amputated. The surgeons were so skilled at amputation that they thought they'd just whack off my foot and give me a wooden one—problem solved! My protests carried no weight with the medicos. Sanity prevailed, however, and the X-rays showed just some cracks and a few simple fractures. So they strapped me to a bed and yanked joints and bones around so as to cause me maximum eye-popping pain. Then they put the whole foot in a cast up to my knee. They made the cast nice and heavy so I wouldn't be able to move the leg very much.

"After that, seven or eight weeks of lying on my backside in bed. Which, when you cannot move or itch your *verdammt* foot is not nearly so relaxing as you might imagine. Eventually, they chiseled off that cast. They took some more X-rays and pronounced me on the mend. Three more weeks in a lightweight walking cast. I got to stroll around the grounds. I got to walk down a long corridor to the mess hall for meals. Of course, the lightweight cast allowed me to stand at a washbasin in the lavatory and wash myself with soap and a cloth. This put an end to the most pleasant part of that hospital stay: long, slow, thorough sponge baths every morning by a very attractive seventeen-year-old blonde Czech nurse named Eva.

"Eventually they pronounced me completely fit. Once again, I was shipped back to my outfit. While I'd been mending, Company 'B' had fought their way eastward across Polish Galicia toward Lublin. Eventually our boys—not to mention, the rest of the 84th Regiment and a whole lot of panzers—had taken Lublin. Afterwards, Company 'B'—not to mention the rest of the 2nd Battalion—was left to invest this important city. This was about the time the Russians jumped in, and seeing as nearly all the remaining Polish forces had withdrawn into tight little pockets around strategic cities that we Germans had surrounded and were in the process of crushing like robin's eggs in a fist, the Russians had very little opposition advancing to their prearranged boundaries of occupation. All those details had been secretly agreed upon between Ribbentrop and Molotov, back toward the end of August. Less than a week later, Warsaw surrendered. So you see, Company 'B' had been snugly bedded down in Lublin for about two months when I was ordered back into Poland to join up with them.

"Surprise! In September, several of my old comrades from the diesel engine servicing squad in Ostrava heard that my battalion was serving garrison duty near where they were setting up a panzer maintenance facility, in the East Polish city of Zamosc. Inquiries were made, strings were pulled, and I was once again detached from Company 'B' to temporarily take up duties as a diesel mechanic! I got to stay in decent quarters in Zamosc, working on tanks and trucks and the occasional halftrack, most of them diesel driven, some of them gasoline. Whenever a Sd.Kfz. 10 came through, I'd privately climb down into the greasepit, tell the grease monkey to go get himself a mug of tea, and scratch '*grosses Stück Scheisse*' on the undercarriage."

"Big Piece of Shit? Did it make your foot feel better?"

"*Ja-WOHL*! *Viel besser*! Anyway, we all knew what was going on. Just like before Poland, we were getting our transport and armor in shape for another big push!"

"Russia?" I asked. Rhetorically.

"Russia! But, it didn't happen for more than a year."

+ + + + + + + +

The reasons for the delay in the *Wehrmacht's* bold conquest of Mother Russia were many and intermeshed. First was the fact that anyone who had ever heard of Napoleon Bonaparte was intimately familiar with what a *frosty bitch* Mother Russia can be in the wintertime, without even the participation of the country's military forces. It was the end of September 1939 before the Germans got Poland sorted out...winter right around the corner. And remember, a large contingent of Russian armed forces had clumped into the eastern parts of Poland. These Russkies were pretty much unscathed and enthusiastically belligerent after advancing against fading or nonexistent Polish opposition, and would have had to be overcome first thing when the Germans tried to jump Russia. The Russkie troops occupying Poland had Russian tanks and Russian artillery and Russain fighter aircraft…pretty much full kit. In addition to worries about the Russian neighbors on the eastern side of the River Bug, once the winter of 1939-1940 was over and done with, there were serious events underway in *western* Europe…events that demanded a lot of German attention and resources.

After the defeat of Poland, the French Army and British Expeditionary forces in continental Europe, recalling how events had proceeded a scant twenty-two years past on the Western Front, were not keen on getting into it again with the Germans. The two sides began maneuvering, growling at each other, perhaps a little shadowboxing and sparring…but not what you could call *combat*. This went on from the fall of 1939 through the spring of 1940. The world's press derisively called this stretch of time 'The Phony War', or '*Sitzkrieg.*' But all that changed in May, 1940.

The Germans initiated *Fall Gelb,* 'Case Yellow.' An advance into the Netherlands, Luxembourg, and Belgium. From 10 May to 28 May the *Wehrmacht* and the *Luftwaffe* trounced the Belgians, along with such elements of the British Army as weren't occupied with advancing smartly to their rear. The Low Countries capitulated. Between 27 May and 4 June 1940, Britain executed Operation Dynamo. The gist of this optimistically named operation was to abandon British heavy armaments and British armor, retreat posthaste to Dunkirk, and absquatulate as thoroughly as possible in whatever boats could chug, sail or be rowed back westward across the North Sea carrying evacuated troops from Dunkirk back to England. Amazingly, our old acquaintance Field Marshall von Runstedt halted the German blitzkrieg for a few days.

This breather permitted 350,000 British and French soldiers to live to fight another day.

In June the Germans executed *Fall Rot*, 'Case Red.' During the 1920's and 1930's, the French had constructed a massive wall of 'impenetrable' fortifications: the Maginot Line. Its purpose was to guard against the Germans repeating their 1914 advance into France and the Low Countries, an advance which had resulted in the butcherous meatgrinder of the Western Front. *Fall Rot*'s cunning method of penetrating the Maginot Line was threefold. First, armored columns came busting into France out of the Low Countries, going around the north end of the Line, construction of which had not been continued northwestward along the French border with Belgium for fear of offending the jingoistic Belgians. Second, German armor and infantry speared through the Ardennes Forest, which had been declared 'impenetrable' by highly placed French officials and therefore had not been heavily fortified with Maginot Line emplacements. And third, *Luftwaffe* aircraft simply winged their way high over the Maginot Line, which had not been equipped with much in the way of antiaircraft guns. France fell in less time than Poland had.

Okay, now it was England's turn. Hitler was out to humiliate every opponent that had clobbered Germany in the Great War. It cannot have been Germany's aim to gain *lebensraum* from France, the Low Countries, or Britain...these countries were pretty densely populated in their own right, and *not* with Slavs and *Untermenschen*, like Poland and Russia. It cannot have been that Hitler's heart ached to repatriate good German expatriates, isolated, abused and oppressed in these western European nations, such as had been his rationale regarding Austria and the Sudetenland, because there weren't many such. It came down to retribution, plunder, dominion and naked conquest.

The Nazi strategy was to utilize the *Luftwaffe* to bomb Britain into such submission that they could be persuaded to timidly negotiate a peace settlement with the Reich. Such a treaty would free Hitler to go ahead and invade Russia, undoubtedly his master aim all along.

In the event the British proved too stiff-backed to capitulate in the face of Blitz from the air, there was a plan for seaborne invasion. *Unternehmen Seelöwe,* 'Operation Sea Lion.' This adventure had tentatively been scheduled for September 1940. Hitler would throw a hundred and fifty divisions across the Channel and conquer England like the Normans had, a millennium earlier. A vanquished England would be plundered for her riches. It is rumored that the Monarchy of Edward VIII was to have been restored, on the hypothesis that the abdicated monarch and his American wife Wallis, in 1939 the Duke and Duchess of Windsor, were friendly to the Reich—which was not particularly true. The planning documents further stated that all British males from 17 to 45 years of age—one-quarter of the population—would be deported to the Continent, earmarked for slave labor. In the planning documents, Operation Sea Lion had already named command staff for *Einsatzgruppen* ('task forces'), whose duty would be the liquidation of some 300,000 British Jews. Fortunately, this insane plan depended on establishing complete German air and naval superiority. Well, the British Navy continued to "rule the waves," at least in the vicinity of her island nation's shores, and was not likely to be soon dissuaded in that status. As for the skies, the Battle of Britain, bitter airborne combat lasting from 10 July to 31 October 1940, failed to go Germany's way, preventing the *Luftwaffe* from accomplishing its air superiority goals. Not to mention, costing the *Luftwaffe* a lot of its best pilots and aircraft which might have come in handy for invading Russia.

And there was yet another piece of business preventing Germany from getting things on quite so soon with her archenemy Russia. Starting in June 1940, Hitler's war machine commenced activities in North Africa with the objective of sweeping eastward through British-occupied Egypt and up the Middle East into the oil-rich regions of the Caucasus and the Caspian Sea. Several things were to be gained. Petroleum was high on the list. Seizing a preliminary foothold in the underbelly of Russia was another thing. But again, it didn't go as well as hoped...resolute, effective opposition from those pesky British again. So, commencing in February 1941, the German High Command initiated *Unternehmen Sonnenblume*, 'Operation Sunflower...the creation of an entirely-new Army Group designated '*Afrikakorps.*' This was intended to be a "blocking force" whose purpose as an expeditionary power was to defend the western half of North Africa against seizure by the advancing British. The *Afrikakorps* was to be garrisoned in Tripoli, Libya. An energetic, aggressive young general officer by the name of Erwin Rommel was placed in command. He arrived in Tripoli on 12 February, 1941. *Afrikakorps* contingents began arriving in Tripoli on Valentine's day, 14 February, 1941. Coincidentally, this date was Hans Raufer's twenty-first birthday, which was celebrated for him in Poland with a lot of the Polish version of *slivovitz*, a dozen of Hans's *Wehrmacht* mates in attendance.

So it can be seen from all this furious military activity why the forces of the Third Reich did not leap to take on the Russians in 1939. Add to that, the pervasive fear of a two-front war, like the hellish logistics of the Great War two decades earlier. The result was that Hans Raufer enjoyed a respite of almost two years' duration, getting comfortable in one place, messing about with the repair and outfitting of diesel engines, refining his tradecraft in a well-equipped maintenance shop in Zamosc. During this leisurely time, Hans was promoted to *Unteroffizier*, a rank roughly equivalent to 'corporal' in armies of other nations.

+ + + + + + + +

"Why do you suppose you didn't get reassigned to France? Or North Africa?" I questioned.

Hans waved airily. "A few units did. But it was obvious that sooner or later we were going for Moscow. All the time I was in Zamosc, there was a slow, gradual buildup going on. Over the winter of 1940-41, they started shifting whole divisions from Western Europe into Poland. We'd gone at France with 140 Divisions! I don't know what the count was in Divisions, but I think they wound up throwing nearly *four million* of us German troops at the Russians! There was no more ground war going on in the West, and Hitler had abandoned his plans for invading England—*Gott sei Dank*, because it would have been a gigantic fiasco that saw us all slaughtered like lambs on market day. And I could *count* the heavy panzers, brand-new, right off the traincars, that came through our shop alone, every day. Lots of them! A buildup, for sure."

"Operation Barbarossa, 22 June, 1941."

"*So!* You know your history, Lewis. Then, you know how it went. I was only on loan to the maintenance shop, and at the start of June, they began setting up to move with the advance: field maintenance groups and mobile repair-and-retrieval squads. So, like before Poland, I was ordered back to Company 'B' to make ready for action."

"Where was your Company at this time?"

"Out in the sticks. Jammed up into this big point of the General Government Area that poked eastward into the Russian zone of occupation. You could see that someone was going to have to lurch out of this beak to take Lvov

94

first thing. From there, the obvious objective was Kiev. Which was a *ficken* big city! People were going to get *hurt* trying to take Kiev!"

"So is that what Company 'B' did?"

"*Nur genau!* You know how it went...our well-oiled machine of war swept over the steppes, invincible, bravely destroying all opposition as we went! Just like in Poland. The Russians were no match for us, their command staff was inept, they were getting most of their orders directly from Stalin, who wasn't much of a strategist in the first place, and was nearly delirious with rage from the first shot fired, so all he could do was scream "Not an inch backward!" and have his own field commanders shot for trying to pull a few *tovariches* back out from under the treads of our panzers. Then things came to a crunch for us at Kiev."

"Tell me about the encirclement."

"Here's how it went. As you know, I'm part of Army Group South, *Feldmarschal* von Runstedt commanding. Okay, okay...I'm a *very small* part. We are advancing south of Kiev. Infantry, panzer divisions. To the north, Army Group Center under *Feldmarschal* Bock is advancing directly towards Kiev on a wide front. His Group's got Panzer divisions grinding across the countryside that start moving around the north of Kiev. The Kiev area has about 850,000 Russian troops with lots of artillery and a few tanks of their own spread around the city and its environs. We start really pushing on Kiev on 7 August. Things heat up. The rate of advance slows. A lot of high-level arguing goes back and forth between the Army Group commanders and Hitler, back at his command headquarters in East Prussia. Well, you don't argue with Hitler. The subject of the discussions is, do we stop the drive on Moscow until we get Kiev taken care of, or do we just bypass Kiev and go hell's-bells for Moscow? If we slow down on Moscow, there's a *verdammt* fine chance we won't take the capital before the autumn rains arrive. But if we leave Kiev in our rear, with nearly a million crap-hot patriotic Russian soldiers there, well, that could be major trouble in our rear. Keep in mind that we've got other problem areas, which Hitler keeps insisting are 'opportunity' areas. Leningrad in the north. And in the south, the Crimea, the Don River valley, the Caucasus. Oil ...manufacturing ...coal. Hitler wants those resources like crazy. So it's agreed, sort of, that Kiev gets priority for now. Bock keeps pushing around the city in the north, von Runstedt in the south. Eventually, the pincers close on 16 September. More than 800,000 Russkie troops bagged! Including *all* their army-group staff! Including *Kommissar* Nikita Khrushchev! Of course, all the Top Brass gets rescued, flown out. Can you imagine what the middle part of the Twentieth Century would be like if Nikita Khrushchev had perished? Well anyway, the Red Army commander, Marshal Semyon Budyonny, is brought before Comrade Stalin, roundly cursed and disgraced, then fired as overall commander of Russian forces in the Kiev Encirclement. I think they shot him. Anyway, *Stalin does not assign a replacement!* And so the encircled forces are left to the command of their Divisional senior officers, such of them as haven't made their own escape by personal aircraft. Or to the commandants of lower-level organizations, like brigades or battalions. Talk about *divided command!* That doesn't exactly make the reduction of this massive encirclement a *pushover* for us Germans, but it helps a lot. The outcome is pretty foregone. There are days and days of savage combat, but with horrible inter-Divisional coordination on the Russian side. Kiev surrenders on 19 September. Heavy fighting continues in the outlying areas until the 26th. In the end, about 620,000 Russian troops killed versus about 27,000 German troops. That's a ratio of...mmmm...twenty-three to one! Hundreds of thousands more Russians taken prisoner.

They are shipped back to Poland for internment and slave labor…hardly a one of those POWs survives the war alive. No one can tell how many Russian—well…*Ukrainian*—civilians are killed in Kiev, but the number must be astronomical. Think about it, *mein Freund* …the Kiev encirclement was surely the most gigantic battle with the highest casualty list of the Second World War, up until that time. Not that there wasn't worse to come." Hans stopped, his head bowed, moved by those doleful recollections.

"And now it's time to tell me how you got wounded, as usual!" I joshed.

Hans Raufer looked up at me with heartbroken eyes. "*Nein…nein,*" he answered. "That happened a little later. And it was terrible…terrible."

14

28-29 September 1941

BABI YAR

Hans reached behind him for the bottle of kirshwasser that had rested untouched on the picnic table since we'd sat down. Gazing out across the gravel beach, the gleaming white sheet of ice, the heaped-up, groaning and crackling pressure ridges, he seemed to ponder some long-ago tragedy. He twisted the bottle's stopper, making an incongruous squeak in the icy, still forenoon. He raised the bottle to his lips, tipped it, slowly drank an ounce or so. Sated, he waved the bottle my direction, a wordless invitation.

Naturally, I hesitated. I'd had plenty to drink at the Townshend's the night before. In spite of my performance at that heel punch party, I've never been too much of a drinker. But it occurred to me that there was a certain companionable cordiality implicit in Hans's invitation. So I took the proffered bottle and had myself a very small swig.

After I recorked the kirschwasser, Hans continued his narration. "Well, Company 'B' was thrashed around a lot in the week following Kiev's surrender…lots of combat, all over the landscape. The fourth or fifth day of this action, we advanced on foot against a dug-in battery of truck mounted Katyusha launchers. This deployment was extremely stupid of the Russians, but understandable because our heavy Panzers were going about blasting any enemy vehicle into scrap metal at a distance of up to two or three thousand meters, and Katyusha launchers out in the open were a favorite target of theirs. And because the Russkies were broken up into company-sized or even platoon-sized elements, that battery must have had no contact with any command capable of telling those

Katyushas *not* to dig in. *Fire and move* was their best bet for survival.

"We infantry were terrified of Katyushas! When fired, they made a shriek coming off the launchers like a whole flight of witches riding on leather-winged harpies out of Hades. And also, a battery could fire off a hundred of these things in about twenty seconds, and each one of them packed an immense wallop on impact. But! Once a launcher had fired its lot, it took forever for the rocketeers to reload! So when we got the assignment to take this particular battery out, all we had to do was show ourselves advancing on them, *nyaaa-nyaaa!*, just poor dumb German infantry boys without any panzer cover, and then when the Russkies touched off the first Katyushas in our direction, we crawled into any pit in the ground we could find, or just burrowed ourselves in like badgers, real fast, then assumed the fetal position and kissed our own asses for luck. On this occasion, the rocket barrage cost us eleven killed. But then we knew we had half an hour at least, to charge on in and slaughter those Russian rocketeers, because, you see, it took them at least that long to reload and ready their *verdammt* launchers.

"Well, once things cooled off in the Kiev encirclement, the Battalion C.O. got word of this creative and risky little anti-Katyusha action of ours. Company 'B' was brought into the city—or what *remained* of the city!— for some recognition. This was on the 26th, I think. The city had surrendered on the 19st, and special administrative units of SS and *Waffen*-SS had already come in to take control of the surviving civilian populace…*verdammt* iron-handed control if you ask me. Us Company 'B' boys were to be given five days of R&R while the rest of the Battalion marched off, along with the rest of the *ficken* Division, in the general direction of Moscow. All that R&R thing meant was we could rest up, get clean, chase down some Ukrainian or Russian liquor maybe, and be excused from getting shot at by the Red Army for a few days. There weren't any night clubs or restaurants or music halls or whorehouses currently operating in Kiev, which is what sorts of entertainment we would have normally preferred for a five-day R&R.

"When some of us started nosing around the city, we began seeing these little cardboard notices posted on light-poles and fences, all in Cyrillic script, either Russian or Ukranian language. One of my buddies grabbed the first raggedy bald-headed civilian he could find who spoke any German and stood him up so his nose was ten centimeters from one of these notices. '*Übersetzen!*' my buddy commanded. 'Translate!' The old guy squinted at the bulletin, obviously a directive from the German authorities. 'It says' the old man recited:

All Yids in Kiev must report to such-and-such intersection for resettlement. They are to report on 29 September. They are to bring money, valuables, identity documents and warm clothes. Any Yids not reporting will be shot!

"We thought about this a moment. I asked an incredibly naïve question, 'What's a Yid?' The old man turned sad eyes to me. 'I am,' he replied. 'It is an insulting name for a Jew.'

"Well, our R&R was interrupted the following morning by the appearance of an SS *Sturmbannführer*, bright red Nazi Party armband on his sleeve, and a squad of eight tommygun toting *Oberschütze*—"

"Sorry," I interrupted. "What are those ranks?"

"*Schutzstaffel*...SS. The officer's like a Major. The enlisteds were 'senior riflemen'. Anyway, he calls the Company 'B' men into formation, such of us as were hanging around the warehouse we were bunking in. 'Is this all?' he demands. There were only *sixteen* of us on hand...everyone else is out in twos or threes roaming around the city. I'm a corporal now, remember...the senior man present. So I'm quaking in my boots because this officer is SS, *für die Liebe Gottes*, but I've *got* to answer. 'Our Company is assigned five days' liberty, Herr *Sturmbannführer*...for conspicuous courage in combat. At our present strength, there are a hundred twenty riflemen and NCOs in Company 'B', Sir. I can have them assembled for duty in thirty minutes, Herr *Sturmbannführer*!' I promised, rashly.

"He says, '*Nein, nein.* Sixteen will be enough. Get your rifles and fall back in here immediately.' Well I wasn't going to argue with an SS Major! Everyone snapped-to, made it back to the same spot, field uniforms on straight, weapons gleaming in readiness, in something less than forty-five seconds. One of the *waffen*-SS men passed out a handful of fully-stuffed ammunition clips, enough for each of us.

"I had put on my *Eisernes Kreuz*—my Iron Cross—that morning, and I cannot remember exactly why. Usually it was stowed in the bottom of my fieldpack. The accepted way of wearing the decoration was right at the base of your throat, hanging from a ribbon about your neck. Everyone I knew who had been awarded the Iron Cross disliked wearing it around his neck when in the field...when you had to double-time, which was whenever the *Tovarichii* were firing at you, it rattled against that sensitive hollow of your throat. Also, the ribbon choked and chafed, or wadded up uncomfortably under your shirt collar. It was usually okay with your more reasonable officers to let you hang the decoration from your second-from-top tunic button, suspending it from the stout steel ring at the top of the cross which that *verflucht* ribbon was usually threaded through. That's how they hung it on you when they first presented it, on your second tunic button, and you were expected to buy your own neck ribbon within a day or two after presentation. Or you could legitimately just *forget* the ribbon and use your *top* tunic button, but that meant you had to keep that top button buttoned up...more *ficken* uncomfortable than the ribbon! Well as we formed up, the SS officer gives me a scary scowl and says, 'Where's your medal ribbon, Corporal?' I replied, 'Came untied in battle, Sir. I rescued the medal but lost the ribbon.' A big lie, of course, but it flew. He says, 'Well that's all right then...just see you get another ribbon soon, *ja?*' Comradely, like one decorated hero to another, I guess. As we marched off toward a cemetery next to a big bunch of ravines several blocks away, the Major confided in me that this Company 'B' detail should consider ourselves honored to perform a small experiment for the SS.

"We entered the graveyard, passed among trees with half their limbs shattered by artillery fire, many gravestones here and there tipped or broken or toppled. Over a small rise. There was a crowd of people a hundred meters up ahead. As we neared, it became apparent they were *stripped naked*! They stood in two rows of eight, each separated from the next by the space of perhaps four meters, the rows facing outward from each other. Nearing them, I saw they stood along the very brims of a long trench perhaps two or three meters deep, about the same distance in width. The soil from the trench had been bulldozed into a heap at the far end. A squad of six more tommygun-wielding SS riflemen stood guard. 'Have your men stand exactly six meters away from, and facing, these condemned prisoners!' the Major ordered. 'Each rifleman offset one meter sideways so the two squads are not in each other's line of fire with respect to your targets. *Sehr gut!*' he said crisply when we had accomplished this. 'This instant, you will all insert your magazines, lock and load a round—safeties off! Port...ARMS! On my first command, the *links* rank will aim, then on my command, fire. On my second command, the *rechts* rank will aim, and then fire.' He emphasized that he was or course talking about *his* left and right with casual waves of his hand. 'You will each execute your prisoner with a single round through the heart!'

"*Mein Gott!* Do you know, Lewis, up until that moment I cannot say for certain I had so much as *winged* an Enemy of the Reich! There was that instant in Poland where I had a small crisis of conscience about aggression and killing in warfare. Since that time, I'd enthusiastically and frequently fired round after round in the general direction of our enemies in an attempt to *scare* them, but without the least pretense of taking aim! No one had been the wiser! In my heart, I'd promised myself that when the situation called for it, I would fire lethally at anyone who was for certain attempting to kill me or one of my comrades right next to me. But in that same heart, I was praying all along that I might make it through the War without this necessity arising.

"I had taken a place on the *rechts* side of the trench. The prisoner I faced was a handsome-looking young woman. She bore her nakedness with no trace of shame. She was perhaps twenty, tall and red haired. High, firm breasts, long well-muscled limbs, like an athlete or a gymnast. But in fact, she was probably also a Soviet guerilla, a saboteur...perhaps an assassin. All of these things would make her braver than I, likely a true hero. But a hero of the Soviet Union, my supposed enemy. As I snapped to attention, my weapon at port arms, she gazed across the short distance and into my eyes with defiance and hatred, and I admit to you this day, Lewis, her look made me ashamed! I averted my gaze. In amazement I looked across the trench and recognized the prisoner directly opposite on the *links* side! It was the same bald, elderly man who'd helped us by translating the notice posted on the wall, the day before! A Jew! It all became clear to me: ALL these condemned prisoners must be Jews! The posted order to assemble with cash and valuables was a ruse! There had been a decision made to eliminate Kiev's Jews by firing squad, and our little detail was some kind of trial run!

"I felt like doubling over and vomiting! I considered throwing down my rifle and refusing to shoot. But that SS Major carried a sidearm, a Luger pistol, and he was certainly not above using it in the event of a small mutiny within his firing squad detail. '*Links*, take aim!' The eight-man squad on the left side snapped their rifles up. The Major cried. '*FEUER!*'

"A ragged volley. On the death pit's far side, eight bodies crumpled and fell backward into the trench.

"Amazing! The wrinkled old man I'd seen across from *my* victim was struggling to his knees down in the pit! Blood poured from a hole in his torso, yet he had not been mortally struck! His eyes bugged and his mouth fell open. A shriek like a desert cat escaped his mouth! Another shriek...and another! Furious, the SS Major yanked the sidearm from his holster and strode around to the pit's far side, obviously to deal the old Jew a *coup de grace*. As the Major strode, he ordered us on the *rechts* side to come to aim. I raised my rifle, sighted on the saboteur Jewess's heart. Then I raised my forward sight infinitesimally so the bullet would go over her shoulder and off into far distance. When my shot failed to take her down, she would be shot anyway, but by somebody else, not me. Now as far as *my* case, I would probably *also* be shot by that Luger-toting SS Major, for failing to obey orders and subverting the justice of the Third Reich!

"Across the pit, the Major had reached a spot no more than five meters from the shrieking old Jew. He

104

raised his pistol, took a bead on the old man. *"Rechts*, take aim!' he repeated shrilly. *'FEUER!'*

Eight Karabiner 98k bolt action rifles and one Luger P08 pistol exploded. Seven cal7.98 rifle bullets found their marks in the hearts of seven Kiev Jews, most likely innocent of all wrongdoing except the offense of Judaism. One cal7.98 rifle bullet slipped past the ear of its intended victim, slightly riffling her flame-red hair but otherwise doing her no mischief.

"One cal7.65 pistol bullet, emanating from the barrel of that SS *Sturmbannführer*'s Luger, did something quite peculiar."

+ + + + + + + +

The old man in the Kiev graveyard trench crying out in his death agony was named Shmuel Semyonofsky. His given name was the Hebrew equivalent of *Samuel*. Once earlier in life, when his age was 38 years, he had also been on his knees in a trench, wounded seemingly unto death, crying out in his agony. It had been in the miserable November of 1916, and the trench had been a military defensive earthwork on the Russian side of the Eastern Front, not far from the nearly demolished city of Pinsk.

A huge German railcar-mounted artillery piece had fired a shell. The projectile had arched over the Russian trenchlines and had detonated a hundred meters in the air, spraying the Tsar's Imperial troops with hot, high-speed knives of shrapnel. A piece the size and mass of an antique Ruble, like those minted in the Eighteenth century by Peter the Great weighing twenty-eight honest grams of fine silver, sleeted out of the sky toward the old man's head. The fragment had pierced Shmuel Semyonofsky's steel helmet and continued on to fracture the top of his skull and embed itself in the outer layers of his brain. Blood poured down, like the winter rains had poured down into the trenchworks. As he lay wounded and writhing, Shmuel's brain swelled and became engorged with his own blood, like the soil of the Eastern Front trenches had swollen and become soaked with the winter's downpours of rainwater, mixed with the downpours of blood from maimed and slain Russian peasants dressed up as soldiers. The soil had turned to black mud the consistency of porridge, in which the soldiers, both Russian and German, had had to continue standing, watch on watch, for months on end.

When stretcherbearers got to the body of Shmuel Semyonofsky, they were certain he was slain. But when they lifted him by his elbows and ankles, Shmuel opened his eyes and shrieked. So they took him back to the aid station for triage. Eventually a field medic, recently a third-year student at a renowned surgical college in Kiev when drafted, had gotten around to giving Shmuel a look. At university, the young medic had been the protégé of a prominent cranial surgeon. This proved fortunate for Private Semyonofsky. The lad wrote out a tag directing this fractured cranium victim to the nearest railhead, thence to be evacuated eastward to Kiev for immediate surgery.

The journey was arduous, but Shmuel made it barely alive. When Shmuel's stretcher had fallen under the examination of the admitting NCO, he had read the impressive name the frontline medic had scribbled in his notes on the casualty's routing tag. By this fortunate occurrence, Shmuel soon fell into the hands of renowned surgical staffers, who thought his skull wounds interesting and operable. Shmuel was administered anaesthesia. Incisions were carefully made. His scalp was laid open. Segments of shattered skull were removed and discarded. The piece of shrapnel was skillfully removed and several tiny blood vessels sutured. A disk of purest silver, cut from a thick silver serving tray that had been charitably donated to the hospital by a distant relative of the Imperial Family, had been shaped, then carefully sterilized, and then pinned

106

in place of the removed cap of skullbone. Temporary drains were installed to carry off blood seepage and cranial fluids during the healing process. Then Shmuel Semyonofsky's scalp had been sutured into place.

Semyonofsky slowly recovered. His soldiering days were over. His mental faculties gradually returned, normal for the most part. He was discharged, granted an Tsarist invalid's pension—barely adequate for survival— which pension did not administratively survive the Russian Revolution the following March of 1917. Upon leaving hospital, Shmuel sought out the nearest synagogue in Kiev and raised many fervent prayers of gratitude to the Almighty. He lived another twenty-five years in Kiev, existing on pittance wages from inconsequential labor, but ever a pious and grateful disciple of Judaism. Until one day, another invasion by German armies found him crouched in a ditch in the ground, in a graveyard near some ravines, once again wounded almost to his mortality by a another piece of German metal.

+ + + + + + + +

"Something *peculiar*? The bullet did something *peculiar*?" I yelled at my friend. "Come on now, Hans! You can't leave things just hanging there! You need to tell me more than that!"

"*Ja*, all right. Lewis, do you know how sometimes your thoughts come rushing with blinding speed? Like electricity through a wire? When a sudden, unanticipated event makes time slow down, or almost stop? You see the world lit up like…like lightning is striking and everything is *Kristall*?"

"Okay…."

"The bullets were fired…I saw the rifle smoke jetting from our barrels! I'd fired my *own* rifle! In the thousandth-second the bullets flew, my thoughts raced and

107

my vision was…was like *Allmächtiger Gott!* I realized an ugly, sickening insight: what was going on in this graveyard, over this ditch, was vicious and patently evil! It was *my people* perpetrating this revulsion! Germans! Our nation and race had produced scholars, geniuses, statesmen, composers, artists, authors, poets, theologians, actors and actresses, singers, inventors, athletes! A hundred categories of meritorious and heroic men and women. And, us sixteen meritorious and heroic Germans, we were standing here murdering innocents whose religious beliefs we perhaps took a few meaningless exceptions to! All Hitler's lies revealed their falseness to me—ALL of them! The smug racism, the delusions of National glory, the invincible superiority of the Aryan Germanic peoples! I personally was embedded in this wickedness—my participation in the battles and conquests, my *arrogance*, and this thing regarding the Jews, the magnitude of which I'd just now seriously glimpsed for my first time. And…and I was *trapped* in this wickedness—for me or any other good German citizen, there was *no way out*! I saw the woman's fierce eyes while she waited for my bullet to pierce her heart and destroy her young, heroic life. In a consummational, instantaneous transfer of ideals and emotions those eyes of hers spoke to me these words:

Never forget me! As I have for you in this my terrible mortal instant, you must purge hatred from your heart as my heart's blood unites with yours! I will become you, be in you, be part of you…with my aid, you are never to be the same man, beyond this instant! Hide your secret transformation from all eyes, for all time, from this second forever after!

"I wondered what those inscrutable phantom words meant to me. And in the next millionth-second, I could *see* my bullet sing over her shoulder, past her head, riffling her

108

hair. And then I could *see* the *Sturmbannführer*'s luger bullet, a projectile with far less muzzle velocity than the one from my rifle, travelling more or less toward me, askew at a small angle, a head shot taken at the bald old man shrieking in the pit, speeding toward me at only 350 meters per second, striking the old Jew in the head, but higher than the SS officer would have intended. His bullet *glancing off the old man's skull instead of penetrating, as if a miracle from the Bible*! Continuing on a deflected trajectory upward! Penetrating the back of that woman in front of me, entering between ribs next to her spine, passing straight through her heart exactly where my shot should have passed in the reverse direction, if I'd been attending to orders. Killing her instantly! The luger bullet exited her chest at a point in the cleft between her lovely breasts, a spray of bone fragments and blood accompanying the now-tumbling projectile, flying even slower now for its transit through the girl's body, all this—gore and tissue and bone and bullet—flying directly toward me where I stood frozen and rooted in my footprints! The slug struck me directly over my heart! Gouts of that woman's blood struck me as well, splattering, penetrating lacerations on my chest, her blood mingling as the woman had prophesied with my own heart's-blood! I felt intense pain! I felt my heart's rhythm falter in my chest. And, though I was surely dying, Lewis, I discerned as clearly as ever I had known anything in life that by her blood I was changed, never to be the same beyond that instant, ever in life or in death."

Hans Raufer bowed his head and fell silent.

I must admit, I was struck dumb myself. I reached behind Hans for the kirschwasser and helped myself to a generous swallow. "Shot through the heart, man! How did you...What did you—"

109

Hans Raufer doffed his glove. He lifted up the hem of his heavy down parka and rummaged in his pants pocket. He dredged up an object and handed it to me.

An Iron Cross, Second Class. A malformed dimple right in the center, obliterating the swastika that once had appeared there. A dimple in the iron, a metal wound left by the impact of a cal7.65 bullet from a Luger P08 pistol.

Well. Hans told me some of the rest. He'd been thought dead. Evidently what the SS *Sturmbannführer* was seeking to demonstrate was that it would work acceptably and efficiently to line Jews up on *both* sides of their mass graves and execute them with *two* ranks of *Waffen*-SS troops and *Sonderkommando 4A* specially trained murderers. The experiment failed...Hans's death proved that. One couldn't have good German executioners accidentally *shooting each other*!

Some time later, one of Hans's mates sent him a letter which explained that the disgusted *Sturmbannführer* had immediately taken his SS *Oberschützen* and left the Company 'B' detailers to deal with Hans's body themselves. Departing, the officer had stiffly said he would have an aide contact the field medics with an ambulance to reclaim the corpse. Hans confided in me that he was surprised the SS squad, before they marched off, hadn't just kicked his mortal remains into the pit along with the Jews. "Actually..." Hans reflected, "That would have been an honorable rest. And, if I'd come to rest up against that red-haired, heroic Jewess *Valkyrie*, my heart's blood and hers could have spent Eternity mingling, as she wished."

When, a day later, the mass murders of Jews at the ravines of Babi Yar, "Grandmother's Pits," began in earnest, thirty-three thousand seven hundred and seventy-one Jews naïvely reported for relocation, were robbed of their cash and valuables, then stripped naked, then marched

110

to the ravines, and there they were machine-gunned to death by *only one* rank of soulless, blackhearted murderers. You need to see that number again:

33,771

That is how many Jews, innocent of any crime, were murdered in shifts, over the space of *two days* by the SS at Babi Yar, Kiev, Ukrainian SSR.

Corporal Hans Raufer, having eventually been recognized by a couple of stretcher-toting medics as not being quite dead after all in spite of a gruesome wound that appeared like a gunshot through his heart, was comatose for days as he lay in a Kiev hospital ward alongside several hundred other of his brigade's wounded. He lay mercifully deaf to the volleys of gunfire emanating from Babi Yar. Unconscious, his heart was embarked on slowly mending. And on slowly losing whatever traces of Nazi blackness with which it may have been tarnished. And on slowly developing a soul worth cherishing.

Hans stopped talking. He silently held his own counsel for maybe ten minutes, gazing out across the Arctic ice. I was compelled to let the silence linger. After a while, he groped for the bottle and took a hit of kirshwasser. Then he half turned to me and in a low voice, recovered a bit, half smiling, he observed, "Babi Yar, *mein Freunde*! *Grosser Gott*, what a mess that was! Gruesome, totally gruesome!"

I couldn't agree more. "Sounds completely grim and grisly!"

A third voice expressed its opinion: "*Grrrrowlf!*"

We both swiveled our necks around. At our backs, an eight-hundred-pound polar bear had its front feet up on our picnic table, sniffing at us.

Hans snatched the kirschwasser and we leapt up and bolted the *scheisse* out of there. Both of us sprinted for the Mercedes. As I ran, I recalled some sage advice I'd heard one time about when you and your hunting buddies are being chased by an angry bear: you don't have to be the *fastest* guy trying to flee. You only have to be the *second slowest!*

On the fly, I wondered whether polar bears might have a thirst for kirschwasser?

15

14 February 1942
AFRIKAKORPS

The Mercedes started right up, thankfully. When we got the glass defrosted and gazed out the windows, our bear friend was nowhere to be seen. *Verdammt!* He—or she—hadn't even been pursuing us!

Hans dropped the big sedan into gear and slowly rolled out of the car park. "Have you ever tried talking to anyone about those disturbing experiences?" I asked him gently.

"What, you mean like a *shrink?*"

"I was thinking more like a counselor. A regular M.D., even. Or, yes! Maybe a psychiatrist!"

"Nein! Niemals! Absolut nicht!"

Whoa...*three* strong denials! "What about Anna... have you ever told her about Kiev and Babi Yar?"

Hans took his eyes off the road to give me a momentary bug eyed gawk. "Are you *CRAZY*?! *Nein*...not a word have I told to Anna!"

"I was just going to say—"

"I've never talked about any of that to *anyone!*"

"Well you just now talked about it to me!"

His sidelong glance was more contemplative this time. *"Ja*...I guess I did."

I wasn't going to push it. Perhaps it was having first established that warrior connection thing, he and I. After his questioning me about the Viet Nam experiences, maybe there was a bond of confidentiality established that had allowed him to open his floodgates. In any case, he seemed somewhat cleansed, purged, some level of self-absolution having been accomplished. Wouldn't that be the best result any counselor or post-trauma therapist would hope for? I thought it appropriate to change the subject. "So how did they fix your bullet wound to the heart?" I asked him.

"Okay. First thing, they kept me doped up with sleeping pills and tranquilizers and pain meds. In Kiev, the local *Wehrmacht* docs were hardly *heart* specialists! They were Sawbones and Stitchers and Shrapnel Pluckers, for the most part, but they knew they had to keep my heart on an even keel. So in four or five days, after they got me stable and when they were pretty sure I was not going to cork off in the next ten minutes, they got me on a transport train back to Germany. That train was probably packed with wounded, since they were sending a couple thousand back home every day. But I was completely out of it, so I can't say for sure.

"Here's what the scorecard on me said. I had a splatter of lacerations across my entire upper chest. Caused by bone fragments from that Russian Jewess. And also little hunks of lead from the Luger bullet, breaking up and splashing sideways from impacting my medal, you see? A couple big tears in my pecs from little chunks of the edges of the Iron Cross itself. My sternum was cracked in two places. But my heart was the worst of it. As the cardiac specialists once I was back in Berlin described it, the heart muscle was traumatized like a big bruise. Some minor internal bleeding and tissue contusions to various chest wall muscles. Thankfully, no cardiac arteries ruptured. Everything would heal in time. For a few weeks, I would have a lot of pain unless they kept me on constant high octane painkillers. So, that's what they did, and I was mostly in Dreamland for all of October and into November. Then they started me on therapy and gentle gymnasium exercises. By Christmastime though, I was very nearly a hundred percent. I was so bored with life in that hospital, I actually *asked* when they were going to send me back to my unit on the Russian Front!"

"And did they do it?" I prompted him.

"Couldn't."

"Uhhh…why not?"

"There *was* no Company 'B'. Wiped out. Every man, every officer."

"*How?*"

Hans shrugged. "The usual way. It started raining nonstop in October. Everything on the Russian Front turned to mud. The boys couldn't make hellbent dashes forward in among the protection of Panzers any more, and the Russians got a lot better at coming against us in waves, firing off Tommyguns like lunatics.

"Then it got cold in November. All that muddy slop and sloppy mud turned half-frozen *crunchy* slop. Diesel engines don't like to start up or keep running when it gets cold. Gasoline engines have cooling systems that freeze and crack engine blocks when it gets cold. So…the boys were on their own. On foot. In boots that weren't particularly waterproof. Weren't *cold*-proof at all! Company 'B' is pared down to about one-third our full component, and starting to lose boys to pneumonia as well as Russian bullets.

"Then it gets *ficken cold* in December, and it starts to snow. All the crunchy slop turns into iron-hard frozen dirty ice with snow on top. It goes down to minus-30 at night. The boys don't all have winter kit yet…supposed to come out from Germany, but the lines of supply aren't working very well for some reason. Losing boys from frostbite and from just freezing solid in the snow at night on sentry duty, waiting for the Russians to make a crazy charge again. Manpower down to about one-fourth a standard Company.

"And then, on Christmas Eve, up to their eyeballs in snow and stalled only about twenty kilometers from

Moscow City Limits, a big human wave of Stalin's Best washes over Company 'B' foxholes. Not a one of my old chums survives...not a one of the NCOs, not a single officer. They couldn't send me back to Company 'B' because *there was no* Company 'B' anymore."

"Was that about the time Operation Typhoon was abandoned?"

"Slowed to a stop, decimated, beaten by General Winter and *eine enorme Masse* of Russians. Hitler's big-deal Operation Typhoon failed in its bold objective to seize Moscow. But that's all right...Herr Hitler himself was snug and warm back in Berlin."

"So what did the *Wehrmacht* personnel people do with you?"

"Well, it seemed to have made it into my personnel folder that I was something of a diesel mechanic. They had need for some of those! Someplace where a lot of dust seemed to be clogging up the panzer engines. They sent me to join the *Afrikakorps* in Tripoli. That's in Libya, North Africa!" Hans paused, then added, "*Ach, ja!* One other thing: just about the time I was on a train passing through southern France so I could climb onto a troopship bound for Tripoli, some orders came through for me. That would have been the beginning of February 1942. They'd decided to advance me to *Unterfeldwebel*! That means, *Sergeant*!"

Hans pulled in to the car park at the DOT Hilton. He slammed the driver side door. Like every resident of Churchill, as near as I could figure, he didn't bother to lock up. We trudged upstairs, stamped the mud and ice off our feet. The door to Unit 218 wasn't locked either. Anna had left a note on the kitchen table explaining she was going Sunday visiting. Hans dug around in the pantry and came back to the table with six or seven half liters of Molson.

"Let's see…" he pondered. "We were talking about North Africa!"

+ + + + + + + +

North Africa! In many respects, a splendid place to fight a war! A million square miles of almost nothing! No forests, farms, or rivers to slow down the panzers! Clear skies nearly the whole year around—perfect for air operations! Precious few pesky cities or towns to bother with, damned little population in most of the place. Hardly any Jews, and Herr Hitler was getting annoyingly insistent about frontline soldiers becoming involved with what he glibly called the Jewish Question. Now, if only back in 1940 there had been Nerf® ammunition or paintball guns to minimize the casualties and decide the outcome, North Africa would have been an almost perfect battlefield for a million troops to have a go at one another.

Well, that's on the optimistic side. There were also several *drawbacks* to practicing no-holds-barred combat in North Africa. These included:

Sand. More accurately, dust. Fine, gritty, deep, pervasive dust. Nearly the entire million square miles was sparsely vegetated at best, and composed of depressions or plains or wadis or hills or ranges or dunes or entire mountains of dust. Occasionally, the terrain was punctuated by steep and non-navigable crags of solid rock. If you were *Panzerarmee Afrika*, the armored wing of *Afrikakorps,* and you went hell-for-leather after those nasty Brits with four hundred panzers and six hundred trucks full of storm troopers, you raised a *massive* amount of gritty, sandy dust. First off, this spoiled the element of surprise and obscured the view. Second, it made breathing rather a challenge for the guys crewing the panzers and the guys riding in those trucks. Third, it made breathing rather a challenge for the diesel engines of all those panzers and

117

trucks themselves, not to mention playing Hob with tracks, wheel bearings, and miscellaneous lubricants [The astute reader will apprehend that this is why Hans Raufer, Diesel Mechanic, enters the North African scenario!].

Heat. It's a *desert*! It's hotter than blazes in the day, even though it drops down to colder than ice at night. The wild fluctuations in temperature reduced the comfort of all those million or so soldiers. Modified uniforms were necessary. Sunstroke and sunburn were no minor concern. Soldiers had to lug more kit to survive both day and night. But this drawback worked evenhandedly, both sides in equal measures.

Water. Crucial lack of fresh water. It's a *desert*!

Flies.

Scorpions.

Snakes. *Venomous* snakes!

So why did Adolf Hitler dispatch a lot of valuable troops to North Africa early in the War? Troops that he could have been using in Western Europe, where he was contemplating a cross-channel invasion of the British Isles? Troops he could have been positioning for use in Operation Barbarossa? To begin with, Adolf Hitler *didn't* dispatch many troops to North Africa. Until 1940, most of the Axis presence in North Africa were *Italians*. On the opposing team, the British presence was because the British were heavily involved in Egypt, almost colonially involved. The British valued Egypt highly because of that *canal* thing. As the War proceeded to get serious, Hitler realized he could depend very little on the Italians. Their air, transport, armor and combat equipment was so-so. Their enthusiasm for world domination was lukewarm at best. Their field commanders and their High Command staff were inept. *Il Duce* was a nutcase, even by Nazi nutcase standards. After a few Avaricious Dictator conferences between the two, Hitler had quickly come to loathe and mistrust Mussolini.

So, initially, the German military presence was to shore up the Reich's Italian allies, and then to provide theater-wide strategic guidance in the form of good iron-fisted German command authority for all Axis elements in North Africa.

As the Nazi geopolitics of Europe started to evolve, Hitler must have certainly realized the value of dominating North Africa. He would secure the Mediterranean! Note that he had made heavy investment, militarily speaking, in Greece, in several of the larger Mediterranean Islands, and in the Balkans. Earlier on, Germany had honed its warcraft in Spain, and could count that country as within the Nazi sphere of influence. Italy was a second string Axis power, but pretty much on board with the German world domination scheme. In North Africa, Morocco and Algeria were already Vichy French colonies and hence under Hitler's thumb. If German adventures in North Africa could secure Tunisia, Libya, and Egypt, they would in essence ring the entire Mediterranean...with the notable exceptions of Turkey and the Levant. And those nations would fall like ripe pears, once the rest of the Mediterranean rim was in German hands.

Consider what success in North Africa would gain for Hitler! Control of the Mediterranean shipping lanes! Control of the Suez Canal! Control of the Arabian Peninsula—hiding under those sands, oil galore! If Turkey fell without too much squabble, an open pathway to the Caucasus! An open pathway to India! A powerful presence in Russia's underbelly, cheaply bought: the South Asia -*stan* SSR's ...Turkmenistan, Uzbekistan, Kyrgyzstan and Kazakstan! *Mein Gott*, North Africa, gotten without huge sacrifice, would be well worth the trouble, no matter how busy Germany's hands were in Poland, the Low Countries, and France!

Well but however. Those British were deuced fond of their Canal, and were dratted reluctant to give it up without a fight. In 1940, the Germans had worked their way eastward from their bridgehead in Tripoli, consolidating against British interference, pushing their Italian associates to take firm possession as far east as the grimy eastern Libyan town of Tobruk, just a little shy of the Egyptian border. But by January of 1941, British and Australian Divisions had retaken Tobruk, seized right out of Axis hands. By February 1941 the British (actually, the Australians, for the most part) had pushed the Germans 450 kilometers farther westward, as far as Benghazi, which grimy central Libyan town the British had also seized out of Axis hands. It appeared possible that the Germans, as well as their Italian cronies, could be pushed right off the North African continent by the intrepid Brits (and their ANZAC, Indian, South African, etc. etc. allies, let's not forget!). All the Germans' adventurous fantasies would gurgle down the drain. So that's why, in early 1941, Hitler repurposed a bunch of his Divisions, labelled them *Afrikakorps*, and had them shipped on out to Tripoli. *Generalfeldmarschall* Erwin Johannes Eugen Rommel commanding.

Tobruk and Benghazi. It pays to consider the Wartime histories of these two coastal cities. Here's a little table showing who was in charge of Benghazi and/or Tobruk, and when they changed hands:

Date	City	In Control
To end of 1940	Benghazi	Germans and Italians
6 Jan 1941	"	Seized by British
4 Apr 1941	"	Retaken by Germans
24 Dec 1941	"	Re-retaken by British
29 Jan 1942	"	Re-re-retaken by Germans
20 Nov 1942	"	Re-re-re-retaken by British
To end of 1940	Tobruk	Italians and Germans
22 Jan 1941	"	Seized by British (Aussies mostly)
10 Apr 1941	"	Besieged by Axis (Italians mostly)
16 May 1941	"	Partially seized by *Italians!*
7 Dec 1941	"	Retaken by Brits+Colonials (NOTE THIS DATE!)
21 Jun 1942	"	Re-retaken by Germans
13 Nov 1942	"	Re-re-retaken by British (last time! promise!)

If you look at all this on a map, you will realize what was going on. The Germans and their Axis colleagues were pushing eastward out of their garrison base in Tripoli, Algeria. Then, after reaching some eastward high-water mark, they were being pushed back westward by the British and their Commonwealth colleagues. This happened THREE TIMES! Spanning east-west distances of many hundreds of kilometers! Try to imagine how little of Western Europe would have been left standing if this seesaw of warfare had swept back and forth across *that* terrain three times! Of course, on the third seesaw, there had been American landings in Morocco and Algeria in November of 1942. The Germans were caught in a nutcracker between the British and the Americans, and that was that for the likes of them!

Whew! A pretty well educated novelist could go a lifetime casually absorbing factoids about World War II in North Africa and never figure that all out. It helps to take extensive notes, draw pictures, and scribble on a map!

+ + + + + + + +

'Whew!' I thought. Hans's background on North Africa was a lot to absorb! "So…," I asked him. "When did you arrive in Tripoli in the middle of all this mess?"

"Easy! On my twenty-second birthday! Fourteen February, 1942! Both sides declared a truce in my honor! *Nein*, just joking! That was just when Erwin 'Desert Fox' Rommel was getting the third of those big eastward pushes underway, the one that took us all the way into Egypt, to El Alamein. *Ja, ja*…another of those grimy little coastal towns, but this one grimier and littler than either Tobruk or Benghazi. So, here's how things went for me.

"My orders were clear and unmistakable. I was identified as an '*Erfahrenen Diesel-Techniker.*' 'Skilled!' I liked that! They could have identified me, those orders, as 'Disposable Accident-Prone Frontline Cannon Fodder,' except that specialty was highly in demand on the *Russian* Front, which is where they would have once again sent me in that case. Midwinter 1942 was a *very bad* time to be sent to the Russian Front, my friend! In Tripoli I was handed over to *Panzergruppe Afrika*, the 'armor' side of *Afrikakorps.*

"Now, slinging panzers was Rommel's specialty. Hitler loved meddling with his general officers' assignments. I always supposed he thought it prevented them from consolidating power and forming cabals against him. Well, he allowed Rommel to 'consolidate power' concerning all the bits and pieces of Panzer Divisions that had been surplused to *Afrikakorps*, and eventually a 'cabal' of Divisional and Army Group commanders had formed, clustered around the real, underlying chain of command for *Afrikakorps*. Once the commanders' cabal figured out how they'd actually like to run things, they left it to Rommel to petition *Der Führer* for the high level Command restructuring, since all the generals knew that Hitler showed great favoritism for his popular, heroic *Generalfeldmarschal*. Rommel got the armor: *Panzergruppe Afrika*. Other German and—believe it or not!—*Italian* generals got other titles. But I suspect everyone deferred to Rommel. He was the only one in the bunch with a respectable pair of *Hoden*!

"All right, so since *Afrikakorps* was far enough from Berlin as to not be under constant scrutiny to conform to their requisite one-plan-fits-all organization structures, Rommel had seen to the creation of a bunch of small, semi-independent ancillary units which performed certain

122

unique, specialized roles—roles that required a high degree of mobility and didn't necessarily hew to the restrictions of exclusivity as to serving only the Divisions that 'own' them. Like, field-hospitals for example. Or water treatment units. Well, diesel engine maintenance units worked much like that, and I was assigned to a mobile squad in one of these units at the Divisional level. We had a nice go-anywhere halftrack with a hoist that could yank a *Mittelpanzer* out of a ditch. Did I say 'assigned?' Better than 'assigned'…as a new minted *Unterfeldwebel*, I was *put in charge* of that squad!

"In desert conditions, panzer engines failed at an appalling rate! Routine servicing had to be done eight times more frequently than in the Western European Theater or on the Russian Front. 'Routine servicing' is a joke, sort of, because the *verdammt* things usually broke down out in some wadi somewhere, a thousand kilos from any actual service facility. Usually, under combat conditions.

"The problem with engines was, in spite of the best air intake filters we could obtain, the fine, gritty dust just got right through! Injectors clogged. Pistons scoured. Fuel pumps got jammed up. Fuel lines got blocked. Engine oil turned to thick, abrasive mud gruel. Bearings failed. Operating on a diligent schedule of air filter servicing or replacement was a sufficiently simple procedure that the panzer crews could handle it themselves. But it was never enough, and in the heat of battle, you couldn't expect the boys to stop and change air filters when the odometer clicked over to some arbitrary number!

"Then take the *verdammt* tracks! Tank jockeys could never go ahead at a nice moderate twelve or fifteen klicks per hour…it was balls-to-the-wall or nothing, and that's exactly how Rommel liked to see things run. Grit got in the track bearings and trammels, the bogies and pinions and drive sprockets, and just ate their bearings alive.

Craaack! Off would fly an entire track, and that panzer was a sitting duck until one of our mobile service vehicles got to it and fixed it. You ask me, servicing panzer *tracks* is not exactly in the job description of a 'skilled diesel mechanic!' But we did it anyway...*somebody* had to.

"So I arrive in February 1942. For the next few months, it looks like Poland, France and the early days of Russia all over again! Hell-bent German advances against ineffective resistance. All this time, me and a squad of five are following the *panzergruppe*, cobbling together field fixes for rapidly aging engines. Pulling panzers out of holes, ditches, and wadis. Jury repairs on cooling systems. Slinging tired out treads back onto worn sprockets and tightening them up a notch or two. The troops on the Russian Front are in big, desperate trouble right about then, so Hitler, who is deeply involved in losing the war for us in a thousand ways in Russia, scrimps and denies us in North Africa. We fail to receive replacement Panzers and relief troops. And even parts and spares and tires and spark plugs and fan belts that we on this forgotten front might have found very handy in keeping our advances moving.

"So. Through the spring, Rommel uses what we have to spearhead our advance eastward. In spite of the perilous condition of our armor and transport, things look glorious here in Africa for the Reich! Earlier, a couple weeks before my arrival, Benghazi had been recaptured. In May, we seized Bir Hakeim! Thirteen June and Rommel crushed a British armored column in head-to-head combat out in the desert...hundreds of Allied tanks destroyed! Twenty-one June: Tobruk recaptured! Twenty-eight June, Marsa Matruh fell to Rommel...and now we are *in Egypt*! Two days later, 30 June 1942, we reached El Alamein!

"...And El Alamein is where everything turned to *Ratte-scheisse.*

"The German war machine just seemed to have a knack for doing this! In Western Europe: we stampede across mainland Europe, pull up short at the English Channel and then throw everything we've got in the way of air-power against the English...who refuse to go down. And we are stopped in our tracks. Moscow: we stampede across the steppes and pull up short at the gates of Moscow. Can't seem to carry off that last push that would take the capital and deliver us all of Russia! The Russians use *our* favorite blitzkrieg tactic and almost surround us. They make us reverse our march, and they kick our German asses right back across those thousands of kilometers of steppe. Stalingrad: same thing. Leningrad: same thing. El Alamein...pretty *Gott verdammt* near the same thing.

"The worst of it is that with the greater part of the *Panzerarmee* and a whole lot of Italian auxiliaries coming close to being encircled by the British Eighth Army, Rommel takes seriously ill. On 23 September he's flown out of the pocket, home to Germany. A general from the Russian Front, Georg Stumme, is flown in to take control. Things just go from bad to worse as the British noose tightens. Supplies are critically low, two fuel transport ships are sunk by Allied aircraft, which further worsens our already desperate diesel and gasoline situation. There are adequate supplies of food, ammunition and fuel at Benghazi...but that's a long distance from El Alamein, and the fact is we can't keep the requisite 1200 supply trucks making that arduous trip every day to keep El Alamein in supplies.

"On 26 October, Rommel, in somewhat improved health, returns! At this point, Rommel displays the one little difference between himself and Paulus or Guderian. Rommel is in constant touch with Hitler, begging for critical supplies, fuel, vehicles and reinforcements. He figures—erroneously—that eventually Paulus will succeed in taking Stalingrad and will start driving south into the

Trans-Caucasus. The British will have to back off at El Alamein so as to divert troops to northern Persia in defense against German advances southward into the Middle East. All *Afrikakorps* has to do is stick it out until that happens. But, in response to Rommel's pleas, Hitler is screaming at Rommel that, no, he doesn't have any tanks or troops or bullets he can spare."

Hans stopped, took a gulp of Molson, stood up. "Wait here a minute!" he cried. Then he hustled off toward the bedroom. He was back in a flash with a book.

He fumbled for a dog-eared page. "Okay...Here's a message that Hitler sent Rommel at midday on 3 November 1941. Listen to this!"

> **To Field Marshal Rommel. It is with trusting confidence in your leadership and in the courage of the German and Italian troops under your command that the German people and I are following the heroic struggle in Egypt. In the situation which you find yourself there can be no other thought but to stand fast, yield not a yard of ground and throw every gun and every man into the battle.... Your enemy, despite his superiority, must also be at the end of his strength. It would not be the first time in history that a strong will has triumphed over the bigger battalions. As to your troops, you can show them no other road than that to victory or death. Adolf Hitler**

Hans set the book aside. "'A load of *Quatsch*!' says Rommel. Not to Hitler, of course. He knows when he's in a pincer that's about to be sprung. He knows that Hitler won't hesitate to write him and *Afrikakorps* off rather than make big sacrifices to effect some kind of rescue.

126

Guderian should have known as much, standing outside the gates of Moscow. Paulus should have realized as much, standing in the ruins of Stalingrad.

"Rommel salvaged what he could from the debacle. He sent a fluffy message back to Berlin assuring his Führer the *Panzerarmee Afrika* would do their duty, fight to the last shell, to the last man. Then he set about seeing how many of his men and panzers he could get the *Hölle* out of there."

I found myself itching to know how *Hans* had fared through all of this! "So how about *you*?" I insisted. "Where were *you* during El Alamein? How did *you* make out?"

"Me? I and my little squad were driving back and forth along the coastal highway between Sirte and Ajdabiya Junction, 400 kilometers of shitty road. There were literally hundreds of trucks every hour going eastward loaded, headed for El Alamein, and westward empty. We'd get a radio distress call and a milepost number, then fight our way east or west, whichever, to find the broken-down truck. If it was fixable, we'd fix it. Otherwise, we'd use that crane to jerk the derelict well off the highway, and sabotage the engine so no one else could use it under any circumstances. We did that eighteen hours a day, from August until November. Cooked rations over a campfire…slept under the halftrack. Early on 4 November we get the word on the radio that Rommel's organized a retreat, which has broken out of the British ring and is fleeing El Alamein westward. British tank columns are sure to be in hot pursuit! Evidently all those transport trucks get the same message, because all the eastbound ones have slammed on their brakes and executed three-point U-turns in order to flee back toward Tripoli. Naturally, a good number of them wind up in the road-ditches. There are crashes and tipovers, and the highway is

like a vehicular insane-asylum. That's no problem for me and the squad...our vehicle's a halftrack! Halftracks don't need any stinkin' highway! Won't be too much of a problem for the panzers because a panzer doesn't need any stinkin' highway either. So me and the diesel mechanics talk it over and decide we ought to start heading west ourselves. We pull off the highway and start rolling westward at a moderate rate. Next thing you know...
Ka-BLAM!

"*What?* What happened?!" I shouted
"Anti-tank mine. Could have been one of ours, could have been one of theirs...that highway had changed hands six times! We just clipped the mine with the back end of the left-side track. Flipped the truck over, shrapnel everywhere. I'd been riding shotgun, up front. Three guys in the truckbed. My corporal was driving."
"Were you guys all right?"
"Well *scheisse* no, Lewis! All the rest of the squad, killed dead! I was rapped pretty good across the skull with a piece of shrapnel...only a scalp wound, but bleeding like anything. Bits of shrapnel in the meat of my right arm, where I'd had it hanging out the window. I had an awful struggle getting out of that upside-down truck cab, climbing over the body of my corporal. Just a good thing we didn't hit that mine with a *front* wheel! That truck would have been engulfed in flames, and I'd have been killed for sure!"
"God, man! What did you do?"
"Found the first-aid kit. Stuck adhesive plasters on the bloody places. Then I found a couple canteens and hooked them on my belt. Started heading for the highway. We'd strayed maybe a hundred meters off the track. Plenty of traffic, all heading west. Not a *ficken* one of those bastards would stop and pick me up! Pretty soon, the

traffic flow peters out and I'm all alone on that sand-surface highway."

"So what did you do then?"

"What else? Started walking! Well, about midafternoon, here come the first panzers rolling west from El Alamein. You could see how beat-up those tanks were! Twenty-liter fuel cans strapped down on every rack. Exhausted, hollow-eyed troops who'd thrown away their rifles clinging on every remaining square centimeter of the hulls, jouncing up and down as the monsters treaded west. Sure as fate, some of those boys were going to spill off and get chewed to hamburger by the next pair of treads to come up the road, but they looked as if they didn't give a damn. Those tanks, they just sped on by me, like the transport trucks had done."

"You didn't plan to *walk* all the way back to Tripoli, did you?"

"Lewis, I hadn't really worked it all out. I was not thinking too clearly, and I was doing a lot of bleeding. Pretty soon, the sun went down and it started getting cold. I didn't have anything on but my desert uniform …undershirt and cotton button-up blouse on top, light cotton trousers on the bottom. Lightweight desert cap. Stupid, useless, dented Iron Cross hanging from my second shirt button!

"I hiked all night. Couldn't stop…too cold. Every so often I'd have to bail off the road so I wouldn't get squashed by a panzer or a halftrack or a utility truck towing a field gun. The sun came up and it immediately started getting warm, then hot. Along about mid-morning I came over a rise and here's a Panzer III Medium Tank…a newer model with the 50mm main gun. It's stopped right in the roadway. The driver's in there cranking the starter. The *panzerkommandant* and crew and a bunch of infantrymen—doubtlessly external hull-clinger passengers—are standing around scratching their asses.

Engine won't start, no pre-ignition smoke at all coming out of the exhaust.

'Injectors clogged!' I yell out as I approach.

'What the *scheisse* do you know!' growls a filthy rat-faced *Soldat*.

'That would be, What the *scheisse* do you know, *UNTERFELDWEBEL*!' I answer. 'I am a skilled diesel technician. Perhaps your *Panzerkommandant* would like me to take a look? Tell the driver to stop grinding the starter…it sounds like he's got about twenty seconds of battery life left, and it's never going to start with clogged injectors!'

"The crew commander was more than happy to let me take a crack at it. I crawled into the engine compartment. One of the more on-the-ball tankers, the gunner I suspect, acted as my OR nurse and smartly snapped the correct tools into my outstretched hand as I called for them. Sure enough, little globs of oily dirt on the injector ports.

" 'Crank it over!' I called out, once I got things cleaned up and back in place. The engine fired on the first revolution!

" 'Herr *Oberleutnant*,' I call out. 'Mind if I hitch a ride?'

" 'Sorry. Can't be done. No room. Full up.'

" 'Mind telling me which hanger-on is going to clean your injectors, next time they clog?' I ask politely.

"The *Oberleutnant* glanced from man to man. The infantrymen were in the process of struggling up the flanks of the softly throbbing panzer, reclaiming their previous perilous perches. His eyes lit on one. Wordlessly, the officer gave a jerk of his thumb, and the filthy, rat-faced trooper disconsolately slid off onto the sand. 'Be my guest!' the *Oberleutnant* smiled. He actually bowed from the waist and smartly clicked his booted heels together!

"It took several days for that Panzer III to get back to Benghazi. While we were on the road, on 8 November, the Americans were making massive landings in Morocco and Algeria. That meant that the battered remains of Rommel's *Afrikakorps* was all-of-a-sudden in a *two-front war*.

"When I got back to Benghazi on that Panzer III, the place was like a kicked anthill! Rommel himself had fallen back this far. But he was organizing things to establish a defensive line somewhat farther east, hopefully Tobruk where we still had a pretty substantial garrison. His hope was to consolidate something of the terrain he had gained since the start of the year. I actually saw him, Lewis! Saw the renowned *Generalfeldmarschall* Rommel. I must say, he looked as haggard and filthy as any common soldier who'd bailed out of El Alamein and fled westward. And all his frantic preparations came to nothing. Within eight days, Rommel was barely holding a line at Tobruk. And on 13 November the British took Tobruk back again— third time—and we swiftly lost all the intervening ground right on back to Benghazi. On 20 November we lost Benghazi too. Rommel began pulling us back toward Tripoli. Armored panzer elements had been dispatched westward in preparation to face the Americans. I spent my days and half my nights frantically working on very beat-up, barely running panzers in an improvised shop in Tripoli. We lost Tripoli to the Brits on 23 January, 1943, and left a lot of equipment and vehicles behind. Westward, US forces were moving toward us. We met them at the Kasserine Pass and kicked their inexperienced asses! Our celebrations were short lived and not to be repeated. Eisenhower promoted a general we hadn't yet heard of, a guy named George Patton, and as a tank commander, he was the worst news yet for the Third Reich. Well, it was Patton advancing from the west, Montgomery from the east. Anyone with half a brain knew we were finished in North Africa. They started pulling personnel out on ships, mostly to Italy and Southern France. But crossing the Mediterranean was chancy, with both British and American destroyers prowling the water. I got orders saying I was to evacuate out of Tunis, 5 May, along with a bunch of other support specialists and mechanics. We were designated 'critical-skill' specialists. Me! A critical specialist!"

16

HANS ESCAPES TO SICILY

It was getting on toward the middle of the day. Hans volunteered that Anna might have left something for us to lunch on, in the fridge. He rustled around, bending over at the waist to access the lower shelves. "Aha!" he cried in triumph. A moment later, he had hauled a couple of delicacies over to the dining alcove table: a foil-covered platter of crispy potato latkes with pickled seal meat, and a reeking bowl of kraut. Four more half liters of Molson, to be sure. All this provender, perfectly edible when cold.

We pitched in. After a while, sated, Hans tipped his chair back and took up the tale of his escape from North Africa.

"Well, I turned up at the appointed pier in Tunis. I figured it would be a mistake to miss that particular sailing, since I could hear British cannonfire in the near distance. The evacuation vessel was moored dockside. From what I could make out in the dark, it was an aged rustbucket patrol boat about ten meters long! I went aboard and a seaman checked me off on his clipboard. That seaman and a helmsman of obscure rank...they were the entire crew. It was assumed we would make the crossing to southern Italy in only about twenty hours, so there were seven of us crowded on an open-air deckwell...no classy staterooms or bunk facilities for us! We waited and waited for the go-ahead to sail. That little deathtrap boat pushed away from the pier in Tunis harbor at about 11 p.m. Pitch dark, not a light showing on board. There was a wind, and the water was choppy. The boat bobbed like a cork. The only other time I'd been on a ship was the great big troopship that had brought me to Tripoli, and it was as stable as an iceberg. Pretty soon I was hanging over the lee rail and puking in the ocean!

"The wind rose and rose. It was so black I couldn't imagine how the helmsman could tell anything about our course or position. But what did I know? About four in the morning, we all discovered that my suspicions were right! The boat, churning ahead at what I thought was a pretty good clip, ran right over a jagged underwater coral ridge, or something very much like it! The impact threw us all off our feet. It didn't quite rip the entire bottom out of the boat, but the crewman came back to where all us evacuees were huddled and said the boat couldn't float very long and we ought to get into life jackets. No worries, he informed us—only a precaution. If the helmsman was correct about our position, we were only half a mile from a nice, gently sloping sandy shoreline. He was going to execute a turn to port, give the engine all the speed she had, and run us softly ashore.

"When that boat ran up on the sand, it was about as gentle as running into a brick wall."

I had to laugh aloud! Judging from Hans's previous wartime adventures, a shipwreck was just about par for the course. "So I take it you walked away from that one?" I asked.

"Didn't walk...waded. Swam a bit. Got rolled in the surf, and a lot of sand wound up in my clothes. I took a big crack to my ribs when the boat hit the beach. Hurt like fire for weeks! Later, I found out I'd broken three ribs. They pretty much healed by themselves...only left some odd lumps under my chest muscles. Well, there was only me and four others. Three *Wehrmacht* and the nondescript crewman. We had no idea where we were. The helmsman had stuck his head through the windscreen when we impacted, killing himself, so he was not able to share his opinion about where we had encountered land. The other troopers must have drowned. When the sun came up, I selected a trooper and the deckhand to come with me toward some buildings a short way inland.

"There was a damned fine chance we were on Allied terrain, in which case we'd shortly be POWs. My guess was Malta, but my knowledge of Mediterranean Islands was sketchy. If it was Malta, we were screwed! The *Kriegsmarine* and *Luftwaffe* had pulverized the *scheisse* out of Malta for two and a half years without succeeding in breaking the British Maltese spirits and getting them to surrender. We had given up on trying to persuade them with artillery, after the fall of El Alamein. The place we were didn't look very pulverized, however, so I suspected it wasn't Malta after all.

"We got up to the buildings, and the place actually looked kind of nice. Lines of dark-green cypresses along the roads. Tidy rectangular stone-walled fields filled with wine grapes, the vines neatly pruned and leafing out nicely. Stone walls, little stone houses. We picked out a medium-sized house with red tile roofs, a villa almost, and prowled around to the front. There was a handsome wooden front door with grapeleaf carvings and brass fittings. No smoke from the flue, no sound other than roosters greeting the dawn, and a faraway dog barking. It was still pretty early. I knocked on the door panels and waited. Knocked again. The door creaked open! An elderly woman wrapped in a black shawl stood peering out through the narrow gap. *'Sì, chi sei?'* she said. Seeing us all bedraggled from the sea, she stepped out onto the flagstones. Well, Lewis, I recognized her words as Italian, but that's about as far as it goes! I asked the other two guys if either of them spoke any Italian. No and no. I thought hard about how to proceed, and then…Aha! Considering the circumstances, one single useful Italian word occurred to me! *'Dove?'* I asked her, *'Dove?'*—'WHERE,' as in, 'Where in Hell are we?' I looked pathetic, like I was seriously lost.

'Oh sì! In questa direzione è Likata, e laggiù è—'

"I'm sure she would have gone on and on in high-speed Italian, but I hushed her with my finger to my lips. I pointed to my ear, then shrugged both shoulders eloquently. Too stupid to understand plain Italian. I repeated my one-and-only word of her language nice and slow: '*Dove?* Dough-VAY?'

"The old lady got the hint. She pointed in a direction right up the beach. '*Likata! Lee-KAH-tah!*' she enunciated carefully, like to a three-year-old moron child. I'd never heard of Likata, so I kept looking stupid. She got that hint too. She swiveled about and pointed one-eighty in the other direction. '*Ragusa!*' she informed me. Well, Lewis, I had heard of Ragusa but I couldn't tell you where it was...I thought maybe Greece or Finland or somewhere else far-away, so Ragusa didn't help. I tried looking even stupider. '*Buon Dio, ciò che un grande idiota!*' the old crone mumbled to herself. Then she made a big swooping "over-the-mountain" gesture with her hand. '*Catania! Catania!*' Then another gesture just like it, but in another direction. '*Palermo! Palermo!*'

"That one I knew!"

"Christ, man!" I yelled. "What luck! You ran aground on Sicily! A nice Italian province. Under Italian Army control. With a substantial German garrison, am I right?"

Hans nodded agreement. "*Ja.* Axis territory. Until, as you no doubt know perfectly well, *Klugscheisser*, Patton and Montgomery landed on this lovely Sicilian south coast no more than two months later, the bastards! With a couple hundred thousand troops between the two of them."

"What did you and your fellow marooned survivors do?" I asked.

"Well...we were in pretty poor shape. We took inventory, and found we had about 120 soggy Reichsmarks pocket money among us. We were getting pretty hungry, and I didn't see how we were going to talk that old Sicilian lady out of provisions and drink, in view of the language barrier. So we thought we would walk until we found the nearest village, and see if we could buy some bread and sausages or something there...and maybe some beer. I had it in mind to see if I could contact some German military authorities. But first, something for our stomachs!

"We picked up the other two fellows from the beach, who reported that no one at all had walked, driven, or sailed by and taken note of our wrecked boat a hundred meters out in the surf, getting pounded to fragments. We all five regained the road. I, *Unterfeldwebel* Raufer, was in command by unspoken acclaim. I looked east along the road, then west. West was where the old lady had indicated 'Likata' was. I figured we might as well try west.
"We walked and walked. The sun climbed up. Our clothes dried out, leaving salt and sand to annoy the *scheisse* out of us. It got hot! My bruised ribs ached. The others found their own collection of annoyances to gripe about. Eventually, after maybe five or six kilometers, we came into the outskirts of a town.
"One of the first roadside businesses we came to was what the Sicilians call a *Taverna*...except, unlike 'taverns' in lots of other lands, which are more like booze-dispensing nightclubs with music and bar girls, in Sicily these establishments are usually open all day. Usually the host lives in quarters attached to the back. Usually the host has little, if any, hired help. The menu is meager and unvarying. Coffee and bread for breakfast, cold pasta for lunch, whatever hot dish the host (who is also the cook, scullion, sommelier and cleanup crew) decides to whip up for dinner...it's usually sea food of some kind, prepared

with hot Moorish seasonings. Wine all day and well into the evening. Beer? *Pah!* Go find a *Kraut* drinking hole!

"We commandeered a table, ordered by waving a couple of 10-Reichsmark notes and pointing at what local patrons were having. After a while I was sufficiently sated. I flagged the host over. *'Sie haben ein Telefon?'* I demanded, figuring that last word would be pretty universal.

"He gives us a slackjawed gaze.

'Uno Telefon-o? Rrrring-Rrrring?' I mimicked finger-dialing in thin air.

"A glimmer of recognition. The host raised his hand and, hollow palm upward, rubbed his thumb across his index and middle finger. The international signal for 'Give me a lot of money!' I handed him a fiver. He sniffed, stood undecided for a moment, then jerked his head sideways...the international signal for 'Follow me, jackass!'

"With a phone receiver in my hand, it occurred to me I didn't have any idea who or what to call, nor any notion of how to make a phone call on the Sicilian system, undoubtedly degraded by the vagaries of World War II. I just dialed 'O' and hoped for the best.

'Opera-TOR-e! Buon-GIOR-no! Che NU-mero, per favo-RE?' a female voice chirped.

'Wehrmacht! Wehrmacht! Wehrmacht!' I yelled. I kept it up until some forwarding clicks and clacks sounded over the receiver.

"The next voice answered crisply, loudly, and almost without punctuation:

Fünfzehnten Panzergrenadier Division Büro des Kommandanten Oberstleutnant Zeigler zu sprechen wie kann ich Ihnen helfen MEIN HERR?

"Uh-oh! I believe I'd been put through to a number a little higher up the chain of command than I'd intended to shoot for. I put the best face on things, and explained that I and four other soldiers, having evacuated from Tunis, had had our very small transport craft run aground in the dark, and that the boat's helmsman and another four soldiers had perished in the sea. 'Er...I guess we are reporting for duty, *Herr Oberstleutnant*," I concluded. That rank is like Lieutenant Colonel, by the way, Lewis.

'Name, rank, identity number and unit, soldier!' the officer barked.

'*Unterfeldwebel* Hans Raufer, Sir!" I rattled off the rest of it.

'All right, Sergeant,' the officer said soothingly. 'Let's get you five sorted out, then. Anyone injured?"

'*Keineswegs*!' I lied. 'Not at all!'

'Good...good. Where are you, Sergeant Raufer?'

'A town named Licata, Sir. A *taverna* on the edge of town...*Taverna Magnifico*, it's called.' I eyed the grubby, fish-smelling kitchen and dirty-pot-stacked scullery, which is where the wall phone was to be found...*Ja*, real *magnifico* all right!

"By now the Colonel had transformed into a pretty nice guy. He took a minute to explain that many ships carrying thousands of German troops, also refugees from *Afrikakorps* units, had made harbor in Palermo, which is where the 15th *Panzergrenadier* Division was positioned at present—but none yet had found their way to Sicily by the expedient of running their keels up onto a remote beach. Things were incredibly busy just now getting these troops cleaned up, re-equipped and reassigned. He advised me to linger at the *taverna* until midday, two or three hours after which time a vehicle would arrive to give us a ride back to Palermo. He suggested that at midday we switch from coffee and bread to one of the local pasta specialties along with some south coast Sicilian wine. He recommended

Arancine con Calamari with *Saracena* olives, and a nice, crisp Ragusa *Cerasudo*. 'Run a tab, lad! The driver I'm dispatching will have orders to pick up the bill. It should be about four hours!' The officer rang off.

$$+ + + + + + + +$$

Allied High Command knew by late April they were going to succeed in defeating *Afrikakorps* in Tunisia. They knew that Sicily was going to be the next campaign, a stepping stone into Italy and a foothold onto the European mainland—what Winston Churchill had erroneously called "the soft underbelly of the Reich." Air attacks had commenced to soften up likely targets. Bombers flew out of newly captured airfields in Tunisia, dumping their explosive loads on Messina and Palermo. These were crucial north Sicily ports by which the Germans were reinforcing their Italian colleagues. But also, by targeting north Sicilian cities, Allied strategists hoped to divert Axis attention from the planned landing sites on the island's *south* coast. Messina drew extra attention because it was only a couple miles across the strait to Italy—a certain route for escape, once the Allies had Sicily's Axis troops in a vice. The British 8th Army under Montgomery would be landing at dispersed locations around the extreme southeastern tip of the island. US forces—the 7th Army— were under the command of Omar Bradley, seconded by the terrifying George Patton, whose very name seemed to inspire German dread. These forces would make their amphibious landings along the South-central coast…at Cassibile, Torre di Gaffe, and the port of Licata.

Fortunately for Hans Raufer, he and his other castaway buddies had not been left to idle away a month or two in Licata. Because on the night of 9 July 1942, paratroops of the US 82nd Airborne Division made their first-ever combat drop into the valley farmlands just to the East of Licata. By early morning, American troopships overran the miniature harbor facilities of Licata and, spoiling for a fight, combat teams had stormed ashore against disappointingly meager resistance. The Italian commander had anticipated heavy landings, and had repositioned his forces a long distance back from the coast. Within two days, both the American and British landing forces had pushed well inland.

Where was Sergeant Raufer at this time? He had been reassigned to a unit of the 15th *Panzergrenadiers* as emergency on-call diesel field-repair specialist. Suspecting, however, that Sicilian combat was going to be quick, hot and nasty, it was made clear to Hans that when he *wasn't* called for mechanic duties, he was expected to be leading a platoon of riflemen. And getting his ass shot at, just like the rest of the field grade cannonfodder.

Very soon after the Allied landings, 15th *PzGd* Division moved out from Palermo. The troop transports and supply trucks and panzers raced eastward on the north coast highway. The distance was about 230 kilometers, not very far compared to North Africa vastnesses Hans had grown used to. A defensive line was established fifty kilometers out from Messina. Its purpose was to guard the Straits of Messina, across which the German and Italian forces on Sicily would no doubt have to retreat. The German High Command was becoming heartily sick of losing hundreds of thousands of experienced combat troops at a crack, disarmed and disconsolately marched off as POWs.

+ + + + + + + +

"Did you get into the thick of it against Patton's 7th Army?" I asked. Obviously, I wasn't too certain who was where in the Sicilian Campaign.

141

"*Nein*…it was Montgomery on the east flank, not Patton. The British…the 8th Army. Patton was already all the way to Palermo by 22 July, thoroughly in control of about three-fourths of the island. Monty had sent columns around both sides of Mount Etna. It's surprising he didn't send a Division *over the smoking top* of Etna, just for the sake of thoroughness. Into the first week of August, Patton got tired of waiting for Montgomery to finish up with Messina, so he points his armor eastward from Palermo and they charge off toward Messina. So it's a horse race for glory between two would-be conquerors of Messina. Well, slowly and meticulously, Monty's 8th Army advanced up the east coast toward Messina. And at the same pace, implacably we got our asses shot off and our defensive lines pushed back toward the port city.

"On 15 August, the inevitable happened. I got wounded."

"My god, Hans!" I exclaimed. But I'd been expecting it. "How?"

"Well, I got my ass shot off."

This revelation caused me to spew a mouthful of Molson across the Raufer dining-table. "*Gawd!*"

"It wasn't as big a deal as you are probably thinking. I was dashing from position to position, keeping my men alert, making sure they were aware of targets, keeping them behind cover. I'd just leaped up to move position when a bullet came along and clipped *mein Hintern*. Hurt a lot, but didn't even bleed that much. Most of the round went right on through. That evening a field medic tweezered out a couple of bullet fragments and poured some antiseptic on it. A stick-on bandage and a couple of aspirin and he declared me fit for combat.

"But, everyone knew it was just about over for us. That included the Brass. Company by Company, our guys were pulled back into Messina for evacuation.

"Now, the Allies didn't *want* us to evacuate! They had almost complete air superiority, so they tried bombing and strafing the port and city of Messina round the clock. But! We had pretty good air defenses going, at least in daylight hours. We brought down a *lot* of American bombers and British fighters! So after a couple days of big losses, they switched to *night-time* bombing. So we switched to night-time lying low and *day-time* evacuating! Only problem was, the people doing the load coordinating and troop embarkation people had to work like crazy to get twice as many troops and twice as many tons of valuable war material onto the ships and out of port, in half as many hours. The trip across the strait to the Italian side was only about 20 kilometers, so shipborne travel time was *not* the problem."

"Where were you being evacuated to?"

"Reggio. That's in Calabria. The 'toe' of the Italian boot."

"Okay, so how did *you* get out?"

"Typical screw-up. My Company is holding down a defensive line against probably a couple battalions of Brits, also dug in. About six in the morning, 16 August, we get the word to break off contact…later in the morning there will be a transport ship with us on the manifest. My wounded ass is aching like a rotten tooth, and I'm bringing up the rear. Not a pun! Up ahead, the Company *Hauptmann* stops, waits for me to catch up to within twenty or thirty meters of him. 'We are missing a rifle squad!' he yells. 'It's one of those from 3rd Platoon that was out on that ridge, extreme right of the line…they must not have gotten the word!' Well I know perfectly well what he's asking me without him actually saying the words, so I save

143

him the trouble. 'I'll go back for them!' I holler, then I turn around and take off.

"It takes me fifteen or twenty minutes to get back to the foxholes we had just abandoned. *Danke Gott* the Brits hadn't figured that out yet! I scramble from cover to cover, moving right, until I reach the forgotten rifle squad, who are pouring fire into the Brit positions, pretending they are an entire Company. Preserving the fiction, you know. 'Let's crap on outta here!' I yell. There's only eight guys, but they don't argue with me. 'Time to evacuate!'

"We are triple-timing down the coast highway for the Messina harbor, maybe three more kilometers away, and a latecomer British Hurricane comes screaming over the ridgetop, its four 20mm wing cannons spitting fire nonstop. That *verdammt, ficken* pilot strafes the whole strung-out running line of us from one end to the other. Kills every last one of that rifle squad! Me, I pick up a little shrapnel, because a 20mm projectile just bursts into pieces when it hits anything hard. But nothing serious, just some red hot bits of metal in my flesh. I'm the only lucky one left alive when that son-of-a-bitch pilot breaks off!"

Once again, is it Hans Raufer *good* luck or Hans Raufer *bad* luck? "Okay...I suppose you missed your evacuation timeslot."

"By a mile. But it turned out all right."

"How did you get out of Messina?"

"I commandeered a submarine."

144

17

I GO TO THE MOVIE WITH HANS AND ANNA

I feel certain Hans was on the point of explaining that comment about stealing a submarine when the telephone rang. Hans answered. "It's Canada National," he said. He handed the receiver to me.

"Mr. MacLeod?" a polite male voice asked. I didn't recognize the voice. "I have a note here that you were to be informed whether the tentatively scheduled weekly Monday Winnipeg-to-Churchill flight is on for tomorrow. Unfortunately, only two northbound passengers booked seats. Winnipeg has canceled the flight. Our sincere thanks for selecting CanadaNational as your airline of choice." Click!

Just as I was hanging up, the front door banged open. It was Anna, back from visiting. Evidently she'd done a little shopping, too. Hans helped Anna with the bags of groceries in her arms, then offered to fix her a cup of tea. Anna declined, since this would entail Hans's trespassing upon her Sacred Culinary Precincts. "What's wrong?" she asked me, reading my expression.

"That Monday flight from—and *back to*—Winnipeg has been cancelled. No big thing…I expected as much. Hans, can I use your phone to leave yet another despairing message at my engineering firm? I'll bill the charges to the business number."

"*Ja,* sure…go ahead! And hey, before you make that call…Anna asked me to take her to the movie tonight. *Star Wars*! *The Empire Attacks,* or something like that. You want to come?"

"Sounds fine!" I agreed.

Anna added that there was another phone call I might want to make, to someone who was probably sitting by her own telephone chewing on her fingernails. She added that I could invite her to the movie with us if I wished. It was like a gentle trap snapping closed! I fumbled out the piece of paper Anna had given me, and dialed Qilqiq's number.

And so that's how all four of us came to be sitting side-by-side in a row of theater seats, halfway down, right in the middle, at about six-thirty on Sunday evening. The theater was pretty full. Only average sized, and the one and only movie house in Churchill, the theater could still have accommodated half the town's population at any one time. It looked like half of Churchill *was* here. I'm sure I recognized a few faces from the party at the Townshend house. Qilqiq Sidney, wiggling with delight that I'd invited her to the flicks, clutched my arm possessively on my right side. Anna and then Hans sat to my left. The lights went down. We watched half a dozen previews. Then a jingle cartoon pitching popcorn and soft drinks on sale in the lobby.

Odd thing about the soft drinks! It appeared to be the usual range of pop: cola, orange soda, grape, root beer, lemon-lime. But the snack bar sold this stuff in *glass bottles*! With a straw, if you liked. Oh yeah, I remembered…soda pop in glass bottles was the cargo in the belly of the good aircraft *Miss Piggy* when it went down on the tundra out there. A Canadian thing. I wondered if the cargo plane had been heading north to resupply a *movie theater* in Chesterfield Inlet.

Time for the feature! When the Twentieth-Century Fox art-nouveau theater logo with searchlights came on and the familiar orchestral theme began, the entire audience *trilled right along*! Singing dum-da-dum-dum scat syllables accompanying the orchestra! Like they'd *practiced* it together! I glanced rightward at Qil, participating like the best of them, and she glanced back as if to ask, "What? What? We *always* do this!" I had an inkling that here in Churchill, Far Frozen North, Manitoba, I was *not* in Kansas anymore.

Star Wars Episode V—The Empire Strikes Back commenced. Everyone—the whole theaterful!—read the familiar block letter overlay in unison, out loud:

A LONG TIME AGO IN A GALAXY FAR, FAR AWAY

Things got a little raggedy for the dramatic public unison mass-reading of the usual slopey, sliding yellow letters spelling out the backstory. At the mention of the villain, Darth Vader, there was a chorus of **BOO!** and *hisssss!* like you'd expect to hear in an old-time vaudeville opera house.

Wait a minute! That's <u>exactly</u> how this crowd was behaving! That realization crashed me through my haze of mild irritation and got me into the mood. It was a goofy mood of collective semi-participation, almost as if an invisible Interlocutor were holding up ornately lettered instructional signs for the audience's delectation:

Our Hero!

CHE VILLAIN!

How SAD!

The root of this was *not* a single, isolated, yakky, rude theater patron. Instead, it was a cozy small-town community spirit the like of which I had never experienced before in a movie theater. I decided to relax and enjoy it.

The Ice Planet of Hoth, ass deep in snow, appeared on the Big Screen, and a voice from the audience sang out, "Hey! That's *Manitoba!*" Luke Skywalker riding across the snowfields on a curly horned tauntaun: "Yay! Our Hero!" Clap-clap-clap-clap! When the tauntaun emitted a string of incomprehensible, gargly noises, someone postulated, "Is that *Inuktitut*?" This was evidently someone named 'Jimmy' speaking, because another voice responded, "Yeah! It's saying '*Jimmy's a jackass!*'" ...followed by sounds of a brief scuffle in the dark. A hideous Ice Creature had hung up Luke Skywalker by the heels in his cave for our boy's flesh to age a bit before the Creature devoured him, and the voiced opinion of right-thinking Churchilleans was that the Ice Creature was a discreditable Hollywood misrendering of a *polar bear*! A bit later, when Han Solo light-sabered open the belly of his deceased tauntaun and the beast's grotesque guts spilled out onto the snow, several Inuit-sounding voices, life-long epicures of weird, semi-cooked animal substances, chimed, "Oooh! Yummy!" Every time Chewbacca emitted a comment in wookiee-speak, the entire audience had to reply. In fluent wookieeese, of course. Ah, but when the Imperial Walkers came striding toward the rebel base to destroy it, the Churchillians were unanimously *outraged*! "Those are *mechanical POLAR BEARS*!" an alert viewer declared. "But stupider!" he was seconded. "Less dangerous than *real* polar bears!" another opined. Two seats over on my left hand, I heard Hans volunteer, "A *Wehrmacht* Tiger Panzer with an 88-millimeter antitank gun could take out any one of those...." Amicable agreement from several male voices:

"Yeah!"

"Damn straight!"

"*Ja-WOHL!*"

"You betcha!"

It was at this point, not very far into the flick, that the first pop bottle made its desperate run for freedom. You see, the theater floor sloped down, back to front, like you'd expect. When constructed, the concrete auditorium floor had been poured in steps. The floor covering was cheap but durable linoleum. The chairs were old style padded theater seating, where the springloaded bottom snapped up with a thump when the patron stood up. Four seats in a block, one set of cast metal legs on each end of the block, bolted to the floor. So, lots of open space at floor level between the legs. Way up in the back, some guy had finished drinking his soda and had placed his empty glass bottle on its side, parallel with the movie screen, on the floor under his feet. He'd given it a small shove with his toe. The bottle rolled audibly across the linoleum—a little rr-rr-rr-rr sound—moving downhill toward the screen. It encountered the first step, fell four inches with a little *clink*, then kept on rolling. The pop bottle repeated this maneuver. Rr-rr-rr-*CLINK*!-rr-rr-rr-*CLINK*! all the way down. This particular pop bottle made it to Row One, fell into what must have been an orchestra pit, and shattered with a satisfying breaking-glass *pa-ding*! Wild, celebratory cheers! Then everyone settled down so a bit more of the movie could be watched.

Except for the occasional further pop bottle making its run for freedom and glassy suicide, the audience settled into the magic of the fantasy film. At the scary parts, Qil hugged my arm, seeking some Big Strong Man comfort. All in all, the circumstances, astonishing and eccentric as they might have been to the likes of me, made for a delightful, quirky screening.

The four of us walked through the icy evening back to the Mercedes. Qil and I, as the youthful guests, naturally took occupation of the back seat. Qil did not hesitate to snuggle right up close to me. Earlier at the movie, we had passed on lobby snacks, all of them too sugary or buttery for our tastes, which must have been the incentive for Qil to suggest we drive uptown and have an ice cream at a well frequented café. Anna protested. No...no, she and Hans were tired. "Hans will drive us home and you two kids can take the car yourselves." Hans rolled his eyes over the

seatback.   Like   me,   he'd   perceived   the   cleverly
camouflaged ambush of Anna's ulterior motive.

Instead of the café, Qilqiq gave directions at various
intersections and I found myself directed out to the picnic
ground where that very morning I had watched the bears
frolic and prowl while Hans had recounted the horrors of
Babi Yar. All the bears were gone now, off to bed
somewhere, not a one to be seen. In their place, dancing
curtains of aurora washed the entire starry northern
horizon, battling with a dazzling-bright gibbous moon,
vying   for   Mother   Nature's   trophy   for   nocturnal
splendorousness. Far into the distance, unending ice on the
vast surface of Hudson Bay, lit green and magenta by
aurora, pearly-white by moonshine.
       "*Aqsarniit!*" Qil informed me, gazing with every
bit as much rapture as myself. "Awk-SAHR-nee-eet.
Northern Lights!"
       "Mmmm!"
       Qilqiq came into my arms, kissed me softly. "I
don't suppose you watch movies in quite that way back in
Boston," she ventured, when we came up for air.
       "No…no. New England audiences are too starched
to misbehave like that."
       "*Misbehave…!*" she protested. I figured the right
strategy for avoiding a heated argument would be a little
more kissing.
       After a while, we paused. "So, you aren't going
back on the Winnipeg run tomorrow!" She stated it with a
hint of relief in her voice, maybe even triumph. "You
know, the replacement parts are going to be here first thing
tomorrow morning, so I'm told they will fly your wounded
turboprop on south Tuesday afternoon. You with it! But
never fear, it might not be until Wednesday."
       "Who told you that?"

"I've got my spies! I *work* at CanadaNational, remember?"

I *hadn't* remembered! She must have told me at the party. I'd had too much heel punch and Islay single malt to retain every conversational detail I'd heard at that party. An interesting question popped into my mind, and I just had to ask her. "You didn't tell me that you're an *aircraft engine mechanic*, by any chance?"

Her laughter was like silver bells! "No, of course not! I'm a Cargo Dispatcher! I'm *Chief* Cargo Dispatcher!" She laughed more, and I had to stop her mouth with kisses.

We talked endlessly. About her job. Her life. Her younger days, and her school years in Winnipeg. "I went to the same college as Auntie Anna," she told me. It was an institution that Northern First Peoples children without the means for higher education might attend at government expense.

"Wait! AUNT Anna?"

"She's my great-aunt. Her brother is my Gram-pop."

I tried to work out the generational ages. Anna was about fifty-seven or fifty-eight, Qil was twenty-four. Yeah, given the Inuit propensity for youthful parenthood, it could work. If Qil's Gram-pop was Anna's *older* brother, it would work *easily*. "I didn't know that!" I admitted. "So then...your clan name would be same as hers?"

"Yah!"

"Utkuhiksalingmiut?"

"How can you say that?"

I gulped. Had I committed some ghastly *faux pas*? "I...I—"

"No, I mean...how is it that you can *pronounce* it? I never met any *qallunaq* yet who could! Oh Lewis, *I adore you!*" More kissing ensued.

The Mercedes' cabin was getting cold. There was a folded wool blanket on the far-back window ledge. I stretched to reach it. An old-fashioned fringed lap robe, I unfolded it and spread it over the two of us. This was not difficult because Qil snuggled *very* close.

We talked and talked. She asked a million questions about Boston and my life and my job. About my family and my growing-up. About my hobbies. About what books I liked and what music I favored. She was delighted I played Irish whistle and frequented Boston area Irish pub *sessiuns*—the Inuit persona runs toward one making one's own melodies, and unaffectedly sharing one's talents with the community. At one point she somehow steered me onto my misadventures in Viet Nam, gently urging me to tell her about things I don't usually speak of. At one moment as I talked of grim, far-off times in Southeast Asia, I glimpsed the glint of an empathetic tear trace down the sweet curve of her cheek.

I steered the topic back to her. How had she avoided the usual young female Churchillian routine of marrying young and having a lot of babies? What might her hopes and aspirations be? Did she dream of travel? Was she content here in Churchill, or did she long to venture into the broader world? Had she ever yet vacationed in exotic places? Europe? The tropics? Did she aspire to further her education? Did she have strong political leanings, or adamant views as to the social issues of the day? A propensity for activism in current Canadian concerns, or in affairs of worldwide interest?

Then we came spiraling back to the two of us, from different worlds, yet cuddling together romantically, wrapped in a blanket, on the night-time edge of an ice-covered Arctic sea.

"So that dratted engine-repair might take until *Wednesday*?" I asked. (Good going, Lewis! Great *non sequitur*!)

152

"Yah. Wednesday, maybe."

"If I'm stuck here in Churchill much longer, my boss is going to cut off my pay and tell me not to bother coming home!" I grumped.

"That wouldn't be so bad...." Qil murmured. Her tiny words were like knives in my heart.

"It's just that there's a lot waiting for me in Boston. You understand, Qil?"

She pulled back into the blanket up to her eyes, like a ptarmigan chick half-hiding beneath its mother's feathery breast. "Do you have a girlfriend waiting in Boston, maybe?" she murmured.

"No, Qil. No girlfriend. I've been pretty much without a girlfriend for four years. Went through a bad breakup back then. Haven't even dated much."

"Wife, maybe? And five kids?"

"*Nooo*! No wife, no kids!"

"A *boyfriend,* maybe?"

"*Qil!* Stop! *No boyfriend*!"

"Sorry. I can't believe you don't have a girlfriend, is all."

"Maybe the right lady hasn't come along. Maybe not until now."

This comment made Miss Qilqiq Utkuhiksalingmiut melt into hot, romantic taffy. I was overwhelmed with a big, torrid, prolonged kiss. Then she suddenly broke off, laughing, and bashed my arm ineffectually with her fist.

"*Ow!*" I protested. She must have decided I was pulling her leg. My 'right lady coming along' comment is a very Inuit sort of tease.

...But I don't think I was kidding. To prove it— well, to prove *something*!—I engulfed her in my arms and we kissed, hard. Then the kiss dissolved into something softer, sweeter. Our embrace turned some subtle corner onto perilous ground. We both felt the rapid lift of passion, of ecstasy taking possession of us, and hazily I realized that we were drifting beyond our limits of control. In the next moments, garments would become unbuttoned, underclothes slipped, tantalizing sexual boundaries crossed, restraint abandoned, then loving interminglings, lips exploring forbidden terrain, and intense, ardent penetrations…all of that and more would become inevitable, then become sweet, steamy reality. In that moment I desired her utterly, as she did me….

…But there was a tiny morsel of restraint left somewhere deep within us both. By mutual consent, unspoken and agonizing, we backed away from the moment. Too soon! Too fraught with hazard!

"Sorry, Qil."

"No! Don't be sorry! *I'm* not sorry! Dear one…it will happen for us when it's supposed to. We don't have to hurry."

My rueful smile admitted my doubts. I was leaving soon…too soon! It was a long way from Churchill to Boston, in more ways than just the miles. "When I go home—" I began.

"After you go home, will we see each other again?" she begged, racked with apprehension.

I nodded my own affirmation of this fear. "Qil—"

"I'll write you!" She said it with panicky desperation. "You write me back, okay? Send me some pictures of you! And, we can telephone! And, didn't you say, your engineering company sends you north all the time? And—"

"And maybe I could come visit on my vacation?"

"Yes! Yes, and maybe I could come visit YOU on *my* vacation! I get two weeks! In June!"

"You? In Boston?"

"Well why not?"

I stopped to think this through. Why not indeed? I'd find her a nice affordable hotel nearby, and…. No! No hotel! Bad idea! I'd clear out my treadmill and my

154

drafting table and my TV and stereo and all my posters and sports gear and the musical instruments and the untidy heaps of masculine clutter out of the...the MAN room! The lease papers trumpeted it as a 'spacious second bedroom with separate bath', but that's not how I thought of that room! Still...I could rearrange it into a *proper* guest room for her! Maybe repaint, even! Buy a daybed or a sofa bed for the room. Some nice art for the walls, some patterned bed linens and throw pillows and drapes to match. And she could stay *there* instead of some cold, stinkin' hotel!

I tried to enthuse. "You know, I'd *like* to show you around Boston! I'd *LOVE* to! Listen, Qil! Give me some dates and maybe I can—"

"Lewis..." she interrupted. "Lewis, maybe we shouldn't make plans. Dear, I want to beg a favor."

"Anything."

"I...I just want to see you one more time. Alone, you and me together. Let's meet for coffee at the café we're supposed to be at right now. Auntie Anna will tell you where it is. Tomorrow, when I'm done work. Or later, maybe. How about nine o'clock? Or Tuesday morning, even. Call me when you've got your departure time. But...one more time, before you fly? I have something to give you, Lewis. Let's not make promises we might not be able to keep."

She sounded so disconsolate. I nodded acceptance. To my further disappointment, the Mercedes started up cooperatively. And so I drove her home.

18

HANS ON THE RUN: ITALY

I awoke Monday morning to muffled sounds of bustle. Anna and Hans had obligations waiting, working hours to compel their presence. Unlike myself! The inconvenience of my unplanned airborne stopover coming when it had, I'd foregone what would have been a nice, idle post-mission weekend in Boston for this unforeseen Saturday and Sunday in Frozen Manitoba. Not that the stopover had been so arduous or anything! Quite the opposite...nothing less than completely entertaining.

Today, however! A Monday...and normally I considerably despised Mondays! But today I was completely at liberty. The Raufer apartment to myself, a far-north winter sun in the sky. *Low* in the sky, to be sure, and late to rise. And a sun not likely to have much in the way of warmth to it! But sunshine for the day instead of sleet, snow and ice-boned raindrops.

Anna had left me coffee and *Apfelkuchen*. I breakfasted unhurriedly. Then I showered, toweled myself dry, put on my change of work clothes that Anna had laundered for me. I had a rugged outdoor coat I always took on trips like this, for prowling about on construction sites. But I opted for Hans's loaned parka—in spite of its overgenerous roominess, the thick filling of goose down was a comfort in the biting breeze coming off of Hudson Bay. I wandered downstairs and outside. I meandered along the road, then angled off into the tundra, sticking to the firmer spaces between bogs and iced-up lakes and suspicious peaty marshland.

A few of hardier species of ground dwelling mammals were astir in the snapping-cold air. *Shouldn't they still be hibernating underground?* I reflected. Perhaps, like myself, these early risers felt the stirrings brought on by a day of tenuous late-winter sunshine. A fat white grouse-like bird took to panicked flight, startling me, whirring away from me close to the ground. What was it called? Willow ptarmigan! No...*Qilqiq*! As the bird flew, its whirring wings seemed to caution me, **Watch out for bears!**

Was Willow Ptarmigan my *Spirit Guide*?

I crossed a rough pan of stone, the primeval, monolithic gneiss of the Laurentian Shield, deeply scored where long-ago glaciations had dragged boulders across its surface. The rock rose in low hillocks. As I topped a rise, one of Churchill's ubiquitous polar bears gave me a cautionary *growlf* from two hundred yards away. Just as my Spirit Guide had cautioned me! I took the hint and executed a quick one-eighty.

Back to Apartment 218. I spent the balance of the morning poring through the eclectic selection of books comprising the Raufer library. A range of novels, many in German. Picture books from exotic locales the world over, to which, I suspected, the Raufers had not likely traveled themselves. A lexicon of Inuktitut. Words, phrases, nuances of meaning, the dazzling complexities of pronunciation and grammar. I made myself comfortable and spent an hour browsing its contents. As Anna had hinted, one probably had to be born into some particular dialect of this language to claim anything but the most rudimentary mastery. Nonetheless, I checked on the word for 'ptarmigan' and found it very like the name for my little fuzzy-ptarmigan-chick lady friend. Then I searched out one particular short phrase that interested me, and labored over it until I had it to memory. The phrase was *Nagligigitvit*...Nahg-LEE-gee-zheet-vit.

I had kicked off my sturdy low-topped workboots when I'd come in after my walk, and after perusing weird

Inuit words, the pronunciation of which I could only guess at, my eyelids were growing heavy. I decided on a little lie-down on the embracing softness of my *qiviut* bedcover. Lack of sleep due to two evenings in succession of Churchill late nights lulled me gently into an unintended slumber. I dreamed nebulous dreams, a mix of Lucasfilm space opera, dusty Panzers in the Libyan desert, and Polar Bears on Parade. A door banged, and I awoke.

It was Hans, home for a midday meal. Traditionally, Anna packed him a hearty pailful, and he lunched at the Gradge with the guys. But today he had thought he might drive on home to see how *my* day was coming. He clanked open his tin pail while I rummaged in Anna's fridge.

"*Zwei Bier, bitte!*" Hans requested when I was in mid-rummage, and I fished out a couple of cold Molsons. Rendering good Canadian beer ice-cold was a monumental travesty to Hans's German warm beer sensibilities, but he'd made the sacrifice for my benefit. We munched and drank in companionable peace.

"I suppose you are anxious to know about that submarine?" Hans asked, his eye atwinkle.

"You stole a submarine in Messina. Am I right?"

"*Durchaus nicht!* I never said I was *stealing* it!"

"Okay then…*borrowed* a submarine!"

"I think I said *commandeered* it."

"How's that different from stealing?"

"Well, no one was using it! Nice big submarine, moored bow and stern to the pier. At this minute, Messina is a madhouse, people running everywhere, antiaircraft guns firing bursts into the sky, artillery pounding, gunfire out at the edge of town. Trucks speeding past, troops in irregular bunches dashing for the last remaining transport ships. And this sub, its hatches thrown open and nobody paying it any attention! I'm standing there a minute, still in shock at having my rescued rifle squad shot to *scheisse* by

158

a fighter plane, thinking, *Why isn't that submarine getting ready for sea?* Then a couple guys come out of nowhere, each carrying a pair of cases, and they jump off the pier onto that submarine's deck. 'Hallo!' I yell. 'Is that U-boat heading out?' '*Nein!* It's heading *down!*' one of them laughs. 'What the hell?' I demand. He hoists one of those cases. 'Scuttling charges! Ten-minute fuses…you'd better clear out!'

"I demand to know why they are scuttling a perfectly good submarine! The guy rapidly explains that the engines are *kaput*. Don't want to leave a perfectly good submarine with possibly fixable diesel engines for the Brits!

" 'What kind of engines?' I insist. The guy shrugs …he knows nothing.

"Well, there's this *Kriegsmarine* officer I hadn't noticed, about twenty meters away, loitering in the shadow of a bombed-out building on the dock fronts. 'She's a Type VII U-boat,' he calmly tells me. 'She's got dual Germaniawerftt F46 diesels. Four-stroke, six-cylinder supercharged engines. Forward engine is completely blown…gaskets, piston-rings, bearings gone. Aft engine won't start. She could run on one engine if she needs to. You know anything about diesel engines?' he asks.

" '*Jawohl, Kapitänleutnant!*' I answer snappily. '*Unterfeldwebel* Hans Raufer, Sir. Critical specialist in diesel mechanics!'

" 'Do you know anything about *marine* diesels?'

" '*Nein, Herr Kapitänleutnant.* Panzers only. But a diesel is a diesel. May I ask, where are your boat's mechanics?'

'See that cantina down there?' he asks, pointing to a smoking pile of rubble. 'The four of them decided to take a quick *vino*-break a couple hours ago. Abandoned their post after trying—unsuccessfully!—after trying all night long to get my boat running again. Just about dawn, a British

159

aircraft blew that cantina to bits, and the entire staff of both my diesel watches along with it. Blown to bits! I devoutly hope the bastards hadn't gotten to take their first gulp of wine yet! So, *Unterfeldwebel*, you are hired. Pay: one free ride to Italy. Jump down that hatchway and see if you can get the aft engine to fire up. You two sappers! Go ahead and plant your scuttling charges, but don't you dare prime those fuses!'

"Well, Lewis, I'd never been anywhere near a submarine! The whole idea of a boat that sinks itself on command makes me want to pee in my pants. There's this scrawny seaman in a greasy undershirt and dungarees at the bottom of the ladder. 'Engine room!' I bark at him, and he heads off aft, leading the way.

"I have to tell you, a marine diesel is nothing like a Panzer engine! Even a fairly compact U-boat engine is a pretty huge thing! I take a quick look around. Tools are strewn everywhere, valve covers and bolts are scattered on the deckplates where the engine room crew had left them. If four experienced marine engineers couldn't fix this big bastard, I wondered if I could! 'Turn it over!' I ordered the miniature sailor.

"He yanked a lever back. He turned a handle from horizontal to vertical. He flipped a switch.

"A powerful electric motor turned the aft diesel's crankshaft. Valves lifted, pistons rose and fell. Nothing fired off.

" 'Again!' The sailor cranked the engine over, while I listened. There was a whistling noise somewhere in the machinery. 'Hold it!'

"I stuck my head down behind the engine's mass and under a bunch of piping. 'Once more!'

"A definite whistling! 'Flashlight!' The sailor slapped a torch into my outstretched hand. 'Now, crank it until I say Stop!'

"I played the light's beam over the tubes back under there while the starter-motor made the engine groan and whine. I turned my head this way and that, searching for the source of the whistling. Surely those experienced submarine mechanics had tried this! The searching flashlight revealed nothing...nothing.... Wait!...THERE! A brass pipe had ruptured, a thin longitudinal crack no more than ten centimeters long. 'STOP!' I yelled, and the cranking ceased.

"I pointed at a heavy casing at the front of the engine. The casing bristled with boltheads and tube fittings. 'What's that thing?' I asked the grubby seaman. I suspected the answer already.

" 'Supercharger pump!' he responded. Well... panzer engines have *turbo*chargers. A *super*charger differs from a turbocharger in that it is driven directly off the crankshaft. A turbocharger, on the other hand, is spun by the engine's exhaust stream. So, the *gott-verdammt* engine has to be *running* for a turbocharger to do anything, but *not* a supercharger! In fact, the extra cylinder pressure from this supercharger was *necessary* if the fuel was ever going to ignite. The Gas Law: $PV=nRT$. Lewis, this is absolutely the *only* physics equation I know! High pressure—that's the 'P'—produces high temperature—that's the 'T'. Hot enough to ignite atomized diesel fuel without need for a spark plug and a distributor and a bunch of wires and timing linkages and spark gapping and all that gasoline-engine *Dummheit*! That crappy little split in the pipe wasn't letting the pressure boost get from the supercharger into the cylinders! *Verstehen*, Lewis? Just then, the skipper stuck his head through the compartment hatchway to see if I was making any progress.

'Got it, Sir!' I exclaimed. 'Crack in a supercharger tubing! No high pressure air getting into the cylinders...they cannot fire compressively, even so much as to start the engine!'

161

'Can you fix it?'

'I think so…it will be a juryrig repair but it ought to hold!'

'How long to make the fix?'

'Ten minutes with a brazing torch!' I boasted.

"The captain disappeared. In a moment I heard him roaring at the sappers to get those *verdammt* explosives the *scheisse* off his *ficken* U-boat, and, while they were at it, tell his Mate to get his *Gott-verdammt ficken Scheisse-essen* crew back on board!

"Fortunately, my fix worked! I brazed up that crack and clapped the covers back where they probably belonged and twisted in as many bolts as I could make fit in various bolt holes. 'Fire it up!' I yelled at my grubby assistant. The engine caught on the first revolution! While it rumbled and warmed up, we hugged each other and jumped up and down, yelling in triumph. When the *Leutnant* dashed through the engine room hatch, he hugged us *both* and we *all three* jumped up and down!"

I reveled with Hans, thirty-eight years after the event. "He got you out of Sicily on that sub?"

"You bet your ass! Not a moment too soon! Monty and his gang had the eastern part of Messina in their hands by that afternoon. Before they did, though, the *Leutnant*'s crew rounded up about sixty other *Wehrmacht* stragglers, crammed them into various compartments in that U-boat, and we limped off toward the Gulf of Taranto under a single engine. Ran on the surface until there was a bit of a battery charge, then flooded tanks and dove! Down we went, gurgle-glug-glug! I nearly pissed my pants!"

"You got to Italy safely?"

"*Ja*! There was a medic on board who'd spent the whole night before, pouring down *Sizilianische Rotwein.* He figured that he was a goner, with the U-boat out of commission, and he figured he might as well die drunk.

Drunk or no, he did a pretty good job pulling a few stray bits of shrapnel out of my hide. The bullet wound in my ass had gone a bit septic, as if I couldn't feel that for myself! So by the time we got to the sub pens and graving docks at Taranto, I was pretty well patched up. Oh *scheisse*...look at the time! I got to get back to the Gradge! See you this evening, Lewis!"

I goofed around for the rest of the afternoon. At five o'clock, Hans got home. "Where's Anna?" I asked. I'd assumed he would have picked her up at the Hospital.

"She had to stay late at the RHA. There's a pregnant woman being flown in from Rankin Inlet. Complicated birth, going to do a C-section. Anna's setting up the Obstetric O.R. for the surgery and then she is going to assist. So, my friend, we are on our own for dinner! There's a café downtown on Kelsey Avenue. How about we go into town and see what special delicacies deep-fried in heavy seal oil they've got on the menu tonight?"

The cuisine was not that bad. After we'd eaten, when the soiled plates and condiment bottles were cleared away, we ordered another Molson. "Hans, I'm going to meet with Qilqik about nine o'clock, and—"

"Where meeting her?"

"Well...right here. She'll drop me at the Dot Hilton after, so...."

"So I, *Mensch Nummer Drei*, ought to get out of here?"

"If you don't mind. No hurry, though! We've got more than an hour...should be time for another beer or two. Well...so, Italy! I've got you as far as the port of Taranto, Hans," I reminded him. "Now, I know Italy was a godawful mess! Winston Churchill had visions of just dashing up the Big Boot and kicking Germany in the belly. But if I've got my history straight, the Allies bogged down there and didn't get out of Italy entirely until Germany surrendered in May 1945."

"*Ja*, that's about right. But things didn't last that long for me. Here's what happened.

"I was ashore in Taranto, which is a smallish port right in the 'arch' of the Italian 'boot'…over in the Puglia Region. The Italian Army is just about done for by this time. Their morale is through the floor. They had had two hundred thousand troops taken POW in North Africa, another hundred thousand in Sicily, and the whole Fascist thing was losing popularity more and more every day. So the German military presence in Italy knew it was going to have to carry the ball. The 10th Army had staff set up at every Italian port where evacuated troops were coming in from Messina. That was mostly Reggio, on the Calabria Peninsula, but they were cobbling together units from evacuees in Taranto as well. They grabbed me right away. Stripped off my uniform, which was reduced to tatters, mostly. Then they hosed me down, disinfected me, and gave me a new set of field grays to hang my battered Iron Cross on. They handed me a *Karibiner* and I became part of a Rifle Company in the 315th Infantry Division.

"We billeted in Taranto while they fleshed out our Company and a couple others as well. The best they could do was about 170 men per unit. Being an *Unterfeldwebel*, I got put in charge of a 40-man platoon. Every one of my men was well seasoned, so we got along fine. We spent our days seeing to our equipment and toughening up a little more. Hikes and physical training…that sort of thing. We spent our nights drinking local *vino* and getting plenty of sleep.

"On 3 September, the British 8th Army made landings in Calabria. The bastards hadn't wasted much time taking it easy in Sicily, had they? Our Companies were ordered north to join up with larger elements of the 10th Army. We got out of Taranto just in time! The Brits

164

jumped across the Gulf and seized the port on 9 September, same day the American 5th Army made landings at Salerno. Same day, by the way, the Italian government agreed to an armistice with the Allies, leaving the Reich holding the bag in Italy!

"We joined up with our brigade outside of Bari. Naturally, the Brits attacked Bari immediately! We were in some hot exchanges for awhile! My platoon took losses, but we held our own for several weeks in the uplands west of Bari.

"In mid-October we bailed out of there and headed northwestward to Foggia. What do you know, the Brit 8th Army followed, and soon pushed us out of Foggia! I spent two weeks trying to keep my boys from being murdered by artillery as we moved backward every day. Then we gave the Foggia region up as a lost cause and hastened farther northwest.

"It's early November 1943 by this time. Hitler had a big plan that we were supposed to establish iron-hard, multiple, parallel defensive lines right across the width of the Italian Peninsula, east to west. This would keep the Allied armies penned up in the south of Italy. He wrote this terrain off as not of any particular strategic value. This plan, *der Führer* insisted, would keep the Allies from establishing airfields within bombing range of southern Germany, or from their land armies breaking out northeastward through the Alps and invading the Balkans. All we had to do was keep about a million Allied troops bottled up, indefinitely.

"The defensive barriers were collectively called the Winter Line. Guess what kind of weather we had to build the damned defenses in? The Apennines aren't very high, but they are high enough for snow, sleet, and a shitload of rain! My brigade fell back northwestward to Campo Basso and went to work digging-in on the southeasternmost defenses: the Volturno Line. Soon, the Brits started hammering away on us. My platoon lost more men, and there weren't any replacements forthcoming. Altogether, the lads took a lot of wounds. Myself, I got peppered with still more shrapnel a couple of times, and I just had to pluck out the bits myself. Either that, or slap dressings on and hope they wouldn' get too badly infected.

"End of November they pulled us off the Volturno Line and trucked us back to Isernia, high up in the Apennines. This put us on the next defensive line northwestward, the Barbara Line. Same story: incoming artillery every day and every night. Air raids with bombing and strafing and damned few German fighters to chase the Hurricanes off. British infantry getting right up close and blazing away at us. For the first time for me in the War, masses of *Canadian* troops started coming against us! One morning I took a rifle bullet through the bicep, upper right arm, courtesy of some Canadian sharpshooter, I'm sure. Pretty serious wound, but back at the aid station they sprinkled some kind of powder into the wound, stitched it right up, and wrapped the whole thing up in gauze. Patted me on the ass and told me to get back to my platoon. Earlier in the war, a wound like that would have gotten me transported to the rear and given a little hospital time. But the *Wehrmacht* couldn't afford the luxury anymore.

"By Christmastime, we were really getting worn out, our Company. My platoon's down to twenty-four men, counting myself. Brigade command decided to take us off the Barbara Line and move us a good way back westward to the next string of defensive works. It was called the Gustav Line. I was told we would be billeted in a nice comfy, safe town being paid very little attention by the Allies where we could rest up, maybe take on some replacements, have a few nights on the town. There was a real ancient monastery on a hill right above the town, full of Medieval art and sculpture and stuff. Right after we arrived, I went up there a couple of times to look around,

166

enjoy the quiet, and listen to the monks sing liturgy. It's a place you've probably heard of, Lewis."

"What was the monastery called?"

"Monte Cassino."

19

HANS ON THE RUN: THE APENNINES

How many times was this going to happen? Hans winding up in some hellish hotspot focal point of World War II, getting shot or blown up or run over? I had lost count! But the ability of his experiences to knock me off my feet seemed to be never-ending!

Like anyone who ever paid the smallest attention to the events of the War, I was familiar with the tragedy of Monte Cassino. The massive mountaintop Abbey dated to the Sixth Century. It housed frescoes and mosaics and priceless works of art from every age between that century and the present day. In fact, the Nazis had plundered a lot of Medieval and Renaissance art from around about Italy, so it was believed, and had stockpiled it in the Monte Cassino Abbey for safekeeping.

There is uncertainty as to whether German troops had taken up defensive positions inside the Abbey itself. The valley town of Cassino was another matter. The town and its immediate environs were unmistakably occupied by thousands of *Wehrmacht* soldiers. But on 15 February 1944, suspecting that there were indeed German guns or German observers in the Abbey, and unwilling to risk the questionable veracity of those suspicions, Allied Brass ordered bombers to destroy the Abbey. Fifteen hundred tons of high explosives were dropped on the venerable structure. It was leveled, blasted to rubble.

Notice that, once again, this noteworthy date was within a day of Hans Raufer's birthday. He was twenty-four years of age and had been a combat storm trooper for fully one-quarter of those years.

"Cassino and the Gustav Line must have been a bitch!" I offered. "How did that go?"

"About as bad as anything I'd experienced. From the first of the year, the Allies were determined to overrun the town. You can't call those clashes 'engagements'…it was more like a series *pitched battles*, one after another. Curtains of artillery, waves of advancing enemy. You see, Lewis, the Allies were convinced the town of Cassino was the key to the Gustav Line, and thus the key to the entire defensive complex of the Winter Line. Bust through in Cassino and there would be no fixed German defenses for the entire rest of Italy. Well, the historians count four distinct Allied combat pushes for possession of Cassino, but it didn't seem to stop or slack off between campaigns from my point of view!

"By March, there was nothing left of Cassino for the Allies to take possession of. The Abbey had been reduced to rubble, but the town had been reduced to *gravel*…to *dust*! On about the 14th, the Allies went all-out: three straight days of non-stop bombing raids. What was left of the German defenses gave it up and backed out of there on 17 March. Do you know, Lewis, of the 175 troops my company had started out of Taranto with, there were THREE of us left alive? My platoon was gone entirely…killed, to a man. Me and two other guys from my Company crawled out of the rubble early on 17 March, and briskly determined we'd better get what was left of our sorry asses out of there!

"There was no one to link up with. German survivors of Cassino were either so badly wounded or so completely dazed that they just lay down their rifles, sat in the rubble and waited to be taken POW. A few, like the three of us, headed north at a high-step run, hoping to stay ahead of pursuit, and somehow to connect with more organized German units. We three beat it up the *Via Forca d'Acero* toward the town of Belmonte Castello, fifteen klicks distant, up into the Apennines. We jogged a kilometer, then walked doubletime a kilometer, over and

169

over. By late in the day, we passed through the edge of the town. No sign of any German concentrations. But *plenty* sign of foes! Rumble of trucks and armor...crack of gunfire down along the river. We were buzzed by Hurricanes or P-40s a couple times, but I guess three isolated German soldiers running for their lives weren't worth wasting a couple hundred rounds of machine gun ammo on at that particular moment, so they kept their thumbs off their trigger buttons.

"A klick or two beyond Belmonte Castello there was a spur of rock coming down across the roadway. The two-lane went through a short tunnel. Well, there were about fifty Allied Mountain Infantry hidden very effectively, lying in ambush on both sides of the road. They were defending that highway at the tunnel, a chokepoint to be sure. They were excellently camouflaged...I never suspected a thing. "Through the tunnel!" I yelled, when the other two guys seemed to hesitate. We were five jumps from getting inside that tunnel when a machine-gun opened up on us.

"The other two went down right off, killed, shot to shit. I felt three hits diagonally across my backpack: rap-rap-rap! At least two of them punched through the pack and into my back muscles. I was going on pure adrenaline by that instant so I just kept on running. Then there was an unbelievable noise:

whssssssht-WHOMMM!

"Must have been a bazooka round or a mortar shell. A big flash! Rock splinters flying everywhere. Huge rocks started tumbling down from the arched stonework entry of that tunnel. One grazed the side of my head and slammed into my shoulder, knocking me flat. Another great big one landed across both my legs, and I swear I heard the bones snap! That was it for me. I blacked out.

170

"When I came around, there were some guys lifting boulders off of me. Some more guys pointing rifles at me. Canadian guys.

20

P.O.W. HANS RAUFER

"The Prisoner of War protocol was that you were interned by whatever nation's troops had captured you. You catch him, you keep him! I'd been taken by a bunch of Canadian Mountain Grenadier Infantry. So they tossed me onto a stretcher and detailed a couple of chaps to trot me down circuitous pathways back to Belmonte Castillo. There, in a khaki tent with a big red-cross symbol on its top, a doctor turned back the blanket that had been pulled up over me. I was conscious but groggy as he took his first look. 'Sweet Jesus!' he said. 'This one's a goner!'

"How's that for bedside manner? Well, he wasn't too busy at the moment, so he thought he would have a go at me anyway. The bullet wounds were pretty serious. No important arteries nicked, but still pretty bloody...and the slugs still in there somewhere. He put compression bandages on them to save the probing and stitching for later. He examined the head wound that first falling rock had given me, manipulating my jaw and skull for the crepitation of broken bones. Put a temporary dressing on that bleeding laceration as well. Then he turned his attention to my legs.

" 'Broken right through! Both bones, both legs!' he murmured. When he manipulated a leg, bolts of searing pain shot through me like I'd never experienced. I screamed like a banshee!

" 'Does that hurt?' the doctor asked. A dumb question, Doc!

" '*Christus! Schmerzte wie Feuer!*' I said. At some level we must have understood each other. Next thing I know he's sticking my arm with a big hypo with something orange in it, and I drift off to Dreamland.

"It was days and days before I came back to rational consciousness again. When I did, I found I was strapped to a canvas bed. I was in a vehicle, like maybe a van or an enclosed truck or something. There was a lot of noise, a steady droning. Things smelled funny, like strong antiseptic mixed with odors of blood and dirty, sweaty bodies and sickly decay. My eyes were caked slits, but I forced them open.

"Racks and racks of wounded. Stacked three high on bunks. I was on a bottom bunk. Daylight filtered in through small windows. Three or four nurses were moving up and down a narrow aisle, one of them with flame-red hair, another one who appeared Asian. There was a doctor in hospital-whites, bloodstains down the front of him. It came to me that I was in a transport aircraft. I was being evacuated somewhere. I wondered where it might be that I was being taken.

"I took stock of myself. Everything hurt! A deep, pervading ache, punctuated by flaming soreness in my back and lower legs and skull. A transfusion bottle hung just above my head, dripping clear fluid into my arm. My head was thickly bandaged. My right arm was immobilized by mummy-bindings of adhesive tape, wrapped around and around my torso. Both my legs were encased in plaster casts. Waves of nausea washed over me, and pain as well. I groaned in my agony.

"A soft hand floated into my vision from beyond my head, and lay coolly for a moment on my brow, assessing my temperature. The form of a small, black-haired nurse appeared. It was the little Asian nurse...or perhaps she was American Indian. She brought a cup of cold water to my lips, and I drank gratefully. 'Do you hurt?' she asked, just like the doctor had. But maybe with some genuine sympathy.

173

'*Ja...schmerzte!*' I answered. Well she must have thought I was fluent enough in English to have understood her, because she started telling me *why* I was hurting so much and why she couldn't do anything about it in terms of more medication. Naturally I don't remember what she said, because I couldn't *understand* what she said. But the gist of it must have been:

There is a shell fragment from a bazooka round buried in your humerus – your upper arm bone. It's going to require general-anaesthesia surgery to remove, and to repair the damage, and the doctors don't think you are stable enough to undergo surgery quite yet. Unfortunately, it's pressing against your brachial bundle – that's a bunch of nerves that run down your arm. Painkillers and sedatives are very little help. You just have to be strong until we arrive in Halifax and get you into a proper hospital.

'Do you understand?' she asked me.

"All I could do was whisper, '*Ich verstehe nicht... Ich verstehe nicht...*' Inexplicably, I was overcome with grief. I began to weep silently, tears leaking from my eyes and running down my cheeks into my ears. Me! Weeping like a child! I felt myself slipping into delirium. I was certain I would lapse from this into coma, and then death.

"I felt the nurse lay a cool, moistened cloth across my forehead, and I opened my eyes again. She kneeled by my cot. Her small hand, warm and feminine, sought out mine and she began to gently stroke my palm with her fingertips. Then, very quietly, she began to sing to me. A simple song, in major thirds only, very rhythmic. I could not place the words. Certainly not German. Nor Polish, nor Russian. Not French either, and certainly not English. That exhausted my nodding familiarity with foreign languages. The words didn't sound like an Oriental language either. But…the words were very strange. Comforting. Soothing. I found myself letting go of my anxiety and my pain. I focused on the hypnotic song, and I came to realize there were only five phrases. The little nurse repeated these phrases over and over, each one ending in a short, emphasized word, the first four of them rhyming. To this day, Lewis, twenty-five years on, I can remember those five words:

Dum-dum-dah-dee-dum EE-NOOK
Dah-dee-dum-dee-dum KOO-OOK
Dee-dah-dee-dee-dum TAHL-OOK
Dum-dee-dah-dee EEK-UHL-OOK
Dee-dee-dum-dah AH-NAH-NAH

"Lewis, I don't know how long she knelt by me singing. Maybe ten minutes…maybe a couple of hours. Eventually I felt myself drifting toward sleep.

"A burning question leapt into my mind, and I snapped back from the edge of slumber! I strained to sit up, but the woman gently urged me to lie back. *'Wie nennen Sie dich? Dein Name?'* I asked her.

"The little nurse, obviously unfamiliar with German, repeated the most-recognizeable word she had heard: 'Nahm-uh? Does that mean, *name*?'

'*Ja*! *Name.*'

'Tiriaq. Nurse Tiriaq. You can call me Anna.'

"I drifted into painless oblivion. But neither a coma nor death, to be certain."

Wow! What a surprise! Anna! A World War II Canadian nurse! In 1944, her age must have been only about eighteen or nineteen!

I thought hard about the tonalities Hans had been imitating from her song. Even before he'd divulged that

175

revelation about his nurse's name, I imagined I was hearing Inuktitut! "Wait here a minute!" I begged him. I stepped to the Raufer bookshelf and retrieved the Inuktitut lexicon I'd been leafing through earlier, and a notepad and pen. I asked Hans to repeat those words. I tried transliterating Hans's recollected sounds into conventional Inuktitut spelling using the Roman alphabet. I came up with:

INUK - KU'UK - TAALUQ - IQALUK - ANANA

These words translate as:

MAN - RIVER - ISLAND - FISH - MOTHER

Anyone who lacks sufficient imagination as to be able to speculate what that little nurse's comforting song dealt with, is a pathetic, uncreative soul!

"You'd better tell me about being a POW in Canada," I prompted Hans. "You were taken with something less than fourteen months until VE-Day?"

"*Ja*, a year, a month, and three weeks. The medevac plane I was on turned out to be a Douglas DC-3 Dakota. On arrival in Halifax they transported me to Victoria General Hospital, a big pile of brick that had been in Halifax since the 1880's and had a top-grade orthopedic surgery unit, better than anything the Canadian military hospitals were able to offer. I was there from late March until about 10 July. I had undergone five separate operations to set and pin and straighten and, ultimately, to UN-pin my legbones. They, of course, had early on removed that piece of shrapnel from my upper arm, to my great relief. X-rays had turned up no fewer than seventy-six bits of metal in various places around my body, and they plucked most of them out. I've still got seven they couldn't pluck! Oh...the bullet wounds seemed to be the least of my injuries. But one of them became infected and I got all septic and feverish. They used a brand new antibiotic of some kind that they'd developed in the US, and it saved the day.

"I cannot imagine that I would have received this level of medical attention in Berlin in the spring of 1944. Not because Berlin was receiving twenty-four hour attention from British and American bombers—which it *was*—but because military medical care was stretched to the limit. And it must be admitted that there was a...a hierarchy of medical attention. Higher rank...better doctoring. As a mere *Unterfeldwebel*, I wouldn't have placed very high on that hierarchy, and I'd probably be limping like a paralytic to this very day...if I'd survived at all!

"When they decided I was pretty near fit, it was necessary for me to be taken into the Canadian Prisoner of War camp system. There were something like forty various POW lagers around the country, some very small, some virtual country clubs exclusive to officers, some reserved for interned foreign nationals or interned Canadian citizens of Japanese descent. I was dispatched to a camp called Montieth, also known as Camp 23, way up in the roadless northern wilds of Ontario about 700 kilometers north of Toronto.

"The treatment they gave us wasn't bad. The food was good, and plenty of it. We even got good Canadian beer on occasion! They had us work five days a week, but it was mostly logging, milling lumber, that sort of thing. The biggest complaints were the *bugs* in the summertime and the *cold* in the winter. I was only there for the winter of 1944-45, but it was a wet, cold, windy, snowy, son-of-a-bitch winter!

"There were hardly any guards. There were no barbed wire fences...or fences of any other kind. No trip

177

wires, mine fields, machine gun towers. Where were you going to go? There were no roads and five hundred kilometers of trackless forest in all directions, and we all knew it. Something else we all knew, but didn't discuss openly: if a soldier made it out of there and by some miracle made it back to the Fatherland, we'd wind up on the Eastern Front facing the Russians and certain death...in a war we were losing.

"So I did my time. When occasion allowed, I volunteered my services as a diesel mechanic. We used teams of horses mostly for the logging, but there were a few diesel tractors and road graders and log trucks. I applied myself to learning English, and got pretty good at it.

"After the Allies rolled over the remains of my country, and after the Beloved *Führer* did the world a favor and blew his lunatic brains out in his bunker, they started getting us POWs ready to repatriate. The Canadians made an effort to separate the die-hard Nazi storm troopers from the rest of us. And the rest of us were invited to take classes where the discussion was on the Error of Nazi Ways over the past six wartime years, and how 'good,' reconstructed Germans ought to act in the future. This sounds like sarcastic criticism on my part, Lewis, but it is not...not really. We received certificates attesting to honorable behavior and praiseworthy deportment as POWs, those of us who deserved this recognition. And we were told to retain and protect our certificates in the event we decided to apply for immigration back into Canada at some future date."

21

HOME AGAIN IN DRESDEN

On 25 June, I was issued civilian clothing, shuttled back to Toronto, and put on a ship along with about a thousand other German ex-POWs. The ship made its way down the St. Lawrence River to the North Atlantic, then across the stormy sea to Bremerhaven. After six years, my feet once again stood on the native soil of Germany.

"I think I neglected to tell you that my father died in June 1939 while I was in Czechoslovakia waiting to invade Poland. A stroke. He just keeled over at the dinner table with a forkful of *spaetzle* halfway to his mouth. My mother was left with hardly a pfennig, other than a minuscule widow's pension. So she moved in with her younger sister. Her sister's husband was an oral surgeon, about eighty years old but still practicing, so exempt from military service. They had an apartment just off of Striesener Strasse, eight blocks east of the Frauenkirche. If you've ever gone sightseeing in Dresden, you have probably seen the remains of this structure…it's a renowned landmark in the downtown area along the Elbe River. It was a fantastic pile of Rococo architecture, a Lutheran cathedral. Well you certainly must know about the firebombing of my native city, which occurred between the 13th and 15th February in 1945, culminating on my twenty-fifth birthday. I only got the infrequent letter from my mother…she was not much of a letter writer, and it was murder getting letters out of Germany and into Allied countries. After my capture, the only way I got *any* mail from her was through my status as a POW, by way of the International Red Cross.

"When the firebombing destroyed the center of Dresden, I imagined my mother and her sister had already evacuated the city, like lots of sensible people had in the last few months of the war. Gradually, I let go of that hope and accepted that she had died in the bombing. Nevertheless, I had to see for myself. So I traveled all the way from Bremerhaven to Dresden, five hundred kilometers, diagonally across the shoulder of Germany. Don't imagine this was easy! Germany lay in ruins! Highways and rail lines were barely making their way back into service. There was no air transportation available to civilians, particularly ex-POWs like me. Add to that, Dresden was in the Russian Zone of Occupation! I had to beg and grovel, and call in favors from the very few influential acquaintances I could scrape up, before I was granted a five-day pass into the Russian Sector.

"A single day in Dresden was more than enough for me. Lewis, you cannot imagine the devastation that had been visited on that city. By summer 1945 there had been a lot of effort to clear up the debris...bring down standing walls and open the streets, for example. They were still finding bodies! Lone bodies. Bodies in pairs and small groups. Basements and subway tunnels packed with baked, asphyxiated bodies. Bodies reduced to charcoal. Bodies dessicated by the intense heat until they were shrunken mummies. I have to admit that I had not been close to my mother after the age of fourteen or so. But it made me gasp with revulsion to imagine her death in that fiery maelstrom. I fled back to the American Sector, coming to rest in Munich, a city I'd had some familiarity with eons ago, before the War.

"I had a little money that I'd earned as a kind of prisoner's allotment while I was at Montieth. It wasn't much, it was not going to last me very long, and there was little to buy anyway in the ruins of Germany. There were literally millions of able-bodied German men of about my age, vying for paying work: all the ex-soldiers who had managed to survive the War. For a while, I pursued the idea of putting my diesel mechanic skills to use. But there

180

was no work for me. The only diesel engines in need of maintaining belonged to one or another of the Occupation countries…and they had an abundance of their *own* combat veterans to take those positions.

"In October, once again being disappointed in seeking a mechanicking job that had already been filled, I got a tip from the fellow who'd just turned me down: there was a small diesel engine refurbishment operation being set up in the French Sector, in Koblenz. So I hitched rides across Germany, got entry into the French Sector, and so into Koblenz. A day or two of sniffing around and I discovered that the information had been a red herring…no such factory, and no work otherwise for any broke-down ex-*Wehrmacht* panzer diesel mechanic such as myself.

"What to do? I spent a long evening sopping up beer in a down-at-heel *Bierhalle*, reflecting on my past, my dismal present, my perilous future. If there was no longer a need for my skills as a Critical-Skill Specialist in Diesel Maintenance, what *else* was I any good at?

"I realized I had only one other skill. It was the skill I'd been indoctrinated in as a teenager, and all I'd really ever done in my life:

Soldiering.

"Well, there was a group of seven or eight rowdy fellows in uniform sucking down beer in that hall with me, collected around a table next to the stone fireplace. From their uniforms and insignia, they were not French Army, exactly, and I doubted such an unruly bunch from any other nation would be carrying on here in Koblenz, in the French Sector of Occupation, without getting quickly arrested. Who were those guys? The raucous conversation was mostly— but not exclusively—in French, but I heard plenty of German. And a diversity of curses and obscenities in at least half a dozen other tongues. Who *were* those guys? I bought a big pitcher of suds and carried it over along with my almost empty stein. I clanked the brimming pitcher onto their tabletop.

"Silence from the whole bunch. *'Was ist das?'* a very tough looking individual asked coldly. Well, he spoke German and was still wearing a uniform of *some* kind…that was a good sign.

'Peace offering.'

'You are ex-*Wehrmacht*?' the fellow growled.

'Ja. Afrikakorps.' It seemed like the best name to drop.

"A snaggly smile. He grabbed my pitcher and slopped beer into his glass, then mine. He handed the pitcher off to his left, and it made the rounds. *'Prost!'* Glasses clanked and were drained. In a while we were Old Friends.

"Filthy jokes were told…in German, for my benefit. Boastings and tale telling about horrendous combat and acts of slaughter from the late recent glorious days of warfare. Twice, a pair of brutes got to arguing. The first incident was a dispute over a minuscule bit of trivia relating to the comparative merits of Russian versus German heavy tanks. The second was a standard faceoff over who had shagged whose girlfriend first, most frequently, and most comprehensively. Insults and shouting seemed to suffice the belligerents, and neither squabble escalated into a knife fight or something. Beer flowed like water: in rivers and deluges and bucketsful. 'Hans, you big ugly Nazi bastard…you ought to sign on with *our* outfit!' someone shouted. There were general growls of concurrence. A heated discussion developed on how one such as I might best accomplish such enlistment…what credentials I might need, what recruitment office I might present myself at, how large a bribe I might offer. Joining up with a bold outfit such as this, I considered, might actually have its merits! I slipped a small query into the boisterousness. 'I

182

beg your pardon for my ignorance, gentlemen. I have to ask…what exactly *are* your uniforms, you fellows?'

"All of them, as if on cue, raised their glasses and hollered:

LÉGION ÉTRANGÉRE !
The FRENCH—FOREIGN—LEGION !!!

Hans took a quick glance at his watch. "Quarter to nine! I better go! Eh, Lewis? She doesn't show up, you give me a call and me and the Mercedes, we'll come and get you."

"And you are going to leave me sitting here wondering whether or not you enlisted in the French Foreign Legion?" I demanded, once again thunderstruck.

"I tell you about it tomorrow!" he answered me, waving farewell.

I nursed the remainder of my Molson, then asked the waitress to switch me to coffee. I stared out the steamy window at the occasional car rolling by, sprays of slush roostertailing from their rear tires. The wall clock came up nine p.m. I watched its red second hand rotate around and around. Ten rotations, I counted. Had Qil decided not to come?

At fourteen minutes past the hour, she pushed through the door and shook snow slush off her parka. She gave me a quick and lopsided smile from over by the entrance, then took her time unzipping and doffing the parka and getting it hung up just so on the coat rack down there. She fumbled a small bundle out of the parka's roomy slash pocket. Then she quickly made her way down to my table.

The bundle clunked onto the tabletop. She bent at the waist and gave me a quick kiss on the mouth, then slid onto the red naugahyde banquette across from me.

"Would you like some coffee?" I asked her.

"Mmm-hmm. No cream, please."

I flagged the waitress and ordered her a cup.

"Qil—"

"Lewis, I can't stay too late. I just wanted to bring you something." She picked up the bundle, fumbled with it a bit, shoved it across the pitted formica toward me.

"What is it?"

Words were deserting her. Before she could start, the waitress bustled over with a heavy coffee mug, a fresh napkin, and a steaming carafe, poured Qilqiq a brimming cup, gave us a toothy smile, and left. Qil tried again. "It's a…well, it's just a little…it's something I chose myself. Just something, Lewis. Don't unwrap it here, okay? When you get back to Hans and Anna's."

"But what is—"

"It's just something I want to give you so you will maybe remember me."

"Don't you want to see me again? Like, when we talked about…?"

She sipped coffee, more to hide her emotions than for any other reason. "Look, Lewis. We both know it's not very likely we are going to see each other again. I'm…I'm really happy I met you. And I like you a lot! But—" Her voice trailed off into awkwardness.

She didn't have to say any more. I could guess what conclusions she had come to, and there wasn't any sense trying to bluff our way into some future that was not ever going to be. "Uh…can you give me a lift back to the Raufer's, Qil?" I asked her.

Wordlessly, she nodded.

I slid out of the booth and shrugged into my extra-roomy down parka, which I'd been sitting on all this time. I lay down some bills for the meal and the beers and the coffee. I collected Qil's gift bundle off the tabletop. It was wrapped in light-brown felt or soft-tanned leather, and bound snugly about with some kind of string. The thing was surprisingly heavy. By the time I turned to leave the table, Qilqiq was halfway to the exit.

185

Qil's car was a light-blue Toyota sedan, not very new, banged-about and dented like any other far north car. The conditions of road and life up here were much too chancy to allow maintaining a pristine body or paint job. We got in on our respective sides, pulled our respective doors closed. Qil cranked the reluctant starter, and eventually the engine fired off. The heater came alive and blew frigid air across our knees, taking its time warming up. She drove slowly back to the DOT Hilton. Not a word passed between us. I couldn't think of anything to say, and neither could she.

As I opened my door to exit, I leaned across to kiss her. She leaned toward me too, and our lips met. A brief kiss of farewell. "Good night, Qilqiq," I said.

"Good-bye, Lewis...good-bye!" When I shut my door, she drove away.

I trudged up the stairway to the second floor with Qil's heavy gift in my hand. To be honest, I thought of dropping it in the hallway trash can rather than carrying it home to Boston in my travelbag. I imagined that for the next forty years, I would inadvertently glance at whatever memento she'd given me, maybe taking it into my notice once in every six months or so. And each time, I would have to endure a momentary bittersweet reminder of a long-ago poignant interlude, a charming potentiality that had come to nothing. I wondered how many years it would take before her adorable face would fade from my recollection, or the taste of her kiss die away from my mouth. At the door marked 218, I turned the knob and went on in.

Anna sat at the kitchen table sewing a blouse on a beat-up old Singer portable electric. She had just flipped down the presser foot as I came through the door. I didn't think she had noticed me, so I just stood and watched for a while.

Anna rotated the machine's hand wheel with her right hand, engaging the workpiece. Then she stepped on the floor pedal and began to feed material in under the bobbing needle. The motor whirred and the needle clattered up and down: Clk-a clk-a clk-a clk-a clk-a CRUNCH!

"Drat!" Anna said, very softly. She flipped up the presser foot and poked around under it with a seam picker. Out came a glob of wadded-up white thread, which she clipped off and tossed on the floor. She rethreaded, dropped the presser foot and then started the machine on up again: Clk-a clk-a CRUNCH!

"Drat!"

Anna looked up from her jammed needle and noticed me standing just inside the front door. "Hi!" she greeted me cheerfully, pushing back from her sewing. "Hans is gone to bed! Did he have too many beers at dinner?"

"Sorry Anna…I didn't count," I responded.

"And did you see our Qilqiq?"

"Yeah…I'm pretty certain it was Good-bye Forever." I sighed. I gently set Qil's wrapped gift on the far end of the table. I pulled out a chair across from Anna's sewing, and sat down disconsolately.

"Ohhh. Sorry, Lewis! She can be a little moody. Don't you give up on her!"

I sighed some more, and moped. It didn't seem that way to me, and I was not sure how Anna's gentle chiding could help. "Well anyway…she gave me a parting remembrance of some kind, and I didn't have a damned thing for her." I gestured at the object on the table.

"Let's see what you got there!" Anna exclaimed. "I'm just about fed up with that dratted, beat-up old sewing machine anyway. I've been fighting with that old wreck for…I don't know, thirty years I guess. And it wasn't new when my momma gave it to me."

The string holding the bundle together did not turn out to be string at all, but some kind of natural fiber cord made of fine, loosely twisted strands. I fiddled with the knot. Eventually it came untied.

"Caribou sinew," Anna informed me. "Very traditional cordage! In the old days, it was either sinew or sealskin rawhide lacing. You save that cord, Lewis! You cannot buy it in the Hudson's Bay Store…someone spent a couple hours just hand-twining that piece of string for you!"

As I folded back a corner, the wrapping felt like it had the softness of chamois about it. In addition, the material gave off a scent of woodsmoke and herbs. "What's this leather wrapping?" I asked Anna.

She gave it a sniff, then a quick feel with thumb and forefinger. "Soft tanned moose hide!" she declared. "Not a traditional Inuit product…moose tend to stay farther south. A great material for warm-weather gloves and baby clothes and hood linings. Or mukluks for really cold weather, when the snow is dry and powdery. The People would get moose hides in trade from Southerners …Woodland Cree …Athabaskans and Slavey, further west. Unwrap it carefully…there's probably some beadwork in the corners, or maybe dyed quillwork."

I unfolded the moosehide wrapping and laid it flat. A nice, tidy rectangle, whipstitched all the way around. As Anna had predicted, the diagonal corners were embroidered with colored wild rose blossoms and leafy sprigs.

Anna gasped in delight! "Oh! Oh, look! This is even better! See how it is colored tufts making up these little blossoms? This is vegetable-dyed moose hair tufting! Very rare these days! I only know two old, old women who know how to do that anymore! Lewis, someone went to a *lot* of trouble with your gift, and I don't need to tell you *who!*"

The heavy object that had lain nestled in the moosehide was wrapped in tissue, several layers of it. I carefully laid the paper open.

It was a soapstone carving. Maybe seven inches long, five inches high. An animal. Very short legs and a high, humped back. Head held low with a tapering, almost pointed muzzle. The top of the head was embellished with a set of horns rendered in glinting yellow metal, bronze perhaps, or an alloy of copper. Thick and heavy, the metal horns were centrally parted like an Edwardian gentleman's brilliantined hairdo across the animal's crown, and went swooping down over either side to taper into upswept points. The cast metal had a striated appearance which suggested the natural texture of horn, while the stonework of the beast's body had been polished to a smooth, high sheen. All in all, the carving's subtle curves suggested graceful movement, and a flowing coat of fur, and a wildland beast's vital, natural power. Michelangelo or Rodin would have taken pride is such feral and energetic expressiveness.

"A *musk-ox!*" I exclaimed.

Peering over my shoulder, Anna muttered something terse and sharp in guttural Inuktitut.

"What's that?" I asked.

Anna gave a brief, guilty smile. "Sorry...a naughty word I won't bother translating. That carving surprised me, is all. Yes, it's a musk-ox. Did she tell you about it, at all?"

"No. Not a word."

"Musk-ox is Qilqiq's Spirit Animal. A big female musk-ox appeared to her one time, when Qil was about nine years old. She'd wandered away from her dad's summer fish camp, a long way upriver from Baker Lake, and she had gotten herself a little lost in the early evening,

189

picking berries out in the tundra. This great big momma musk-ox with a calf came protectively charging out of a willow thicket. It's amazing the beast didn't knock Qil flat with those dangerous horns of hers, and then trample her to death. But instead, the animal stopped short. Turned her big shaggy head and gazed off northward, toward the river. Qil turned to follow the musk-ox's gaze and spotted a thin column of smoke rising straight up into the evening sky, so with relief she knew where her daddy's fish camp was. As she was about to run away home, the musk ox spoke."

"It *spoke*?"

"Oh, come on, Lewis! You know how these spiritual encounters work! Of course it didn't speak with its *voice*! Qilqiq received its spiritual message, is what happened. And she received the understanding that, for the rest of her days, Musk-ox would be her Spirit Guide."

"Okay. Uh…Can you tell me what the message was?"

Anna laughed softly. "The usual! Profound Words to Live By! Qil remembers it as:

> ***You can* see *what you want…You must then have the courage to* grasp *it!***

That's usually how spiritual messages sound, don't you find?"

We both laughed together. I hefted the carving in my two hands. "And so…that's why she bought this carving for me?"

"No, Lewis…you don't understand! *She sculpted that herself!* She started the carving when she was fifteen years old and struggling her way through her high school studies her sophomore year. Loused up the first attempt. Worked on it for four months, then got frustrated and took a hammer to that one. Tried four more times, trashing each botched attempt. Until finally she thought she might have

190

it right. That was sixteen months after she started in on the project. Once she got the stonework done, she turned her attention to the horns. She spent ten weeks taking a remote-learning course in lost-wax casting, and had to beg and whine to get the high school art teacher to let her mess with the school's metal casting equipment, unsupervised. At that time, for a couple of years she'd been saving her pennies and nickels in a big jar, pining after a glamorous, high-fashion leather purse she'd seen in a catalog. But she busted that jar open and found she only had eighty-eight dollars. So she borrowed twenty-two more dollars from me. She took that hundred-and-ten dollars to the bank and traded it for a Canadian Maple Leaf…a solid troy ounce of pure gold. Used that as the metal to cast those horns. It took her three tries! First try, the molten gold blasted through the investment plaster and splattered all over the centrifuge shield. I was there! Qil and I *both* jumped in the air when that plaster canister exploded! After that first failure, I watched her picking little specks of hot gold out of the shield tub, tears leaking down her face at the thought of two weeks' work down the drain. Then she tried again—carved and fitted a wax original, attached waxen sprues, set it in plaster, burnt the wax out in a kiln, furnace-melted all those gold drips and drops, then let the centrifugal caster fly. ***Splatter***! That attempt failed just like the first one. And so she started all over again. Third time's the charm! The casting came out perfect. She spent a whole week, polishing and texturing that gold casting. There's the result: solid gold musk-ox horns!"

It was coming home to me just how precious a gift this sculpture was! "Did she—"

"Lewis, listen to the rest…there's a little more to the story. That June, the artwork took her high school's blue ribbon for Traditional Inuit Sculpture for the year. Then, Regional First Prize at the high school level. Then the Winnipeg papers got wind of it, ran a story and a couple

191

photographs. The family scratched up the $75 entrance fee and persuaded Qil to enter that soapstone in the 1971 All Canada First People's Art competition. Again, her sculpture took First in its category…a $1500 prize. After, an Ottawa art collector telephoned and offered her $8000 for the piece. She turned him down. Two days later, he upped the offer to $15,000. And she turned him down again."

"*Why?*"

"It's her *Spirit Guide!*"

I nodded, an inkling of understanding seeping in.

"Lewis, if my grandniece were to borrow one of my really sharp kitchen knives, slit open her breast, cut out her own beating heart and hand it to you, she wouldn't be giving you a more precious object, in her mind, than that sculpture. You need to have an idea how significant a gift that sculpture is. And what kind of value she puts on the receiver."

"Oh…um, okay. I guess maybe I—"

"Lewis, I think you are a pretty intelligent fellow. I'm just an old woman, and I'm her Auntie, and I love her, so I'm not entirely impartial. But you would be a big thick-headed fool if you let that girl slip away from you!"

23

HANS JOINS THE FRENCH FOREIGN LEGION AND GETS SHIPPED TO A TROPICAL PARADISE

In the morning, Hans announced over breakfast that he had arranged with Chuck Townshend, his amiable boss, to take the day off.

"Why?" both Anna and I asked simultaneously.

"Uhhh...well, because Lewis here is going to get flown out of Churchill tomorrow morning. Eight-thirty! I telephoned the CanadaNational. Don't worry, Lewis...they are going to call later and confirm it. Or...we can stop by the airport and make sure you're on the passenger manifest. You and me, we are going to drive around a little bit. Too bad it's not summer, or at least Ice-out on the Churchill River...I would take you fishing for Walleye or Northern Pike. Or Arctic Char! World's tastiest fish!"

Actually, Hans's surprise plans for the day suited me perfectly! I had a couple errands in mind. "And!" I exclaimed, "You've got to tell me about the Foreign Legion!"

"*Ja...*" he muttered. "*That* fifteen-year fiasco!"

Anna, her face buried in her coffee mug, mumbled something about how Hans could otherwise have given up his soldier nonsense in 1945, come back to Canada, and searched her out while she was still in the verdant bloom of her youth.

Well, it wasn't quite as sunny a winter's day as Sunday had been. Snow spat down from a leaden sky, and wind moaned in from the Bay. "Let's take a drive out to the Airport, Hans!" I suggested.

Like before, we abandoned the Mercedes at the white 'Unloading Only!' curb. Sure enough, the agent smilingly assured me, CanadaNational had set itself the goal of getting its thirty stranded travelers back in the air by Tuesday at eight-thirty a.m…dependent on the arrival of an aircrew.

"Wait a minute!" I protested. "Weren't the pilot and copilot stranded here with the rest of us? And I chatted with the Flight Attendant at a party over the weekend. *Danced* with her!"

No, I was informed. The two aviators, at least, were far too important to be left stuck here, with lots of other CN airplanes needing to be flown about. They had been rescued by a special six-passenger Company aircraft and carried back to more civilized parts, 'way back last Saturday morning. All that left little doubt as to where we mere passengers stood!

We walked away from the Departure desk. "Hey Hans…do you suppose Qilqiq Sidney has an office around here somewhere?"

"Cargo hangar!" he exclaimed. "Follow me!"

Qil was leaning over a large table cluttered with piles of cargo manifests. As we approached from behind her, she was slurping coffee. There was a forklift operator out on the hangar floor, shuttling pallets of cartons back and forth. Forty feet away, a couple of guys in overalls and hard hats were vigorously plying hammers to make last-minute adjustments on a large plywood crate. "Hi, Qil!" I said forcefully, over the din.

"Lewis!" she said, startled. She bobbled the coffee-cup, nearly lost it, but succeeded in finger-hooking the handle and regaining control, narrowly averting a messy disaster.

"Hi, Sweetie," I smiled. I caught her free left hand in my right, and pulled her to me so I could give her a friendly buss on her cheek. "I just stopped by to thank you, Qil. The sculpture is fantastic! Anna told me a little bit about its history…it's far too generous of you, Angel. Are

194

you sure you want to send your prizewinning effort off to Boston?"

"Oh…it's all right, Lewis. I…that is, it's—"

"If I can't persuade you to come visit *me*, you need to come visit Miss Momma Musk-ox!"

"Lewis, we—"

"Look, Qil…I'm flying out tomorrow morning. Flight's at eight-thirty. Will you come over to the terminal a little before that and see me off? I'm so stupid…I had a little keepsake I was going to give you. If I'd remembered, I could have given it to you last night. Or right now, if I hadn't forgot!" I put my free left hand, shaped into a finger pistol, to my temple and shot myself in the head to illustrate my remorse. Some of what I'd just told her was not strictly true, but I intended to make it so before she could possibly find out. "It's just a token, Sweetie. Nothing as thoughtful and extraordinary as Miss Musk-ox, but…"

"Okay. Okay, I'll be there, Lew."

I still had her hand in mine. I pulled her close and kissed her on her pretty mouth. She was stiff in my arms at first, but I felt her reluctance collapse and gently transition to tenderness. Her body softened and molded to me, and her arms tightened around me. I could feel her heart racing as she pressed against me. After a long moment, we broke the embrace. Her cheeks flamed scarlet, but I suspect it was because here was the Chief Cargo Dispatcher putting on a Passionate Spectacle in front of her entire Cargo Hangar staff! Not to mention, her great-uncle Hans!

As Hans and I headed back to where we'd deserted the Mercedes, he nudged me. "Did you get what you came for?" he asked me. "…*Sie kluge Teufel!*"

I think maybe I did, whether by sly devilishness or not. I'd given Qil's fingers a pretty detailed quantitative analysis while I had her hand in mine. "I've got one more stop to make in town, Hans," I told him. "Then I'll stake you to lunch and a few beers. You can tell me about the French Foreign Legion."

As Hans drove us slowly down Kelsey Boulevard, I gazed intently out the right-hand window. I was looking for a particular shop. "There it is!" I yelled at Hans. "Swing in there!"

He pulled the Mercedes into a diagonal parking space. Not that parking spaces were in especially short supply! Midday on a snowy Tuesday, not many Churchillians were in their cars, out and about. "What's up?" Hans asked. I just pointed. A narrow windowfront showing trays of silver objects and rings and necklaces. Churchill's one and only jewelry shop, according to the Raufer's telephone directory.

Hans and I pushed into the warm shop. "May I help you?" asked a diminutive, white-haired lady. For a whimsical instant I considered the only *other* conceivable possibility that would bring a couple desperate-looking characters such as us into a jewelry shop on a blustery day like this would be to stick up the joint.

"Yes, please. I'm looking for a nice ring for a lady friend of mine."

"Do you know her ring size?" the jewelry lady asked.

I held up my right fist. I extended my pinkie. With my left index finger, I pointed to the fold of the first joint. "To here is about right."

We fiddled through a collection of sizing loops, slipping them down my pinkie. We settled on size 5½. "An *engagement* ring?" the sweet white-haired lady asked, with a bit of a leer.

"Uhhh…not yet. Maybe what you'd call a nice friendship gift. A *very* nice friendship gift."

We debated silver versus gold. Maybe *white* gold, the jeweler suggested. White gold is a metal I could never

196

see the point in, because it looks just like silver to my eye...but costs twenty-five times as much. Same goes for platinum. For a set gem, we looked at diamonds, and pearls, and precious stones in the corundum family: emeralds and rubies and various colors of sapphire and like that. Then she showed me a tray of rings that had a yellow-gold one with a heart-shaped, faceted stone of deep red. On either side of the heart, a nice brilliant-cut diamond of about a third-carat each. "What's that red stone?" I asked. "The heart?"

"It's garnet," the lady replied. She turned over the little tag so *I* couldn't see the price, but *she* could. It was sufficiently astronomic as to make her blanch. When she had regained her composure, she told me the price. It *was* somewhat breathtaking.

But a garnet heart was perfect! Garnet is my birthstone, and this gem would certainly send a message every time she looked at her finger and glimpsed the thing.

"May I borrow a loupe?" I asked her. This is a pretty good subterfuge, when buying jewelry. If you peer at stones, particularly diamonds, through a jeweler's loupe, you are informing the dealer that you know a little something about discerning the quality of what you are intending to buy. To buy...if the price is right. It helps if you actually *do* know a little something about clarity and color and cut. In retail shops, fine high end jewelry is customarily marked up from wholesale between 200 to 400 percent, so there's usually wiggle room on the sales price. As I peered into the almost flawless interior of the diamonds, the shopkeeper added shakily, "Of course, that is only the manufacturer's *suggested* price! I can make you a nice...er...*discount* on this lovely ring. Say, twenty percent? Or...uh...or maybe *thirty* percent?"

"That's very kind," I agreed. "Can we make sure it's a size 5½?"

She produced a sizing bar and slid the ring on down. Five-and-a-half, on the dot. As a double check, I slid it down my right pinkie. It stuck at the bend of my first joint. "I'll take it!" I said, smiling. "Can I give you my MasterCard on my Boston bank?"

"Of course!"

"Do you have a nice ring box?"

"Of course!"

Ten minutes later, we were out of there. The ring in its little blue velvet snap-box made a small, satisfying bulge in my parka pocket. "Lewis..." Hans asked me with solemnity. "My boy, do you know what you are doing?"

"Absolutely!"

"It's just...that's a *verdammt* serious piece of jewelry, *mein freund*. You have only known her *four days*! You give that thing to her, you are *not* getting out alive!"

"That's the idea! Let's go get a Molson or two!"

You can* see *what you want! I heard Momma Musk-ox whispering as Hans drove. ***You must then have the courage to* grasp *it!***

So after the jewelry store, Hans drove us to the only eatery that presented an alternative to the café I'd already become quite familiar with. It was a simple bar & grill with a view of the snow-slushy street we'd just parked on. Guess what street? Yep...Kelsey Boulevard.

"Is it too early for a Molson?" Hans roared to the bartender as we pushed into the half-lit interior.

"*Never* too early for a Molson!" the bartender roared in return.

We found a table. Studied the menu and the chalkboard of specials. "Look at that!" Hans marveled. "Pan seared Arctic Char!"

"Couldn't be fresh, could it?" I asked.

"Well it was nice and fresh last September! Char freezes just fine! Tastiest game fish on the planet!"

So we ordered two Arctic Char specials. Coleslaw and fries. We munched fresh sourdough bread slices with tinned butter, and slurped Molson while we waited. The Char was worth the wait...tastiest game fish on the planet! In the entire *galaxy*, as far as I could tell!

"So...you were about to join the *Légion Étrangère*, I believe?"

"*Ja*...only when I presented myself at the recruitment bureau, it didn't seem to go very well at first. Something about me being German and ex-*Wehrmacht*. 'But I was never in combat on French soil!' I protested. Made no difference to the recruiting officer. 'See here? I've got a commendatory letter from the Canadian POW authorities! And, I can speak pretty good English! And a little bit of Polish!' Still made no difference. 'I was declared a highly-skilled technician by *Afrikakorps* Command!' Well that caused the recruiting officer to raise an eyebrow. 'What sort of technical skill?' he asked, with a hint of interest. "Repair and maintenance of diesel powerplants! Panzers and transport trucks, and...and *submarines*!' Well that impressed the *scheisse* out of him! 'A skill like that could come in handy!' he agreed. That French officer pulled out a rubber stamp, charged it with purple ink, and stamped my application. I was *in*!

"The next ten weeks was Basic Training...as if I had never undergone such indoctrination long ago! I came in as a boot private with absolutely no recognition of my two years' seniority as an *Unterfeldwebel*. You have surely seen that old movie *Beau Geste*, where the gentle-spirited young fellow enlists as an escape from a blighted romance? And the tough, nasty officer, or sergeant—I can't exactly remember—gets in his face and gives him hell all the time? Well, the NCOs in our training compound had evidently

199

seen the movie too, because that's about how they acted. Why am I telling *you*? You've been through Basic Training too, and we both know it's about achieving the proper attitude and building teamwork, right? And toughening up your hide a little.

"After that, I was assigned to a mobile Infantry Company. The French had a fair number of troops stationed more or less permanently in their Zone of Occupation. The French Zone included the Saar Region, and there was a certain degree of disagreement among the former Allied Powers as to the eventual allocation of this valuable industrial and mining region. The French, of course, would have been happy to retain it permanently. The French would have been happy to see Germany chopped-up into a hundred weak little feudal states, actually...France had been invaded three times by Germanic armies in the past seventy years!

"Well, post-War political tensions put a strain on the Occupying powers. The Soviets, naturally, were uncooperative from the start. They ran East Germany as they saw fit. The British, American, and French Zones operated independently, but with some coordination by way of a Commission. We in the military participated in disarmament, then in denazification, in restoring basic structures and services such as power, water supply, bridges and roads, telephone system. Us troops cleared away many thousands of tons of rubble, and set off demolitions to take down the standing skeletons of many a building. We transported and distributed relief supplies to starving civilians. Eventually, we helped rebuild schools and hospitals and highways. In this fashion, the years began to pass.

"Then in June of 1948, the Russians blockaded Berlin! For a time, the Western Allies believed we might be on the brink of war, only this time with the Russians! We former *Wehrmacht* soldiers who had some Barbarossa experience were pretty sure this was not a good idea. Tensions ran very high for almost a year.

"In September 1949 the Soviets backed off. Once highway access was restored across the Russian Zone into Berlin, we could stand down from our high alert status. One day, a high Legion officer came to address our Battalion, assembled for the occasion on a large parade ground. He informed us that our Zone of Occupation had reached the place where fewer French troops were required. To that end, our Battalion would be one of the first to be repositioned to another zone of French national interest. 'You are not to worry, *mes braves*! Your destination is a veritable Paradise in the tropics! Home to many beautiful women of very friendly disposition!' We ignorant fools all laughed and cheered."

I had a strong notion what particular tropical paradise Hans was referring to. "Indochina?" I asked him.

"*Jawohl!* French Indochina…better known these days in the USA as *Viet Nam!*"

Lord, what an unlucky cuss my friend Hans had been, back in those days!

Hans continued. "We were transported out by ship. A miserable trip…although our troopships were routed through the Suez Canal, sparing us a nice pleasure cruise around the south end of Africa. We sailed upriver to Saigon right at the end of 1949. The conflict against the Viet Minh insurgency had become so unpopular back in France that the press and the citizenry called it *La Sale Guerre*, the Dirty War, and left it largely up to former and current French colonial troops—Tunisian, Algerian, Moroccan, Cambodian and Laotian—and of course us Soldiers of the Legion, to do the fighting. Under French officers, naturally.

"In recent months, the conflict had transitioned from a low-key rural insurgency to a more conventional war. This was because the Viet Minh were suddenly being equipped with modern Chinese and Russian weaponry. Us French fellows should talk...we were being supplied by the Americans, who were perfectly happy to let us be their anti-communist proxies in Southeast Asia, and take all the lumps. Soon enough, your time came around...didn't it, Lewis?

"The French High Command had a favorite strategy: establish a strong, well-defended fortress with secure, short lines of supply, then goad the Viet Minh, at the far limit of their supply lines, into attacking it. They called it 'hedgehog' tactics. The first time I heard this strategy described, it made me think of the Maginot Line. *Ja*, how well did *that* work out for you, Frenchies?

"But, the French did have their successes. I should say, us chore-boys *for* the French had *our* successes. I should point out that I was still operating on my basic reluctance to just *ficken* shoot anybody in the guts, even soldiers from the opposite side. In Indochinese jungle warfare, you rarely saw your enemy anyway. You'd just unload your rifle into the greenery and hope you'd frightened them off. For the most part, it was mortar fire and bombs and artillery that ran up the body count...for both sides.

"As you are learning to expect, Lewis, I took a few wounds. Never anything too serious, never enough to put me out of the action permanently. Every so often, one Legion Company or another would be rotated back to Saigon or Hanoi or Bangkok for a few weeks of drinking, carousing and lechery. The years seemed to roll by.

"Then in March of 1954, we were collected up, shipped north to Hanoi, and then trucked westward about 400 kilometers to a lovely river valley all surrounded by high green mountains. It was another of those well-defended fortresses where we could lure in General Giap's boys for the slaughter. And, while we were at it, deny the Viet Minh access to resupply from Laos."

Oh Christ! Hans wasn't going to tell me he was being sent to *Dien Bien Phu*? I had to ask. "This impregnable fortress...was it—"

"Absolutely it was, *ja*. Dien Bien Phu."

"Man! That was like Firebase Ripcord, *writ large*!"

Hans grinned and nodded. "The problem was those mountains all around. We French were disposed on nine fortified hills spread around the valley. The hills had been given saucy feminine French names, no doubt to arouse our virile fighting spirit by way of tender, gentlemanly feelings of protectiveness. Fortress Gabrielle, Beatrice, Isabelle, and so forth. On the Viet Minh side, up in all those mountains, Vo Nguyen Giap took his time. He built up anti-aircraft batteries and dug endless tunnels and located artillery on reverse slopes or in those damnable rat hole tunnels where they'd arch fire down on the French, but be protected from counterbattery fire. Then he designated experienced, Chinese-trained elements to devote themselves to intercepting and destroying French resupply convoys on the long road west from Hanoi. Then he started pounding away at us, behind our sandbags and barbed wire. After a while, we ran low on things...like, food and bullets and artillery rounds and medical supplies. Truck convoys were not getting through, because Giap's boys were intercepting them, a hundred klicks east of us. The Brass radio'd for air drops. Giap unlimbered those anti-aircraft guns and shot the resupply transports out of the sky. For the first days, the Viet Minh refused to cooperatively come on in human-wave attacks and permit themselves to be slaughtered. At least, until they'd softened us up.

"After a while our situation became serious. Then it became perilous. Then desperate...then hopeless. One by one, those hillocks with the sexy French tart names were attacked and overrun. The first to fall was Beatrice. The Legionnaire commander was Paul Pegot, a Major and a damned hard-fighting man. He and his entire staff were killed instantly when a heavy artillery shell came down directly on his command bunker. A short time later, Colonel Gaucher, the commander for the entire Northern Sector, was killed. We didn't have any more *good* commanders left, but we had an abundance of *bad* commanders. When the Viet Minh came over the Beatrice perimeter in unstoppable waves, almost five hundred Legionnaires were killed, so they say. My Company was not posted at Beatrice...but soon enough General Giap got around to us.

"Dien Bien Phu was surrendered on 7 May 1954. That miserable defeat was, as you well know, the final gasp of French Colonialism in Southeast Asia.

"I made it through to the surrender. Something like twenty thousand French Colonial troops and Legionnaires *did not* make it...killed by the incessant rain of artillery shells or by the surging waves of Viet Minh ground assaults. But things weren't over yet for those of us who survived.
"Approximately twelve thousand surviving French forces were taken prisoner. More than one-third of us were wounded, and the Viet Minh had basically no medical care to spare for us. They divided us into groups. I was not seriously wounded beyond the abrasions and burns and bruises you'd expect, so I was put with the 'able bodied.' We were force marched to prison camps, eastward and north, all the way beyond Hanoi. Six hundred kilometers! Thousands died on the march. In the prison camp, we were cold, rained-upon, abused by our captors, and had very little to eat. I fell ill with dengue fever. There was no medication made available, nor medical staff to care for us.

204

When I was nearly recovered from dengue, I was hit with malaria. Toward the end of our internment, nutritional deficiencies typical of beri-beri were taking hold of me, and I had lost 50 kilos of good flesh when, finally, we were repatriated. Of the eleven thousand of us who had reached the prison camps alive, just a bit over three thousand of us survived, four months later, to be repatriated.

"Well, Lewis…that's my dismal story of my Legionary days in French Indochina. After I recovered my health for the most part, three months later, I and most of my surviving cronies were re-outfitted for reassignment. They had a special treat for us. A place with a warm, dry Mediterranean climate, health-inducing and wholesome. No pesky jungles that enemies might hide in. No boggy rice paddies filled with leeches, no raging rivers swollen by monsoon rains. Just unending vistas, colorful sunrises, and gentle, wave-lapped beaches. As I listened to these glowing descriptions, I got a very bad feeling about where I was heading next. It sounded a lot like somewhere I'd been before!"

Both Hans and I yelled out the same place name simultaneously, in voices loud enough to make all the other lunchers and Molson drinkers turn and stare:

ALGERIA!

24

HANS IS REASSIGNED TO A MEDITERRANEAN GARDEN SPOT WITH A SALUBRIOUS CLIMATE

"The Legion was right in the thick of the Algerian War of Liberation, from the very beginning. Radical Algerian elements had kicked off a bid to free the country from under the French thumb in November 1954…just about the time I was being freed from a Viet Minh prison-camp. So it wasn't until April 1955 that I was transported to Algiers to be reunited with my reconstituted Legion Company.

"It was nonstop bloody warfare from the day we hit the ground. Nominally, we were stationed in Algiers. But we were in the field almost continually. For the first time since I'd enlisted, they called on my mechanicking skills to keep various armored vehicles and transport trucks operating. When things got hot, though, I was expected to drop my wrench and grab my rifle. In the beginning, Lewis, I did not have a lot of animosity toward the FLN— *Front de Libération Nationale.* But that whole conflict became so vicious, so outrageously vindictive, so fraught with racism and spite, that I quickly lost any sense of empathy for *either* side. Sadistic torture was commonplace, both by French military and police forces and by the FLN. Assassinations, atrocities against non-combatants and women and babies, reprisal murders by the tens of thousands! It was the worst of the Gestapo and SS malevolence, revisited! Many Legionnaires of the bottom ranks were sub-Saharan Africans. There were three hundred years of black African slave-exploitation—largely at the hands of Arabic north Africans—in their history. So naturally there was vicious animosity at play there. Well, it all sickened me! I could see that the FLN was as relentless and resourceful a foe as the Viet Minh had been. The eventual outcome would *not* go in France's favor.

"Eventually, circumstances freed me from further personal involvement, although it was almost five years after my taking up duties in Algeria. This happened on 14 February 1959. My thirty-ninth birthday.

"We were celebrating the occasion at a table beneath a canopy outside a restaurant specializing in blazing-hot traditional North African dishes. It was early afternoon, hotter than hell. The establishment fronted on the Rue Debbin Cherff, a boulevard that twists its way across the north end of Central Algiers, just south of the city's ancient *casbah*. Six of my comrades had insisted on treating me to a big, communal platter of Lamb *Shawarma* with couscous, a finger food, but served for the scooping option with *khoubz,* a hand patted Moroccan flatbread. We washed the hot, spicy dish down with endless rounds of arrack.

"We were in pretty high spirits…not paying any attention to the jammed-up vehicle traffic in the street or the swarms of pedestrians along the roadside. A bundle came arching over the iron barricade separating the tables from the street. I never saw who threw it. The bundle thumped onto the tile floor and rolled under the third table away, opposite from where I was seated. Then it exploded.

"I was the only one left alive. All my comrades— killed. Seventeen other diners and three waiters—killed. I took splinters of chair legs and bits of shrapnel from the bomb in both my legs, and in my lower abdomen. When I regained consciousness on a litter, a bloody mess, I was being ambulanced to a French military hospital. Later that evening, I was airlifted north across the Mediterranean to a better hospital in Marseille. I spent six months recovering before they declared me fit enough to walk unassisted. Naturally, my days as a Legionnaire were over and done with.

"The French have a unique legal arrangement which applies to Legionnaires. It is called, *Français par le sang versé.* This means, 'French by the spilling of blood.' Any Legionnaire, no matter what his nationality, when wounded in battle for *la belle France,* can immediately apply for, and be granted, French citizenship. As I lay recovering, I debated with myself as to whether I would want to become a citizen of France, a nation I did not exactly admire. Ultimately, I came to the conclusion that I'd be better off as an honorable French combat veteran than as a rootless German ex-*Wehrmacht* expatriate. I applied from my hospital bed, and the application was granted.

"Well, Lewis! There I was, for the first time since I was eighteen years of age, free from obligation to any country's military machine! It took me another year before I felt myself fully fit again. I lived in Southern France, subsisting on a small pension and on occasional work of my own choosing—usually as an engine mechanic. Naturally, I preferred diesel engines...but I didn't scruple to work on loathsome gasoline engines if it came down to it.
"Once I was feeling hale, I began to feel restless. I suppose I hungered for the adventure and danger of the soldier's life. Not to mention, the camaraderie of soldiering. Toward the end of 1960, I took a radical step! Can you guess, Lewis?"
I hadn't a clue, but I suspected what direction Hans would have jumped. "So, *tell me!*" I urged him.

"I scoured classified advertisements in obscure periodicals until eventually I found what I was looking for. *I signed-on as a **mercenary**!*"

25
HANS GOES INDEPENDENT, AND THEN GIVES IT
ALL UP

A mercenary! That certainly called for one more Molson! When a couple foam topped mugs arrived for us, I asked Hans how this notion to become a mercenary soldier had come about. Who had he sought out to enlist with? Where did he expect to serve, and in what capacity? What happened next?

"You remember all the trouble in the Belgian Congo in the early 'sixties?" he asked.

"Not so much. I was eight years old in 1960."

"Well, all over the world, countries that had been colonies of European nations were getting restless. Some regions had been oppressed and exploited for a couple of centuries. The Belgians had controlled the Congo for, I don't know, a hundred years. Belgium exported lots of valuable minerals and agricultural products out of the Congo. Copper, tin...chromium. Rubber, I believe. Cocoa too. Let's not forget *uranium* ore! They let villages and small provinces enjoy the rule of traditional African chiefs, actually only puppets for the Belgian administration. They kept a heavy foot on the necks of the ordinary Congolese citizens...particularly, those working for Belgian companies. Well, during the War, Belgium was utterly crushed, thanks to me and my *Wehrmacht* buddies. Certain parties in the Congo took note of this, became emboldened, and started to plan and agitate. In the 1950's the *Mouvement National Congolais*, or MNC, became an ascendant power. Its principal organizer, Patrice Lumumba, became an influential man in the drive for independence.

"There was a rival organization to MNC, far more radical, known as ABAKO. Its leader was Joseph Kasavubu. These two factions came more and more into

209

conflict with each other. Riots broke out in Leopoldville, capital of the Belgian Congo, and in the turmoil, native colonial police fired on the rioters, killing at least five hundred people. White business owners, government officials, supervisors, planters and settlers became nervous about strife among black factions, *all* of which wanted to take over the country and throw the whites out anyway. Eventually the Belgians, exhausted from the difficulties of trying to control their fractious colony, called a round-table conference in Brussels to discuss and agree upon Congolese independence. The country became independent on 30 June, 1960 as the Republic of the Congo, with Patrice Lumumba as its president.

"All hell broke loose! Kasavubu demanded—and received!—a role as 'co-president.' Congolese ties were angrily severed with the government of Belgium, which had humbly offered to assist, with money and advice, in the Congo's transition to independence. White residents fled in droves, transferring their capital out of the country. And on 11 July, a scant forty days after independence, the mineral rich province of Katanga seceded from the Congo, proclaiming itself an independent nation under the leadership of a firebrand named Moise Tshombe. Katanga was the southernmost portion of Congo, a pretty sizeable chunk of the fledgling nation. And so that's about the time that various interests in the Congo started looking for a little help from some hard-ass mercenary soldiers for hire.

"This is where a French fellow by the name of Robert Denard comes in.

"Denard! They don't come any harder-ass that him! He was about a decade younger than me. But, like me, he'd served the French in Indochina—a legitimate French military service, not like the Legion. Then he'd served in Algeria for a while. Then he'd become a police agent in Morocco. The rumor is, devoting himself to torturing information out of would-be Moroccan agitators for freedom from French control. Denard had been convicted of participation in an assassination plot against a French Prime Minister—not the sainted De Gaulle, of course! He spent a mere fourteen months in prison, and on his release, went back to work as a French Secret Services agent in Algeria. Does this sound like a *connected* guy, or what?

"Well, in the late 1950s, although I suspect he was still in the employ of the French Secret Service, Denard took on the persona of a mercenary. More than just a mercenary...a *mercenary unit organizer*, a *recruiter*. He never made any particular secret of his affiliations with French and French-connected interests in Africa. So that's the guy whose clutches I fell into.

"I was offered very good wages to help out the poor, struggling, neophyte nation of The Congo. Things were ratcheting-up, conflict-wise, with Katanga Province. It appeared to be heading toward all-out civil war. I was to accompany Denard and a small, vicious band of mercenary soldiers to Katanga, where we would join up with mercenary forces under the control of Roger Faulques, a higher placed French mercenary operating in the region.

"We prowled around on both sides of the northern Katanga border. We clashed with small patrols of Katangan troops on the Congolese side of the line, and small patrols of Congolese troops on the Katangan side. We raided small villages on *both* sides of the line, torturing villagers to reveal weapons caches and information about troop movements. In these raids, we burnt everything we could light afire, killed our share of civilians, raped a lot of their young girls—some of us—and shot all their cattle. On occasion, we rescued white bureaucrats or settlers and their families from peril imposed by one faction or the other. We—"

"Excuse me, Hans!" I interrupted. "Exactly *who* were you working for?"

"Ah, Lewis! That's a damned fine question! We went down to Africa in December 1961. By the first of February, that was a big questionmark hovering over *my* head, too! Denard spoke in generalities and evasiveness. None of my mercenary cronies gave a damn, so long as they were paid. I was paid, too. Generously, in American dollars. I saved almost every dollar, bundled tightly and kept in a canvas belt around my middle twenty-four hours a day. Eventually I figured it out: our clandestine employers were French or Belgian *corporate* interests, still very much desiring control of Congolese and Katangan mineral wealth. Lewis, I never minded being involved with the dirty work of nations and corporate tycoons...but I was getting *verdammt* tired of *being lied to!*"

"So what did you do?" I asked.

"Glad you asked! I bided my time for a few months. During that time, I practiced my usual deception of firing willy-nilly in the general direction of our would-be enemies, while never taking sufficient aim as to shoot anyone through the brain. In late March our band was making a foray beyond the east fork of the Kasai River, very near the Angolan border. It was the chance I had been waiting for. In the middle of the night, I tendered my resignation from Denard's Mercenaries by means of sneaking away. I stole out of our encampment and made off toward Angola.

"At least one sentry was alert. I hadn't made fifty meters beyond the perimeter before someone opened up on me with an AK47. Only hit me in the hand, but the bullet took off the ends of these two fingers."

Hans held up his left hand and wiggled the ring finger and pinkie. Well, I'd been waiting five days for him to explain *that* small double amputation!

"Didn't slow me down, particularly. At dawn, they could have tracked me by the blood, but nobody bothered. I hadn't taken anything that didn't belong to me, and anyway, mercenaries are a pretty freewheeling lot when it comes to self-determination.

"I headed west into Angola. The country was still a Portuguese province in 1961, but was drifting toward a violent transition to independence. I tried to maintain a low profile as I made my way west.

"I had those shot-up fingers wrapped up in a spare sock to slow the bleeding, but the bullet hadn't exactly clipped them off clean. I stopped running through the veldt in late afternoon. I lit a small fire. Took my sheathed bush knife off my belt. Unsheathed the knife and got it good and hot in the coals. I stuffed the leather sheath between my teeth and bit down hard. Then I laid those two wounded fingers on a log, took careful aim, and whacked off the mangled parts in one swift stroke."

"Ouch!" I commented.

"You bet, ouch!" agreed Hans. "But, the finger stumps were pretty well cauterized. The first sizeable village I came to, I tracked down their herb doctor. The Africans have been dealing with much nastier wounds for thousands of years without the aid of penicillin. The old guy accepted ten Yankee dollars and rubbed some kind of brownish poultice on the stumps that killed the pain. He took a stitch or two in each finger stump, pulling the skin together. Then he wrapped both fingers together with leaves! I never got infected, and things healed up quick and neat!" Hans wiggled his stumps to demonstrate.

"It was a few days getting to Luanda. The last hundred kilometers, I flagged down a truck taking sugar cane down to the coast. In sign language and pidgin French, I promised the driver I'd give him my AK47 and all the rest of my ammo if he'd let me ride along with him into the city. He let me ride shotgun, instead of in back on top of that high, itchy pile of cane stalks!

"In Luanda, I headed for the port facilities. I found a shop selling western style readymade men's clothing, and re-outfitted myself. I found an adequate hotel and took a room. I had a long soak in a tubful of hot, soapy water. I lay on an actual bed for the first time in five months, and fell into an untroubled sleep. On awaking, I put on civilian garb and admired myself in the bathroom mirror. Then I rolled up my filthy, bloodstained, tattered field camos, strapped my disreputable boots onto the bundle with my webgear belt, took a short walk to the trash bins just outside the hotel's back door, and dumped all that *scheisse* into a foul-smelling can.

"Lewis, it was a moment of epiphany! It came to me that I had been a soldier in one form or another for twenty-four years, and I wasn't *ever* very good at it. I'd been on the wrong side, ethically speaking, every time. In addition, I'd been on the *losing* side, most of the time. I'd been wounded—slightly or seriously—in every set-to I'd found myself in. Most of all, due to what my superiors would have considered a deficiency of soldierly character, rectifiable by firing squad had they known about it, I'd never to my knowledge succeeded in actually *killing* an enemy in an act of combat. *Wait a moment, Hans!* I said to myself. *Isn't that something to be* proud *of?* With that final self-revelation, I slammed down the lid of that garbage can and said goodbye to soldiering for the rest of my days!

"Well, I had a fine African breakfast. Then I located a barber and had a haircut and a shave. Next, I walked along the quaysides and piers, asking merchant seamen for information about outbound ships. I was hoping for a particular destination. It wasn't long before my search was successful.

"The *Marie des Sept-Îles* was a small French-Canadian freighter of about a hundred twenty meters length, post-War construction. I was fairly certain she was diesel powered. She had taken on a full cargo of sacked Angolan coffee beans, crates of cacao, and steel drums of palm oil. I made my way up her gangplank and asked to speak to the captain. I was directed to the Supercargo instead.

" 'What do you want?" he asked tersely in French, his nose to a clipboard of manifests.

" 'I understand you are bound out for Montreal?'

"The officer looked up suspiciously. 'That's right...'

" 'Would you be willing to take on a paying passenger?'

" 'We have no facilities for passengers!' he snapped.

" 'She's diesel powered? How are her engines performing?'

" 'Yes, diesel-electric. Running well, except perhaps some lubricant leakage, I'm informed. What is it to you?'

" 'I am an experienced marine diesel mechanic,' I exaggerated, not for the first time. 'I will work engine room service for no pay, whatever shift you find convenient, in exchange for one-way passage to Montreal.'

" 'Hmmm, I suppose— Wait! What is your citizenship?' the officer demanded.

" 'French!' I didn't even have to lie about that one! I had obtained a passport in Marseille before flying out to the Congo. I produced my documents.

"The fellow pondered, but not for long. 'Wait here,' he said, with a tiny measure of cordiality. 'I will speak to the captain!'

"And so that is how I came to Canada! As a French citizen by virtue of spilled blood, as a certified Expert Diesel Mechanic—well, certified twenty years earlier, by the Nazi military machine—and as the holder of an affidavit from the Canadian Prisoner-of-War apparatus attesting to my cooperativeness and reliability, I was made welcome. In time, I achieved Canadian citizenship."

"Where did you go, Hans?" I asked. "What did you do?"

"I spent about four months searching for a Canadian nurse named Tiriaq. As I recall, one of the first things she said to me when I located her working in a Winnipeg hospital was, 'It certainly took you a long time to track me down, Hans Raufer!'

"Well, *mein freund*," Hans concluded with a sigh, "I've finished at last with all my boasts and half-truths...maybe we ought to get on home to Anna and see what trouble we can get you into on your last evening in Churchill."

26

I RELUCTANTLY SUCCEED IN GETTING THE HELL OUT OF CHURCHILL MANITOBA

CanadaNational Airlines, as good as its semi-corporate word, had a familiar twin engine turboprop standing by for an eight-thirty departure. At this hour, just a bit after 7 a.m., Wednesday dawn had not quite come upon us, for it was only 18 February, just over halfway from Midwinter's Day to the spring equinox. Full daylight was still ninety minutes off.

A uniformed CN ticket counter girl read the roll. All twenty-eight of us long-marooned travelers were present. I'd said my farewells to Anna Raufer when Hans and I had dropped her off at the Regional Health Authority Hospital. So it was only Hans who had accompanied me to the departure lounge.

Now here's an interesting observation! I noted. Almost every other stranded traveler had two or three Churchillians in company, tearfully seeing them off. One young woman had Mom, Pop, and four assorted kiddies clustering around—she had been fostered by an entire family! The inherent sociability of a small and isolated town! And at that very instant, who should wedge her way through the press and throw her arms around me but Qilqiq Sidney!

"Oh Lewis! I had a wicked plan! I was going to direct about twenty thousand kilos of cargo onto that airplane of yours, so it couldn't get off the ground! But then I decided it would just fail to lift off its gear, crash at the end of the runway, and they'd figure out why and fire me, and you probably wouldn't have survived the crash anyway. So I didn't!" She stopped to kiss me for awhile.

"Do you want to say goodbye to Miss Momma Musk-ox?"

"Oh yes please!"

I unzipped the travelbag. I'd wrapped the sculpture in my spare change of clothes. Gold musk-ox horns glinted when I laid back the white cotton of a t-shirt. Qil reached in and gently ran her index finger down the humped soapstone back. "Will you take good care of her?" she begged me.

"Safe on my lap the whole trip." Then I remembered something. I groped in my coat pocket. Came up with a blue velvet snap-box. *What*, I wondered momentarily, *What was I thinking, giving this bewitching girl a romantic gemstone ring, five days after I'd met her?* I stomped those doubts back down the dark gopher hole they belonged in. "Qil..." I said. Hans noticed what was about to happen and graciously turned away to afford us privacy. "Qil...this is for you."

She took the box from my hand. She snapped the lid open. I could see her eyes widen as she gazed on the ring...its faceted, heart-shaped garnet, red as love...its glinting, exquisite diamonds. She raised her eyes to fix on mine.

I bent to her. "Qil... *Nagligigitvit!*" I whispered in her ear. In case I hadn't gotten the Inuktitut phrase right, and also for emphasis, I said it again: "*Nagligigitvit!*"

"*Oh Lewis! I love you too!*" We had thirty seconds to kiss and then the gate agent called us to board. Hans took his turn at me, throwing both arms around me and beating on my back with life-toughened hands the size of polar bear paws. "*Auf Wiedersehen, mein Freund!* Goodbye, goodbye!"

I took a last look, waved, and trudged up the boarding ramp, leaving Churchill, Manitoba, Polar Bear Capital of the Canadian Arctic, behind me.

Eighteen hours after leaving Churchill International Airport on my restored twin engine turboprop airliner, I slid my key into the doorknob of my Cambridge apartment. The

218

flight had been more circuitous than I'd anticipated: a long airport layover in Winnipeg, and another long break between flights in Toronto. Home at last, I stepped over the threshold and set my travelbag gently on the sofa.

The scent of my home was familiar and comforting. I crossed to the wide glass windows and threw open the drapes. No snow, no icebound Hudson Bay! Yeah...well...no polar bears or ptarmigan either. No Qil Sidney. No half liter cans of warm Molson lager ...although I supposed I could find it in almost any Massachusetts liquor outlet. Out my window, just winter grass and wind-swirled brown leaves, and a hundred-foot vista rolling down across the Memorial Parkway to the Charles River.

I was musing on whether or not I'd told Hans or Qil or anyone at all that my tidy domicile was actually a *Cambridge* address...or had I just taken the usual liberty to say "Boston" in order to keep things simple and comprehensible? As I mused, I checked things out. Potted plants: well tended and healthy! Fish tank: all present and accounted for, down to the least snail! Aquarium water: crystal clear! Mail: tidily piled on the dining table! I made a mental note to take a box of candy or something up to Mrs. O'Hannity upstairs, my sweet septuagenarian acquaintance who insisted she be the one to tend my apartment during my frequent absences. Idly, I poked through the pile of letters, circulars and ads.

Near the top, an International Overnight Letter. Origin: Canada. From Qilqiq Sidney. Posted directly from the Churchill Airport so it would get to Cambridge before I did.

I zipped it open. Sweet, fond words. A few lines of reminiscence: the party at the Townshend's...the Aurora Borealis over the pack ice on Hudson Bay. A goofy sketch of a polar bear attempting to devour a tiny, helpless, parka-clad Inuit girl...Qil herself, no doubt. In closing: sweet, loving, intimate words. Another goofy sketch of a fluffy Arctic ground bird, a Willow Ptarmigan, followed by three letters:

QIL

...And then, a postscript:

p.s.: June 11 to June 25...okay with you? ♥♥♥

A couple weeks after I returned home in mid-February, I went shopping for a particular item. There was a specialty sewing shop in Watertown. I asked the saleslady to show me the most reliable machine she had that was usually intended for home use, a tabletop model that was portable and versatile. Price, I told her, was less of a concern than reliability and ease of use. Any machine intended for US use would be able to function on Canadian power, the familiar 120v 60cycle. Without hesitation, she showed me a Husqvarna Viking Model 6690. She proudly stated that this machine was the world's first computer-controlled sewing machine meant for home use.

"Ahhh...the machine I want is going to be used in a remote Canadian Arctic location. I'm concerned about maintenance and repairs on a machine that's too advanced."

The saleswoman agreed that it could be a concern with the 6690, unless its user was willing to ship the unit to Toronto for any service needs. Then she showed me the simpler unit that the 6690 was intended to supersede: the Viking 2000. "Half the price, plenty of features and lots of power!"

"Can you ship it airfreight to a Canadian address?"

"Certainly!"

I gave her Anna Raufer's particulars, and wrote Anna a brief note to go in the carton.

On my way home, I stopped at Cambridge's largest, most-posh liquor outlet and ordered up a six-bottle case of Glenlivet Single-Malt, aged for sixteen years in French Oak cooperage. The outlet was happy to ship the merchandise to Hans Raufer in Churchill, Manitoba...so long as I was willing to fork over cash for the duties and shipping.

Some months later, on Thursday, June 11th, I cabbed across town to meet Qil at Logan Airport. I met her with flowers and a big kiss at the arrival gate, like you could still do in 1981 when greeting your sweetheart right off the plane. After collecting her luggage, I got us a cab back to Cambridge. Evidently, I'd subconsciously timed it so we would be stuck in godawful Boston rush-hour traffic. That way, it gave us more time in the cab's back seat to kiss and snuggle. I tipped the cabbie plenty for having to put up with all that mushiness.

She loved what I'd done for her in the matter of the guest room. She particularly liked the prominent dresser-top display of my Inuit sculpture...that is to say, *her* Spirit Animal. I had placed the soapstone carving on a rectangular placemat of soft tanned moosehide decorated on its corners with brightly dyed tundra rose blossoms rendered in rare tufted moose hair craftsmanship. I helped her unpack her tight-stuffed suitcase into the dresser and the closet.

At dinnertime, we had a nice, fishy *salade niçoise* and a glass of Chardonnay on the balcony. I cleared away the dishes. Then we poured the rest of the wine in our glasses, and held each other close for an hour or more while the New England sky darkened into evening. When she yawned cavernously, tired from her travels, I suggested we call it a night. I had wild, touristy plans for our tomorrow. I made certain she knew where all the bath linens and scented soaps and toothpastes were kept. I made sure her pillows were fluffed and her duvet was cozily snugged down. And, in gentlemanly fashion, I kissed her goodnight and, exiting, gently closed the door to her guest quarters.

She managed to endure the privacy and coziness in there until about eleven o'clock. Then I heard her knock softly on my bedroom door. She peeped in. "Lewis, there's too many streetlights outside the window, and a lot of traffic noise from the Parkway. Can I sleep in here?" she murmured…a frail rationale. As she crept in and closed the door behind her, in the dim ambient light I could see shimmering highlights from the pale pink silk of her petite, lace-trimmed nightie. She doffed the garment, slipping it over her head with a subtle nonchalance and a shake of her silky black hair. She slid her warm, supple little self into my bed, wherein she slept for the balance of her Boston holiday. Well…such little as we actually *slept*.

Two weeks later, over breakfast on the 25th of June, Qilqiq sat in my sun-warmed dining nook, ignoring her coffee and croissant. Instead, she wrung her restless hands, fiddling distractedly with a slip of paper.
"What is that?" I asked her.
"My air ticket home."
"Is there a problem with your return flight, Dearest?" I asked.
"Only that I don't want to get on the airplane."
"Why don't you stay, then? Here…with me?"
Qil folded the ticket on its long axis. Then she ripped it in half. Then in quarters. Kept ripping until it was confetti.

To this day, we have been together for thirty-five years, Qil and I. During that blissful time, we travelled to Churchill almost every year. By airplane, train or dogsled. The airplanes never lost any engines or crashed. The trains

222

never went off the rails. The dogsleds—okay, that was a bit of an exaggeration.

To this day, I happily remember Hans Raufer, the world's unluckiest soldier but perhaps among the most blessed of men, truly one of a kind, possessed of an exemplary albeit quirky form of valor and with a dented Iron Cross Second-Class to prove it. He was *mein lieber Freunde*. Hans passed away to his eternal rest, gently, in his sleep, at the age of eighty-eight years.

To this day, at age ninety-three, Anna Raufer lives hale and hearty, still sewing garments for the third and fourth generations of her family on that spiffy sewing machine I sent her all those years ago.

And to this day, Qilqiq Utkuhiksalingmiut MacLeod—these days known as *Doctor* Qilqiq Utkuhiksalingmiut MacLeod, M.D.—and I are hopelessly and joyfully in love. I'm pretty certain it is *she* who has been my life's Spirit Guide.

…Which reminds me to share with you, Dear Reader, these parting words of wisdom in hopes that they will help you live a longer and more pleasurable life:

WATCH OUT FOR BEARS!

OTHER NOVELS BY LEWIS MACLEOD

Miss Mai

"Miss Mai" is a romantic memoir set in the final years of the Vietnam War. The author's progress as a naive draftee through the rigors of military training as an intelligence analyst inexorably lead him to the exotic streets of wartime Saigon. He meets Tuoi Mai under accidental circumstances and his life is altered forever after.

Twenty-One Forty-Seven – Book One in "THE SOLAE' series

In the year 2147, humankind has begun to exceed the critical planetary ecological tipping-point in many frightening ways. Global population exceeds nine billion souls. Unspoiled areas on every continent are shrunken, their wildlife depleted. Poverty is rife in every nation. Petroleum reserves worldwide are nearly exhausted. Sources of water for domestic and agricultural use are severely overtaxed. Air quality has never been so compromised. Still, there is hope. Technology has led to stunning advances, and man's ventures into space have proceeded spectacularly. A new faith—that of the Solae—has arisen from the urban slums of South America, promising a new and vital view on human interactions. Perhaps humanity's future is not so grim after all.

On 15 September, in the year Twenty-One Forty-Seven, all that changes

The Solae – Book Two in 'THE SOLAE' series

It is nearly a thousand years beyond the present day. The globe and the human race are slowly recovering from the horrors of a devastating war and plague that occurred in the year 2147. Humanity lives simply, without the technologies of today, for the net of industry, medicine, and science was shattered beyond recovery by the tribulations of that war. Small villages of farmers and herdsmen cluster against the flank of the mountains once known as the Rockies. On the High Plains, a few fiercely protective bands of nomads make their seasonal migrations, practicing their arts and trades with whatever peaceable folk they encounter. Deep in a mountain fastness dwells a secretive sect, whose avowed purpose is to collect and safeguard scraps of scientific knowledge that survived the Laser War...safeguard this knowledge until the Deserving One their faith prophesies will come forward to receive this store of wisdom. And always, bringing terror and death as their ally, the bands of pitiless, thieving murderers wander this cold and terrible world, marauders known by all men as ULTS.

...But a change is about to come upon this savage world.

Solae Inheritor – Book Three in 'The Solae' series

The Union of Eriss has grown and consolidated for more than a hundred years since its founding in the famine-depleted High Plains of the continent. To the east, an implacable enemy stirs: the Atlan Empire, warlike, aggressive, greedy for land, for power and for slaves. The Union is vigorous and vital, but not without its difficulties: one-third of its population are Ults, restless descendants of a conquered race of one-time wildland brigands and marauders on whom the veneer of Erissard civilization lies thin and uneasy. It is the special task of the House of Eriss, descendants of Old Salin lineage, to defend the Union. But the family's elder, the Domin Therisam, is aged, weak and vacillating. It is good fortune that his eldest son and proxy Jericharek is a man of fierce determination, although his character is flawed by the hateful evil of bigotry directed toward the Ultish populace. Jeri's younger brother Mairhos, although not born into leadership, has a gentler spirit and a keen sense of duty and honor. He heeds the call to serve his nation in less-celebrated ways. But another call also rises in his heart: the impassioned love of a girl from the poorer classes of Pikemond City. Karil Feros is innocent, beautiful, skilled, fearless, and kind of heart, but, may the Sacred Solae pity Mairhos, Karil is one thing more.

Karil is Ult.

Solae Redeemer – Book Four in 'THE SOLAE' series
In the months following the defeat of the Atlan Empire, many citizens of the Erissard Union and its allies remained scattered by the dislocations of war. Karil Feros, Ultish paramour of the High Domin of Eriss himself, waits for her lover in the wilderness reaches of the Sulfur Basin, along with the wives, children and oldsters of her Brisach Ult forbears. The Basin is an ancient volcanic caldera, known in earlier times as the Yellowstone.
There is a cataclysmic eruption, as geologists have been predicting since the nineteenth century a.d. By a miracle, Karil and her cousin Rechalas are temporarily absent on a diplomatic mission westward. Their survival is chancy and unlikely, and Mairhos has scant effort to spare in their rescue. But with help and great good fortune, he manages.
...Only, it takes him eight years to find Karil.

Cúc – a short novelette
This novelette explores the tenuous connection between an American GI who spent a year of service in Saigon VN and a two-year-old orphan child who came to believe the man was her father. Central to the narrative is

the child's-eye experiencing of a horrific occurence, historically accurate, which took place a short time before the Fall of Saigon in April 1975...an event which should never be forgotten worldwide in the annals of that doleful chapter called the Viet Nam War.

Proof

56848910R20128